The Revolt of the Angels

Black Curtain Press
P.O. Box 632
Floyd, VA 24091

ISBN 13: 978-5154-2430-7

First Edition
10 9 8 7 6 5 4 3 2 1

The Revolt of the Angels
Anatole France

CHAPTER I. CONTAINING IN A FEW LINES THE HISTORY OF A FRENCH FAMILY FROM 1789 TO THE PRESENT DAY

BENEATH the shadow of St. Sulpice the ancient mansion of the d'Esparvieu family rears its austere three stories between a moss-grown forecourt and a garden hemmed in, as the years have elapsed, by ever loftier and more intrusive buildings, wherein, nevertheless, two tall chestnut trees still lift their withered heads.

Here from 1825 to 1857 dwelt the great man of the family, Alexandre Bussart d'Esparvieu, Vice-President of the Council of State under the Government of July, Member of the Academy of Moral and Political Sciences, and author of an Essay on the Civil and Religious Institutions of Nations, in three octavo volumes, a work unfortunately left incomplete.

This eminent theorist of a Liberal monarchy left as heir to his name his fortune and his fame, Fulgence-Adolphe Bussart d'Esparvieu, senator under the Second Empire, who added largely to his patrimony by buying land over which the Avenue de l'Imperatice was destined ultimately to pass, and who made a remarkable speech in favour of the temporal power of the popes.

Fulgence had three sons. The eldest, Marc-Alexandre, entering the army, made a splendid career for himself: he was a good speaker. The second, Gaétan, showing no particular aptitude for anything, lived mostly in the country, where he hunted, bred horses, and devoted himself to music and painting. The third son, René, destined from his childhood for the law, resigned his deputyship to avoid complicity in the Ferry decrees against the religious orders; and later, perceiving the revival under the presidency of Monsieur Fallieres of the days of Decius and Diocletian, put his knowledge and zeal at the service of the persecuted Church.

From the Concordat of 1801 down to the closing years of the Second Empire all the d'Esparvieus attended mass for the sake of example. Though sceptics in their inmost hearts, they looked upon religion as an instrument of government.

Marc and René were the first of their race to show any sign of sincere devotion. The General, when still a colonel, had dedicated his regiment to the Sacred Heart, and he practised his faith with a fervour remarkable even in a soldier, though we all know that piety, daughter of Heaven, has marked out the hearts of the generals of the Third Republic as her chosen dwelling-place on earth.

Faith has its vicissitudes. Under the old order the masses were believers, not so the aristocracy or the educated middle class. Under the First Empire the army from top to bottom was entirely irreligious. To-day the masses believe nothing. The middle classes wish to believe, and succeed at times, as did Marc and René d'Esparvieu. Their brother Gaétan, on the contrary, the country gentleman, failed to attain to faith. He was an agnostic, a term commonly employed by the modish to avoid the odious one of freethinker. And he openly declared himself an agnostic, contrary to the admirable custom which deems it better to withhold the avowal.

In the century in which we live there are so many modes of belief and of unbelief that future historians will have difficulty in finding their way about. But are we any more successful in disentangling the condition of religious beliefs in the time of Symmachus or of Ambrose?

A fervent Christian, René d'Esparvieu was deeply attached to the liberal ideas his ancestors had transmitted to him as a sacred heritage. Compelled to oppose a Jacobin and atheistical Republic, he still called himself Republican. And it was in the name of liberty that he demanded the independence and sovereignty of the Church.

During the long debates on the Separation and the quarrels over the Inventories, the synods of the bishops and the assemblies of the faithful were held in his house. While the most authoritatively accredited leaders of the Catholic party: prelates, generals, senators, deputies, journalists, were met together in the big green drawing-room, and every soul present turned towards Rome with a tender submission or enforced obedience; while Monsieur d'Esparvieu, his elbow on the marble chimney-piece, opposed civil law to canon law, and protested eloquently against the spoliation of the Church of France, two faces of other days, immobile and speechless, looked down on the modern crowd; on the right of the fire-place, painted by David, was Romain Bussart, a working-farmer at Esparvieu in shirt-sleeves and drill trousers, with a rough-and-ready air not untouched with cunning. He had good reason to smile: the worthy man laid the foundation of the family fortunes when he bought Church lands. On the left, painted by Gerard in full-dress bedizened with orders, was the peasant's son, Baron Emile Bussart d'Esparvieu, prefect under the Empire, Keeper of the Great Seal under Charles X, who died in 1837, churchwarden of his parish, with couplets from La Pucelle on his lips.

René d'Esparvieu married in 1888 Marie-Antoinette Coupelle, daughter of Baron Coupelle, ironmaster at Blainville (Haute Loire). Madame René d'Esparvieu had been president since 1903 of the Society of Christian Mothers. These perfect spouses, having married off their eldest daughter in 1908, had three children still at home -- a girl and two boys.

Léon, the younger, aged seven, had a room next to his mother and his sister Berthe. Maurice, the elder, lived in a little pavilion comprising two rooms at the bottom of the garden. The young man thus gained a freedom which enabled him to endure family life. He was rather good-looking, smart without too much pretence, and the faint smile which merely raised one corner of his mouth did not lack charm.

At twenty-five Maurice possessed the wisdom of Ecclesiastes. Doubting whether a man hath any profit of all his labour which he taketh under the sun he never put himself out about anything. From his earliest childhood this young hopeful's sole concern with work had been considering how he might best avoid it, and it was through his remaining ignorant of the teaching of the École de Droit that he became a doctor of law and a barrister at the Court of Appeal.

He neither pleaded nor practised. He had no knowledge and no desire to acquire any; wherein he conformed to his genius whose engaging fragility he forbore to overload; his instinct fortunately telling him that it was better to understand little than to misunderstand a lot.

As Monsieur l'Abbé Patouille expressed it, Maurice had received from Heaven the benefits of a Christian education. From his childhood piety was shown to him in the example of his home, and when on leaving college he was entered at the École de Droit, he found the lore of the doctors, the virtues of the confessors, and the constancy of the nursing mothers of the Church assembled around the paternal hearth. Admitted to social and political life at the time of the great persecution of the Church of France, Maurice did not fail to attend every manifestation of youthful Catholicism; he lent a hand with his parish barricades at the time of the Inventories, and with his companions he unharnessed the archbishop's horses when he was driven out from his palace. He showed on all these occasions a modified zeal; one never saw him in the front ranks of the heroic band exciting soldiers to a glorious disobedience or flinging mud and curses at the agents of the law.

He did his duty, nothing more; and if he distinguished himself on the occasion of the great pilgrimage of 1911 among the stretcher-bearers at Lourdes, we have reason to fear it was but to please Madame de la Verdelière, who admired men of muscle. Abbé Patouille, a friend of the family and deeply versed in the knowledge of souls, knew that Maurice had only moderate aspirations to martyrdom. He reproached him with his lukewarmness, and pulled his ear, calling him a bad lot. Anyway, Maurice remained a believer.

Amid the distractions of youth his faith remained intact, since he left it severely alone. He had never examined a single tenet. Nor had he enquired a whit more closely into the ideas of morality current in the grade of society to which he belonged. He took them just as they came. Thus in every situation that arose he cut an eminently respectable figure which he would have assuredly failed to do, had he been given to meditating on the foundations of morality. He was irritable and hot-tempered and possessed of a sense of honour which he was at great pains to cultivate. He was neither vain nor ambitious. Like the majority of Frenchmen, he disliked parting with his money. Women would never have obtained anything from him had they not known the way to make him give. He believed he despised them; the truth was he adored them. He indulged his appetites so naturally that he never suspected that he had any. What people did not know, himself least of all, -- though the gleam that occasionally shone in his fine, light-brown eyes might have furnished the hint -- was that he had a warm heart and was capable of friendship. For the rest, he was, in the ordinary intercourse of life, no very brilliant specimen.

CHAPTER II. WHEREIN USEFUL INFORMATION WILL BE FOUND CONCERNING A LIBRARY WHERE STRANGE THINGS WILL SHORTLY COME TO PASS

DESIROUS of embracing the whole circle of human knowledge, and anxious to bequeath to the world a concrete symbol of his encyclopedic genius and a display in keeping with his pecuniary resources, Baron Alexandre d'Esparvieu had formed a library of three hundred and sixty thousand volumes, both printed and in manuscript, whereof the greater part emanated from the Benedictines of Ligugé.

By a special clause in his will he enjoined his heirs to add to his library, after his death, whatever they might deem worthy of note in natural, moral, political, philosophical, and religious science.

He had indicated the sums which might be drawn from his estate for the fulfilment of this object, and charged his eldest son, Fulgence-Adolphe, to proceed with these additions. Fulgence-Adolphe accomplished with filial respect the wishes expressed by his illustrious father.

After him, this huge library, which represented more than one child's share of the estate, remained undivided between the Senator's three sons and two daughters; and René d'Esparvieu, on whom devolved the house in the Rue Garancière, became the guardian of the valuable collection. His two sisters, Madame Paulet de Saint-Fain and Madame Cuissart, repeatedly demanded that such a large but unremunerative piece of property should be turned into money. But René and Gaétan bought in the shares of their two co-legatees, and the library was saved. René d'Esparvieu even busied himself in adding to it, thus fulfilling the intentions of its founder. But from year to year he lessened the number and importance of the acquisitions, opining that the intellectual output in Europe was on the wane.

Nevertheless, Gaétan enriched it, out of his funds, with works published both in France and abroad which he thought good, and he was not lacking in judgment, though his brothers would never allow that he had a particle. Thanks to this man of leisurely and inquiring mind, Baron Alexandre's collection was kept practically up to date. Even at the present day the d'Esparvieu library, in the departments of theology, jurisprudence, and history is one of the finest private libraries in all Europe. Here you may study physical science, or to put it better, physical sciences in all their branches, and for that matter metaphysic or metaphysics, that is to say, all that is connected with physics and has no other name, so impossible is it to designate by a substantive that which has no substance, and is but a dream and an illusion. Here you may contemplate with admiration philosophers addressing themselves to the solution, dissolution, and resolution of the Absolute, to the determination of the Indeterminate and to the definition of the Infinite.

Amid this pile of books and booklets, both sacred and profane, you may find everything down to the latest and most fashionable pragmatism.

Other libraries there are, more richly abounding in bindings of venerable antiquity and illustrious origin, whose smooth and soft-hued texture render them delicious to the touch; bindings which the gilder's art has enriched with gossamer, lace-work, foliage, flowers, emblematic devices, and coats of arms; bindings that charm the studious eye with their tender radiance. Other libraries perhaps harbour a greater array of manuscripts illuminated with delicate and brilliant miniatures by artists of Venice, Flanders, or Touraine. But in handsome, sound editions of ancient and modern writers, both sacred and profane, the d'Esparvieu library is second to none. Here one finds all that has come down to us from antiquity; all the Fathers of the Church, the Apologists and the Decretalists, all the Humanists of the Renaissance, all the Encylopædists, the whole world of philosophy and science. Therefore it was that Cardinal Merlin, when he deigned to visit it, remarked:

"There is no man whose brain is equal to containing all the knowledge which is piled upon these shelves. Happily it doesn't matter."

Monseigneur Cachepot, who worked there often when a curate in Paris, was in the habit of saying:

"I see here the stuff to make many a Thomas Aquinas and many an Arius, if only the modern mind had not lost its ancient ardour for good and evil."

There was no gainsaying that the manuscripts formed the more valuable portion of this immense collection. Noteworthy indeed was the unpublished correspondence of Gassendi, of Father Mersenne, and of Pascal, which threw a new light on the spirit of the seventeenth century. Nor must we forget the Hebrew Bibles, the Talmuds, the Rabbinical treatises, printed and in manuscript, the Aramaic and Samaritan texts, on sheepskin and on tablets of sycamore; in fine, all these antique and valuable copies collected in Egypt and in Syria by the celebrated Moïse de Dina, and acquired at a small cost by Alexandre d'Esparvieu in 1836 when the learned Hebraist died of old age and poverty in Paris.

The Esparvienne library occupied the whole of the second floor of the old house. The works thought to be of but mediocre interest, such as books of Protestant exegesis of the nineteenth and twentieth centuries, the gift of Monsieur Gaétan, were relegated unbound to the limbo of the upper regions. The catalogue, with its various supplements, ran into no less than eighteen folio volumes. It was quite up to date, and the library was in perfect order. Monsieur Julien Sariette, archivist and palæographer, who, being poor and retiring, used to make his living by teaching, became, in 1895, tutor to young Maurice on the recommendation of the Bishop of Agra, and with scarcely an interval found himself curator of the Bibliothèque Esparvienne. Endowed with business-like energy and dogged patience, Monsieur Sariette himself classified all the members of this vast body. The system he invented and put into practice was so complicated, the labels he put on the books were made up of so many capital letters and small letters, both Latin and Greek, so many Arabic and Roman numerals, asterisks, double asterisks, triple asterisks, and those signs which in arithmetic express powers and roots, that the mere study of it would have involved more time and labour than would have been required for the complete mastery of algebra, and as no one could be found who would give the hours, that might be more profitably employed in discovering the law of numbers, to the solving of these cryptic symbols, Monsieur Sariette remained the only one capable of finding his way among the intricacies of his system, and without his help it had become an utter impossibility to discover, among the three hundred and sixty thousand volumes confided to his care, the particular volume one happened to require. Such was the result of his labours. Far from complaining about it, he experienced on the contrary a lively satisfaction.

Monsieur Sariette loved his library. He loved it with a jealous love. He was there every day at seven o'clock in the morning busy cataloguing at a huge mahogany desk. The slips in his handwriting filled an enormous case standing by his side surmounted by a plaster bust of Alexandre d'Esparvieu. Alexandre wore his hair brushed straight back, and had a sublime look on his face. Like Chateaubriand, he affected little feathery side whiskers. His lips were pursed, his bosom bare. Punctually at midday Monsieur Sariette used to sally forth to lunch at a crèmerie in the narrow gloomy Rue des Canettes. It was known as the Crèmerie de Quatre Évêques, and had once been the haunt of Baudelaire, Theodore de Banville, Charles Asselineau, and a certain grandee of Spain who had translated the "Mysteries of Paris" into the language of the conquistadores. And the ducks that paddled so nicely on the old stone sign which gave its name to the street used to recognize Monsieur Sariette. At a quarter to one, to the very minute, he went back to his library, where he remained until seven o'clock. He then again betook himself to the Quarte Évêques, and sat down to his frugal dinner, with its crowning glory of stewed prunes. Every evening, after dinner, his crony, Monsieur Guinardon, universally known as Père Guinardon, a scene-painter and picture-restorer, who used to do work for churches, would come from his garret in the Rue Princesse to have his coffee and liqueur at the Quatre Évêques, and the two friends would play their game of dominoes.

Old Guinardon, who was like some rugged old tree still full of sap, was older than he could bring himself to believe. He had known Chenavard. His chastity was positively ferocious, and he was for ever denouncing the impurities of neo-paganism in language of alarming obscenity. He loved talking. Monsieur Sariette was a ready listener. Old Guinardon's favourite subject was the Chapelle des Anges in St. Sulpice, in which the paintings were peeling off the walls, and which he was one day to restore; when, that is, it should please God, for, since the Separation, the churches belonged solely to God, and no one would undertake the responsibility of even the most urgent repairs. But old Guinardon demanded no salary.

"Michael is my patron saint," he said. "And I have a special devotion for the Holy Angels."

After they had had their game of dominoes, Monsieur Sariette, very thin and small, and old Guinardon, sturdy as an oak, hirsute as a lion, and tall as a Saint Christopher, went off chatting away side by side across the Place Saint Sulpice, heedless of whether the night were fine or stormy. Monsieur Sariette always went straight home, much to the regret of the painter, who was a gossip and a nightbird.

The following day, as the clock struck seven, Monsieur Sariette would take up his place in the library, and resume his cataloguing. As he sat at his desk, however, he would dart a Medusa-like look at anyone who entered, fearing lest he should prove to be a book-borrower. It was not merely the magistrates, politicians, and prelates whom he would have liked to turn to stone when they came to ask for the loan of a book with an air of authority bred of their familiarity with the master of the house. He would have done as much to Monsieur Gaétan, the library's benefactor, when he wanted some gay or scandalous old volume wherewith to beguile a wet day in the country. He would have meted out similar treatment to Madame René d'Esparvieu, when she came to look for a book to read to her sick poor in hospital, and even to Monsieur René d'Esparvieu himself, who generally contented himself with the Civil Code and a volume of Dalloz. The borrowing of the smallest book seemed like dragging his heart out. To refuse a volume even to such as had the most incontestable right to it, Monsieur Sariette would invent countless far-fetched or clumsy fibs, and did not even shrink from slandering himself as curator or from casting doubts on his own vigilance by saying that such and such a book was mislaid or lost, when a moment ago he had been gloating over that very volume or pressing it to his bosom. And when ultimately forced to part with a volume he would take it back a score of times from the borrower before he finally relinquished it.

He was always in agony lest one of the objects confided to his care should escape him. As the guardian of three hundred and sixty thousand volumes, he had three hundred and sixty thousand reasons for alarm. Sometimes he woke at night bathed in sweat, and uttering a cry of fear, because he had dreamed he had seen a gap on one of the shelves of his bookcases. It seemed to him a monstrous, unheard-of, and most grievous thing that a volume should leave its habitat. This noble rapacity exasperated Monsieur René d'Esparvieu, who, failing to understand the good qualities of his paragon of a librarian, called him an old maniac. Monsieur Sariette knew nought of this injustice, but he would have braved the cruellest misfortune and endured opprobrium and insult to safeguard the integrity of his trust. Thanks to his assiduity, his vigilance and zeal, or, in a word, to his love, the Esparvienne library had not lost so much as a single leaflet under his supervision during the sixteen years which had now rolled by, this ninth of September, 1912.

CHAPTER III. WHEREIN THE MYSTERY BEGINS

AT seven o'clock on the evening of that day, having as usual replaced all the books which had been taken from their shelves, and having assured himself that he was leaving everything in good order, he quitted the library, double-locking the door after him. According to his usual habit, he dined at the Crèmerie des Quatre Évêques, read his newspaper, La Croix, and at ten o'clock went home to his little house in the Rue du Regard. The good man had no trouble and no presentiment of evil; his sleep was peaceful. The next morning at seven o'clock to the minute, he entered the little room leading to the library, and, according to his daily habit, doffed his grand frock-coat, and taking down an old one which hung in a cupboard over his washstand, put it on. Then he went in to his workroom, where for sixteen years he had been cataloguing six days out of the seven, under the lofty gaze of Alexandre d'Esparvieu. Preparing to make a round of the various rooms, he entered the first and largest, which contained works on theology and religion in huge cupboards whose cornices were adorned with bronze-coloured busts of poets and orators of ancient days.

Two enormous globes representing the earth and the heavens filled the window-embrasures. But at his first step Monsieur Sariette stopped dead, stupefied, powerless alike to doubt or to credit what his eyes beheld. On the blue cloth cover of the writing-table books lay scattered about pell-mell, some lying flat, some standing upright. A number of quartos were heaped up in a tottering pile. Two Greek lexicons, one inside the other, formed a single being more monstrous in shape than the human couples of the divine Plato. A gilt-edged folio was all a-gape, showing three of its leaves disgracefully dog's-eared.

Having, after an interval of some moments, recovered from his profound amazement, the librarian went up to the table and recognised in the confused mass his most valuable Hebrew, French, and Latin Bibles, a unique Talmud, Rabbinical treatises printed and in manuscript, Aramaic and Samaritan texts and scrolls from the synagogues -- in fine, the most precious relics of Israel all lying in a disordered heap, gaping and crumpled.

Monsieur Sariette found himself confronted with an inexplicable phenomenon; nevertheless he sought to account for it. How eagerly he would have welcomed the idea that Monsieur Gaétan, who, being a thoroughly unprincipled man, presumed on the right gained him by his fatal liberality towards the library to rummage there unhindered during his sojourns in Paris, had been the author of this terrible disorder. But Monsieur Gaétan was away travelling in Italy. After pondering for some minutes Monsieur Sariette's next supposition was that Monsieur René d'Esparvieu had entered the library late in the evening with the keys of his manservant Hippolyte, who, for the past twenty-five years, had looked after the second floor and the attics. Monsieur René d'Esparvieu, however, never worked at night, and did not read Hebrew. Perhaps, thought Monsieur Sariette, perhaps he had brought or allowed to be brought to this room some priest, or Jerusalem monk, on his way through Paris; some Oriental savant given to scriptural exegesis. Monsieur Sariette next wondered whether the Abbé Patouille, who had an enquiring mind, and also a habit of dog's-earing his books, had, peradventure, flung himself on these talmudic and biblical texts, fired with sudden zeal to lay bare the soul of Shem. He even asked himself for a moment whether Hippolyte, the old manservant, who had swept and dusted the library for a quarter of a century, and had been slowly poisoned by the dust of accumulated knowledge, had allowed his curiosity to get the better of him, and had been there during the night, ruining his eyesight and his reason, and losing his soul poring by moonlight over these undecipherable symbols. Monsieur Sariette even went so far as to imagine that young Maurice, on leaving his club or some nationalist meeting, might have torn these Jewish volumes from their shelves, out of hatred for old Jacob and his modern posterity; for this young man of family was a declared anti-semite, and only consorted with those Jews who were as anti-semitic as himself. It was giving a very free rein to his imagination, but Monsieur Sariette's brain could not rest, and went wandering about among speculations of the wildest extravagance.

Impatient to know the truth, the zealous guardian of the library called the manservant.

Hippolyte knew nothing. The porter at the lodge could not furnish any clue. None of the domestics had heard a sound. Monsieur Sariette went down to the study of Monsieur René d'Esparvieu, who received him in nightcap and dressing-gown, listened to his story with the air of a serious man bored with idle chatter, and dismissed him with words which conveyed a cruel implication of pity.

"Do not worry, my good Monsieur Sariette; be sure that the books were lying where you left them last night."

Monsieur Sariette reiterated his enquiries a score of times, discovered nothing, and suffered such anxiety that sleep entirely forsook him. When, on the following day at seven o'clock he entered the room with the busts and globes, and saw that all was in order, he heaved a sigh of relief. Then suddenly his heart beat fit to burst. He had just seen lying flat on the mantelpiece a paperbound volume, a modern work, the boxwood paperknife which had served to cut its pages still thrust between the leaves. It was a dissertation on the two parallel versions of Genesis, a work which Monsieur Sariette had relegated to the attic, and which had never left it up to now, no one in Monsieur d'Esparvieu's circle having had the curiosity to differentiate between the parts for which the polytheistic and monotheistic contributors were respectively responsible in the formation of the first of the sacred books. This book bore the label R > 32I4VIII/2. And this painful truth was suddenly borne in upon the mind of Monsieur Sariette: to wit, that the most scientific system of numbering will not help to find a book if the book is no longer in its place. Every day of the ensuing month found the table littered with books. Greek and Latin lay cheek by jowl with Hebrew. Monsieur Sariette asked himself whether these nocturnal flittings were the work of evil-doers who entered by the skylights to steal valuable and precious volumes. But he found no traces of burglary, and, notwithstanding the most minute search, failed to discover that anything had disappeared. Terrible anxiety took possession of his mind, and he fell to wondering whether it was possible that some monkey in the neighbourhood came down the chimney and acted the part of a person engaged in study. Deriving his knowledge of the habits of these animals in the main from the paintings of Watteau and Chardin, he took it that, in the art of imitating gestures or assuming characters they resembled Harlequin, Scaramouch, Zerlin, and the Doctors of the Italian comedy; he imagined them handling a palette and brushes, pounding drugs in a mortar, or turning over the leaves of an old treatise on alchemy beside an athanor. And so it was that, when, on one unhappy morning, he saw a huge blot of ink on one of the leaves of the third volume of the polyglot Bible bound in blue morocco and adorned with the arms of the Comte de Mirabeau, he had no doubt that a monkey was the author of the evil deed. The monkey had been pretending to take notes and had upset the inkpot. It must be a monkey belonging to a learned professor.

Imbued with this idea, Monsieur Sariette carefully studied the topography of the district, so as to draw a cordon round the group of houses amid which the d'Esparvieu house stood. Then he visited the four surrounding streets, asking at every door if there was a monkey in the house. He interrogated porters and their wives, washerwomen, servants, a cobbler, a greengrocer, a glazier, clerks in bookshops, a priest, a bookbinder, two guardians of the peace, children, thus testing the diversity of character and variety of temper in one and the same people; for the replies he received were quite dissimilar in nature; some were rough, some were gentle; there were the coarse and the polished, the simple and the ironical, the prolix and the abrupt, the brief and even the silent. But of the animal he sought he had had neither sight nor sound, when under the archway of an old house in the Rue Servandoni, a small freckled, red-haired girl who looked after the door, made reply:

"There is Monsieur Ordonneau's monkey; would you care to see it?"

And without another word she conducted the old man to a stable at the other end of the yard. There on some rank straw and old bits of cloth, a young macaco with a chain round his middle sat and shivered. He was no taller than a five-year-old child. His livid face, his wrinkled brow, his thin lips were all expressive of mortal sadness. He fixed on the visitor the still lively gaze of his yellow eyes. Then with his small dry hand he seized a carrot, put it to his mouth, and forthwith flung it away. Having looked at the newcomers for a moment, the exile turned away his head, as if he expected nothing further of mankind or of life. Sitting huddled up, one knee in his hand, he made no further movement, but at times a dry cough shook his breast.

"It's Edgar," said the small girl. "He is for sale, you know."

But the old book-lover, who had come armed with anger and resentment, thinking to find a cynical enemy, a monster of malice, an antibibliophile, stopped short, surprised, saddened, and overcome, before this little being devoid of strength and joy and hope.

Recognising his mistake, troubled by the almost human face which sorrow and suffering made more human still, he murmured "Forgive me" and bowed his head.

CHAPTER IV. WHICH IN ITS FORCEFUL BREVITY PROJECTS TO THE LIMITS OF THE ACTUAL WORLD

TWO months elapsed; the domestic upheaval did not subside, and Monsieur Sariette's thoughts turned to the Freemasons. The papers he read were full of their crimes. Abbé Patouille deemed them capable of the darkest deeds, and believed them to be in league with the Jews and meditating the total overthrow of Christendom.

Having now arrived at the acme of power, they wielded a dominating influence in all the principal departments of State, they ruled the Chambers, there were five of them in the Ministry, and they filled the Elysée. Having some time since assassinated a President of the Republic because he was a patriot, they were getting rid of the accomplices and witnesses of their execrable crime. Few days passed without Paris being terror-stricken at some mysterious murder hatched in their Lodges. These were facts concerning which no doubt was possible. By what means did they gain access to the library? Monsieur Sariette could not imagine. What task had they come to fulfil? Why did they attack sacred antiquity and the origins of the Church? What impious designs were they forming? A heavy shadow hung over these terrible undertakings. The Catholic archivist feeling himself under the eye of the sons of Hiram was terrified and fell ill.

Scarcely had he recovered, when he resolved to pass the night in the very spot where these terrible mysteries were enacted, and to take the subtle and dangerous visitors by surprise. It was an enterprise that demanded all his slender courage. Being a man of delicate physique and of nervous temperament. Monsieur Sariette was naturally inclined to be fearful. On the 8th of January at nine o'clock in the evening while the city lay asleep under a whirling snowstorm, he built up a good fire in the room containing the busts of the ancient poets and philosophers, and ensconced himself in an armchair at the chimney corner, a rug over his knees. On a small stand within reach of his hand were a lamp, a bowl of black coffee, and a revolver borrowed from the youthful Maurice. He tried to read his paper, La Croix, but the letters danced beneath his eyes. So he stared hard in front of him, saw nothing but the shadow, heard nothing but the wind, and fell asleep.

When he awoke the fire was out, the lamp was extinguished, leaving an acrid smell behind. But all around, the darkness was filled with milky brightness and phosphorescent lights. He thought he saw something flutter on the table. Stricken to the marrow with cold and terror, but upheld by a resolve stronger than any fear, he rose, approached the table, and passed his hands over the cloth.

He saw nothing; even the lights faded, but under his fingers he felt a folio wide open; he tried to close it, the book resisted, jumped up and hit the imprudent librarian three blows on the head.

Monsieur Sariette fell down unconscious....

Since then things had gone from bad to worse. Books left their allotted shelves in greater profusion than ever, and sometimes it was impossible to replace them; they disappeared. Monsieur Sariette discovered fresh losses daily. The Bollandists were now an imperfect set, thirty volumes of exegesis were missing. He himself had become unrecognisable. His face had shrunk to the size of one's fist and grown yellow as a lemon, his neck was elongated out of all proportion, his shoulders drooped, the clothes he wore hung on him as an a peg. He ate nothing, and at the Cremetie des Quatre Évêques he would sit with dull eyes and bowed head, staring fixedly and vacantly at the saucer where, in a muddy juice, floated his stewed prunes. He did not hear old Guinardon relate how he had at last begun to restore the Delacroix paintings at St. Sulpice.

Monsieur René d'Esparvieu, when he heard the unhappy curator's alarming reports, used to answer drily:

"These books have been mislaid, they are not lost; look carefully, Monsieur Sariette, look carefully and you will find them."

And he murmured behind the old man's back:

"Poor old Sariette is in a bad way."

"I think," replied Abbé Patouille, "that his brain is going."

CHAPTER V. WHEREIN EVERYTHING SEEMS STRANGE
BECAUSE EVERYTHING IS LOGICAL

THE Chapel of the Holy Angels, which lies on the right hand as you enter the Church of St. Sulpice, was hidden behind a scaffolding of planks. Abbé Patouille, Monsieur Gaétan, Monsieur Maurice, his nephew, and Monsieur Sariette, entered in single file through the low door cut in the wooden hoarding, and found old Guinardon on the top of his ladder standing in front of the Heliodorus. The old artist, surrounded by all sorts of tools and materials, was putting a white paste in the crack which cut in two the High Priest Onias. Zéphyrine, Paul Baudry's favourite model, Zéphyrine, who had lent her golden hair and polished shoulders to so many Magdalens, Marguerites, sylphs, and mermaids, and who, it is said, was beloved of the Emperor Napoleon III, was standing at the foot of the ladder with tangled locks, cadaverous cheeks, and dim eyes, older than old Guinardon, whose life she had shared for more than half a century. She had brought the painter's lunch in a basket.

Although the slanting rays fell grey and cold through the leaded and iron-barred window, Delacroix's colouring shone resplendent, and the roses on the cheeks of men and angels dimmed with their glorious beauty the rubicund countenance of old Guinardon, which stood out in relief against one of the temple's columns. These frescoes of the Chapel of the Holy Angels, though derided and insulted when they first appeared, have now become part of the classic tradition, and are united in immortality with the masterpieces of Rubens and Tintoretto.

Old Guinardon, bearded and long-haired, looked like Father Time effacing the works of man's genius. Gaétan, in alarm, called out to him:

"Carefully, Monsieur Guinardon, carefully. Do not scrape too much."

The painter reassured him.

"Fear nothing, Monsieur Gaétan. I do not paint in that style. My art is a higher one. I work after the manner of Cimabue, Giotto, and Beato Angelico, not in the style of Delacroix. This surface here is too heavily charged with contrast and opposition to give a really sacred effect. It is true that Chenavard said that Christianity loves the picturesque, but Chenavard was a rascal with neither faith nor principle -- an infidel.... Look, Monsieur d'Esparvieu, I fill up the crevice, I relay the scales of paint which are peeling. That is all.... The damage, due to the sinking of the wall, or more probably to a seismic shock, is confined to a very small space. This painting of oil and wax applied on a very dry foundation is far more solid than one might think.

"I saw Delacroix engaged on this work. Impassioned but anxious, he modelled feverishly, scraped out, re-painted unceasingly; his mighty hand made childish blunders, but the thing is done with the mastery of a genius and the inexperience of a schoolboy. It is a marvel how it holds."

The good man was silent, and went on filling in the crevice.

"How classic and traditional the composition is," said Gaétan. "Time was when one could recognise nothing but its amazing novelty; now one can see in it a multitude of old Italian formulas."

"I may allow myself the luxury of being just, I possess the qualifications," said the old man from the top of his lofty ladder. "Delacroix lived in a blasphemous and godless age. A painter of the decadence, he was not without pride nor grandeur. He was greater than his times. But he lacked faith, single-heartedness, and purity. To be able to see and paint angels he needed that virtue of angels and primitives, that supreme virtue which, with God's help, I do my best to practise, chastity."

"Hold your tongue, Michel; you are as big a brute as any of them."

Thus Zéphyrine, devoured with jealousy because that very morning on the stairs she had seen her lover kiss the bread-woman's daughter, to wit the youthful Octavie, who was as squalid and radiant as one of Rembrandt's Brides. She had loved Michel madly in the happy days long since past, and love had never died out in Zéphyrine's heart.

Old Guinardon received the flattering insult with a smile that he dissembled, and raised his eyes to the ceiling, where the archangel Michael, terrible in azure cuirass and gilt helmet, was springing heavenwards in all the radiance of his glory.

Meanwhile Abbé Patouille, blinking, and shielding his eyes with his hat against the glaring light from the window, began to examine the pictures one after another: Heliodorus being scourged by the angels, St. Michael vanquishing the Demons, and the combat of Jacob and the Angel.

"All this is exceedingly fine," he murmured at last, "but why has the artist only represented wrathful angels on these walls? Look where I will in this chapel, I see but heralds of celestial anger, ministers of divine vengeance. God wishes to be feared; He wishes also to be loved. I would fain perceive on these walls messengers of peace and of clemency. I should like to see the Seraphim who purified the lips of the prophet, St. Raphael who gave back his sight to old Tobias, Gabriel who announced the Mystery of the Incarnation to Mary, the Angel who delivered St. Peter from his chains, the Cherubim who bore the dead St. Catherine to the top of Sinai. Above all, I should like to be able to contemplate those heavenly guardians which God gives to every man baptized in His name. We each have one who follows all our steps, who comforts us and upholds us. It would be pleasant indeed to admire these enchanting spirits, these beautiful faces."

"Ah, Abbé! it depends on the point of view," answered Gaétan. "Delacroix was no sentimentalist. Old Ingres was not very far wrong in saying that this great man's work reeks of fire and brimstone. Look at the sombre, splendid beauty of those angels, look at those androgynes so proud and fierce, at those pitiless youths who lift avenging rods against Heliodorus, note this mysterious wrestler touching the patriarch on the hip...."

"Hush," said Abbé Patouille. "According to the Bible he is no angel like the others; if he be an angel, he is the Angel of Creation, the Eternal Son of God. I am surprised that the Venerable Curé of St. Sulpice, who entrusted the decoration of this chapel to Monsieur Eugène Delacroix, did not tell him that the patriarch's symbolic struggle with Him who was nameless took place in profound darkness, and that the subject is quite out of place here, since it prefigures the Incarnation of Jesus Christ. The best artists go astray when they fail to obtain their ideas of Christian iconography from a qualified ecclesiastic. The institutions of Christian art form the subject of numerous works with which you are doubtless acquainted, Monsieur Sariette."

Monsieur Sariette was gazing vacantly about him. It was the third morning after his adventurous night in the library. Being, however, thus called upon by the venerable ecclesiastic, he pulled himself together and replied:

"On this subject we may with advantage consult Molanus, De Historia Sacrarum Imaginum et Picturarum, in the edition given us by Noël Paquot, dated Louvain, 1771; Cardinal Frederico Borromeo, De Pictura Sacra, and the Iconography of Didron; but this last work must be read with caution."

Having thus spoken, Monsieur Sariette relapsed into silence. He was pondering on his devastated library.

"On the other hand," continued Abbé Patouille, "since an example of the holy anger of the angels was necessary in this chapel, the painter is to be commended for having depicted for us in imitation of Raphael the heavenly messengers who chastised Heliodorus. Ordered by Seleucus, king of Syria, to carry off the treasures contained in the Temple, Heliodorus was stricken by an angel in a cuirass of gold mounted on a magnificently caparisoned steed. Two other angels smote him with rods. He fell to earth, as Monsieur Delacroix shows us here, and was swallowed up in darkness. It is right and salutary that this adventure should be cited as an example to the Republican Commissioners of Police and to the sacrilegious agents of the law. There will always be Heliodoruses, but, let it be known, every time they lay their hands on the property of the Church, which is the property of the poor, they shall be chastised with rods and blinded by the angels."

"I should like this painting, or, better still, Raphael's sublimer conception of the same subject, to be engraved in little pictures fully coloured, and distributed as rewards in all the schools."

"Uncle," said young Maurice, with a yawn, "I think these things are simply ghastly. I prefer Matisse and Metzinger."

These words fell unheeded, and old Guinardon from his ladder held forth: "Only the primitives caught a glimpse of Heaven. Beauty is only to be found between the thirteenth and fifteenth centuries. The antique, the impure antique, which regained its pernicious influence over the minds of the sixteenth century, inspired poets and painters with criminal notions and immodest conceptions, with horrid impurities, filth. All the artists of the Renaissance were swine, including Michael-Angelo."

Then, perceiving that Gaétan was on the point of departure, Père Guinardon assumed an air of bonhomie, and said to him in a confidential tone:

"Monsieur Gaétan, if you're not afraid of climbing up my five flights, come and have a look at my den. I've got two or three little canvases I wouldn't mind parting with, and they might interest you. All good, honest, straightforward stuff. I'll show you, among other things, a tasty, spicy little Baudouin that would make your mouth water."

At this speech Gaétan made off. As he descended the church steps and turned down the Rue Princesse, he found himself accompanied by old Sariette, and fell to unburdening himself to him, as he would have done to any human creature, or indeed to a tree, a lamp-post, a dog, or his own shadow, of the indignation with which the esthetic theories of the old painter inspired him.

"Old Guinardon overdoes it with his Christian art and his Primitives! Whatever the artist conceives of Heaven is borrowed from earth; God, the Virgin, the Angels, men and women, saints, the light, the clouds. When he was designing figures for the chapel windows at Dreux, old Ingres drew from life a pure, fine study of a woman, which may be seen, among many others, in the Musee Bonnat at Bayonne. Old Ingres had written at the bottom of the page in case he should forget: 'Mademoiselle Cecile, admirable legs and thighs' -- and so as to make Mademoiselle Cecile into a saint in Paradise, he gave her a robe, a cloak, a veil, inflicting thus a shameful decline in her estate, for the tissues of Lyons and Genoa are worthless compared with the youthful living tissue, rosy with pure blood; the most beautiful draperies are despicable compared with the lines of a beautiful body. In fact, clothing for flesh that is desirable and ripe for wedlock is an unmerited shame, and the worst of humiliations"; and Gaétan, walking carelessly in the gutter of the Rue Garancière, continued: "Old Guinardon is a pestilential idiot. He blasphemes Antiquity, sacred Antiquity, the age when the gods were kind. He exalts an epoch when the painter and the sculptor had all their lessons to learn over again. In point of fact, Christianity has run contrary to art in so much as it has not favoured the study of the nude. Art is the representation of nature, and nature is pre-eminently the human body; it is the nude."

"Pardon, pardon," purred old Sariette. "There is such a thing as spiritual, or, as one might term it, inward beauty, which, since the days of Fra Angelico down to those of Hippolyte Flandrin, Christian art has --"

But Gaétan, never hearing a word of all this, went on hurling his impetuous observations at the stones of the old street and the snow-laden clouds overhead:

"The Primitives cannot be judged as a whole, for they are utterly unlike each other. This old madman confounds them all together. Cimabue is a corrupt Byzantine, Giotto gives hints of powerful genius, but his modelling is bad, and, like children, he gives all his characters the same face. The early Italians have grace and joy, because they are Italians. The Venetians have an instinct for fine colour. But when all is said and done these exquisite craftsmen enamel and gild rather than paint. There is far too much softness about the heart and the colouring of your saintly Angelico for me. As for the Flemish school, that's quite another pair of shoes. They can use their hands, and in glory of workmanship they are on a level with the Chinese lacquer-workers. The technique of the brothers Van Eyck is a marvel, but I cannot discover in their Adoration of the Lamb the charm and mystery that some have vaunted. Everything in it is treated with a pitiless perfection; it is vulgar in feeling and cruelly ugly. Memling may touch one perhaps; but he creates nothing but sick wretches and cripples; under the heavy, rich, and ungraceful robing of his virgins and saints one divines some very lamentable anatomy. I did not wait for Rogier van der Wyden to call himself Roger de la Pasture and turn Frenchman in order to prefer him to Memling. This Rogier or Roger is less of a ninny; but then he is more lugubrious, and the rigidity of his lines bears eloquent testimony to his poverty-stricken figures. It is a strange perversion to take pleasure in these carnivalesque figures when one can have the paintings of Leonardo, Titian, Correggio, Velasquez, Rubens, Rembrandt, Poussin, or Prud'hon. Really it is a perverted instinct."

Meanwhile the Abbé Patouille and Maurice d'Esparvieu were strolling leisurely along in the wake of the esthete and the librarian. As a general rule the Abbé Patouille was little inclined to talk theology with laymen, or, for that matter, with clerics either. Carried away, however, by the attractiveness of the subject, he was telling the youthful Maurice all about the sacred mission of those guardian angels which Monsieur Delacroix had so inopportunely excluded from his picture. And in order to give more adequate expression to his thoughts on such lofty themes, the Abbé Patouille borrowed whole phrases and sentences from Bossuet. He had got them up by heart to put in his sermons, for he adhered strongly to tradition.

"Yes, my son," he was saying, "God has appointed tutelary spirits to be near us. They come to us laden with His gifts. They return laden with our prayers. Such is their task. Not an hour, not a moment passes but they are at our side, ready to help us, ever fervent and unwearying guardians, watchmen that never slumber."

"Quite so, Abbé," murmured Maurice, who was wondering by what cunning artifice he could get on the soft side of his mother and persuade her to give him some money of which he was urgently in need.

CHAPTER VI. WHEREIN PÈRE SARIETTE DISCOVERS HIS MISSING TREASURES

NEXT morning Monsieur Sariette entered Monsieur René d'Esparvieu's study without knocking. He raised his arms to the heavens, his few hairs were standing straight up on his head. His eyes were big with terror. In husky tones he stammered out the dreadful news. A very old manuscript of Flavius Josephus; sixty volumes of all sizes; a priceless jewel, namely, a Lucretius adorned with the arms of Philippe de Vendôme, Grand Prior of France, with notes in Voltaire's own hand; a manuscript of Richard Simon, and a set of Gassendi's correspondence with Gabriel Naudé, comprising two hundred and thirty-eight unpublished letters, had disappeared. This time the owner of the library was alarmed.

He mounted in haste to the abode of the philosophers and the globes, and there with his own eyes confirmed the magnitude of the disaster.

There were yawning gaps on many a shelf. He searched here and there, opened cupboards, dragged out brooms, dusters, and fire-extinguishers, rattled the shovel in the coke fire, shook out Monsieur Sariette's best frock-coat that was hanging in the cloak-room, and then stood and gazed disconsolately at the empty places left by the Gassendi portfolios.

For the past half-century the whole learned world had been loudly clamouring for the publication of this correspondence. Monsieur René d'Esparvieu had not responded to the universal desire, unwilling either to assume so heavy a task, or to resign it to others. Having found much boldness of thought in these letters, and many passages of more libertine tendency than the piety of the twentieth century could endure, he preferred that they should remain unpublished; but he felt himself responsible for their safe-keeping, not only to his country but to the whole civilized world.

"How can you have allowed yourself to be robbed of such a treasure?" he asked severely of Monsieur Sariette.

"How can I have allowed myself to be robbed of such a treasure?" repeated the unhappy librarian. "Monsieur, if you opened my breast, you would find that question engraved upon my heart."

Unmoved by this powerful utterance, Monsieur d'Esparvieu continued with pent-up fury:

"And you have discovered no single sign that would put you on the track of the thief, Monsieur Sariette? You have no suspicion. not the faintest idea, of the way these things have come to pass? You have seen nothing, heard nothing, noticed nothing, learnt nothing? You must grant this is unbelievable. Think,

Monsieur Sariette, think of the possible consequences of this unheard-of theft, committed under your eyes. A document of inestimable value in the history of the human mind disappears. Who has stolen it? Why has it been stolen? Who will gain by it? Those who have got possession of it doubtless know that they will be unable to dispose of it in France. They will go and sell it in America or Germany. Germany is greedy for such literary monuments. Should the correspondence of Gassendi with Gabriel Naudé go over to Berlin, if it is published there by German savants, what a disaster, nay, what a scandal! Monsieur Sariette, have you not thought of that?..."

Beneath the stroke of an accusation all the more cruel in that he brought it against himself, Monsieur Sariette stood stupefied, and was silent. And Monsieur d'Esparvieu continued to overwhelm him with bitter reproaches.

"And you make no effort. You devise nothing to find these inestimable treasures. Make enquiries, bestir yourself, Monsieur Sariette; use your wits. It is well worth while."

And Monsieur d'Esparvieu went out, throwing an icy glance at his librarian.

Monsieur Sariette sought the lost books and manuscripts in every spot where he had already sought them a hundred times, and where they could not possibly be. He even looked in the coke-box and under the leather seat of his arm-chair. When midday struck he mechanically went downstairs. At the foot of the stairs he met his old pupil Maurice, with whom he exchanged a bow. But he only saw men and things as through a mist.

The broken-hearted curator had already reached the hall when Maurice called him back.

"Monsieur Sariette, while I think of it, do have the books removed that are choking up my gardenhouse."

"What books, Maurice?"

"I could not tell you, Monsieur Sariette, but there are some in Hebrew, all worm-eaten, with a whole heap of old papers. They are in my way. You can't turn round in the passage."

"Who took them there?"

"I'm bothered if I know."

And the young man rushed off to the diningroom, the luncheon gong having sounded quite a minute ago.

Monsieur Sariette tore away to the summerhouse. Maurice had spoken the truth. About a hundred volumes were there, on tables, on chairs, even on the floor. When he saw them he was divided betwixt joy and fear, filled with amazement and anxiety. Happy in the finding of his lost treasure, dreading to lose it again, and completely overwhelmed with astonishment, the man of books alternately babbled like an infant and uttered the hoarse cries of a maniac. He recognised his Hebrew Bibles, his ancient Talmuds, his very old manuscript of Flavius Josephus, his portfolios of Gassendi's letters to Gabriel Naudé, and his richest jewel of all, to wit, Lucretius adorned with the arms of the Grand Prior of France, and with notes in Voltaire's own hand. He laughed, he cried, he kissed the morocco, the calf, the parchment, and vellum, even the wooden boards studded with nails.

As fast as Hippolyte, the manservant, returned with an armful to the library, Monsieur Sariette, with a trembling hand, restored them piously to their places.

CHAPTER VII. OF A SOMEWHAT LIVELY INTEREST, WHEREOF
THE MORAL WILL, I HOPE, APPEAL GREATLY TO MY READER,
SINCE IT CAN BE EXPRESSED BY THIS SORROWFUL QUERY:
"THOUGHT, WHITHER DOST THOU LEAD ME?" FOR IT IS A
UNIVERSALLY ADMITTED TRUTH THAT IT IS UNHEALTHY TO
THINK AND THAT TRUE WISDOM LIES IN NOT THINKING AT ALL

ALL the books were now once more assembled in the pious keeping of
Monsieur Sariette. But this happy reunion was not destined to last. The
following night twenty volumes left their places, among them the Lucretius of
Prior de Vendôme. Within a week the old Hebrew and Greek texts had all
returned to the summerhouse, and every night during the ensuing month they left
their shelves and secretly went on the same path. Others betook themselves no
one knew whither.

On hearing of these mysterious occurrences, Monsieur René d'Esparvieu
merely remarked with frigidity to his librarian:

"My poor Sariette, all this is very queer, very queer indeed."

And when Monsieur Sariette tentatively advised him to lodge a formal
complaint or to inform the Commissaire de Police, Monsieur d'Esparvieu cried
out upon him:

"What are you suggesting, Monsieur Sariette? Divulge domestic secrets,
make a scandal! You cannot mean it. I have enemies, and I am proud of it. I
think I have deserved them. What I might complain about is that I am wounded
in the house of my friend, attacked with unheard-of violence, by fervent
loyalists, who, I grant you, are good Catholics, but exceedingly bad
Christians.... In a word, I am watched, spied upon, shadowed, and you suggest,
Monsieur Sariette, that I should make a present of this comic-opera mystery, this
burlesque adventure, this story in which we both cut somewhat pitiable figures,
to a set of spiteful journalists? Do you wish to cover me with ridicule?"

The result of the colloquy was that the two gentlemen agreed to change all
the locks in the library. Estimates were asked for and workmen called in. For six
weeks the d'Esparvieu household rang from morning till night with the sound of
hammers, the hum of centre-bits, and the grating of files. Fires were always
going in the abode of the philosophers and globes, and the people of the house
were simply sickened by the smell of heated oil. The old, smooth, easy-running
locks were replaced, on the cupboards and doors of the rooms, by stubborn and
tricky fastenings. There was nothing but combinations of locks, letter-padlocks,
safety-bolts, bars, chains, and electric alarm-bells.

All this display of ironmongery inspired fear. The lock-cases glistened, and there was much grinding of bolts. To gain access to a room, a cupboard, or a drawer, it was necessary to know a certain number, of which Monsieur Sariette alone was cognisant. His head was filled with bizarre words and tremendous numbers, and he got entangled among all these cryptic signs, these square, cubic, and triangular figures. He himself couldn't get the doors and the cupboards undone, yet every morning he found them wide open, and the books thrown about, ransacked, and hidden away. In the gutter of the Rue Servandoni a policeman picked up a volume of Salomon Reinach on the identity of Barabbas and Jesus Christ. As it bore the bookplate of the d'Esparvieu library he returned it to the owner.

Monsieur René d'Esparvieu, not even deigning to inform Monsieur Sariette of the fact, made up his mind to consult a magistrate, a friend in whom he had complete confidence, to wit, a certain Monsieur des Aubels, Counsel at the Law Courts, who had put through many an important affair. He was a little plump man, very red, very bald, with a cranium that shone like a billiard ball. He entered the library one morning feigning to come as a booklover, but he soon showed that he knew nothing about books. While all the busts of the ancient philosophers were reflected in his shining pate, he put divers insidious questions to Monsieur Sariette, who grew uncomfortable and turned red, for innocence is easily flustered. From that moment Monsieur des Aubels had a mighty suspicion that Monsieur Sariette was the perpetrator of the very thefts he denounced with horror; and it immediately occurred to him to seek out the accomplices of the crime. As regards motives, he did not trouble about them; motives are always to be found. Monsieur des Aubels told Monsieur René d'Esparvieu that, if he liked, he would have the house secretly watched by a detective from the Prefecture.

"I will see that you get Mignon," he said. "He is an excellent servant, assiduous and prudent."

By six o'clock next morning Mignon was already walking up and down outside the d'Esparvieus' house, his head sunk between his shoulders, wearing love-locks which showed from under the narrow brim of his bowler hat, his eye cocked over his shoulder. He wore an enormous dull-black moustache, his hands and feet were huge; in fact, his whole appearance was distinctly memorable. He paced regularly up and down from the nearest of the big rams' head pillars which adorn the Hôtel de la Sordiere to the end of the Rue Garancière, towards the apse of St. Sulpice Church and the dome of the Chapel of the Virgin.

Henceforth it became impossible to enter or leave the d'Esparvieus' house without feeling that one's every action, that one's very thoughts, were being spied upon. Mignon was a prodigious person endowed with powers that Nature denies to other mortals. He neither ate nor slept. At all hours of the day and night, in wind and rain, he was to be found outside the house, and no one escaped the X-rays of his eye. One felt pierced through and through, penetrated to the very marrow, worse than naked, bare as a skeleton. It was the affair of a moment; the detective did not even stop, but continued his everlasting walk. It became intolerable. Young Maurice threatened to leave the paternal roof if he was to be so radiographed. His mother and his sister Berthe complained of his piercing look; it offended the chaste modesty of their souls. Mademoiselle Caporal, young Léon d'Esparvieu's governess, felt an indescribable embarrassment. Monsieur René d'Esparvieu was sick of the whole business. He never crossed his own threshold without crushing his hat over his eyes to avoid the investigating ray and without wishing old Sariette, the fons et origo of all the evil, at the devil. The intimates of the household, such as Abbé Patouille and Uncle Gaétan, made themselves scarce; visitors gave up calling, tradespeople hesitated about leaving their goods, the carts belonging to the big shops scarcely dared stop. But it was among the domestics that the spying roused the most disorder.

The footman, afraid, under the eye of the police, to go and join the cobbler's wife over her solitary labours in the afternoon, found the house unbearable and gave notice. Odile, Madame d'Esparvieu's lady's-maid, not daring, as was her custom after her mistress had retired, to introduce Octave, the handsomest of the neighbouring bookseller's clerics, to her little room upstairs, grew melancholy, irritable and nervous, pulled her mistress's hair while dressing it, spoke insolently, and made advances to Monsieur Maurice. The cook, Madame Malgoire, a serious matron of some fifty years, having no more visits from Auguste, the wine-merchant's man in the Rue Servandoni, and being incapable of suffering a privation so contrary to her temperament, went mad, sent up a raw rabbit to table, and announced that the Pope had asked her hand in marriage. At last, after a fortnight of superhuman assiduity, contrary to all known laws of organic life, and to the essential conditions of animal economy, Mignon, the detective, having observed nothing abnormal, ceased his surveillance and withdrew without a word, refusing to accept a gratuity. In the library the dance of the books became livelier than ever.

"That is all right," said Monsieur des Aubels. "Since nothing comes in nor goes out, the evil-doer must be in the house."

The magistrate thought it possible to discover the criminal without police-warrant or enquiry. On a date agreed upon at midnight, he had the floor of the library, the treads of the stairs, the vestibule, the garden path leading to Monsieur Maurice's summer-house, and the entrance hall of the latter, all covered with a coating of talc.

The following morning Monsieur des Aubels, assisted by a photographer from the Prefecture, and accompanied by Monsieur René d'Esparvieu and Monsieur Sariette, came to take the imprints. They found nothing in the garden, the wind had blown away the coating of talc; nothing in the summer-house either. Young Maurice told them he thought it was some practical joke and that he had brushed away the white dust with the hearthbrush. The real truth was, he had effaced the traces left by the boots of Odile, the lady's-maid. On the stairs and in the library the very light print of a bare foot could be discerned, it seemed to have sprung into the air and to have touched the ground at rare intervals and without any pressure. They discovered five of these traces. The clearest was to be found in the abode of the busts and spheres, on the edge of the table where the books were piled. The photographer took several negatives of this imprint.

"This is more terrifying than anything else," murmured Monsieur Sariette.

Monsieur des Aubels did not hide his surprise.

Three days later the anthropometrical department of the Prefecture returned the proofs exhibited to them, saying that they were not in the records.

After dinner Monsieur René showed the photographs to his brother Gaétan, who examined them with profound attention, and after a long silence exclaimed:

"No wonder they have not got this at the Prefecture; it is the foot of a god or of an athlete of antiquity. The sole that made this impression is of a perfection unknown to our races and our climates. It exhibits toes of exquisite grace, and a divine heel."

René d'Esparvieu cried out upon his brother for a madman.

"He is a poet," sighed Madame d'Esparvieu.

"Uncle," said Maurice, "you'll fall in love with this foot if you ever come across it."

"Such was the fate of Vivant Denon, who accompanied Bonaparte to Egypt," replied Gaétan. "At Thebes, in a tomb violated by the Arabs, Denon found the little foot of a mummy of marvellous beauty. He contemplated it with extraordinary fervour. 'It is the foot of a young woman,' he pondered, 'of a princess -- of a charming creature. No covering has ever marred its perfect shape.' Denon admired, adored, and loved it. You may see a drawing of this little foot in Denon's atlas of his journey to Egypt, whose leaves one could turn over upstairs, without going further afield, if only Monsieur Sariette would ever let us see a single volume of his library."

Sometimes, in bed, Maurice, waking in the middle of the night, thought he heard the sound of pages being turned over in the next room, and the thud of bound volumes falling on the floor.

One morning at five o'clock he was coming home from the club, after a night of bad luck, and while he stood outside the door of the summer-house, hunting in his pocket for his keys, his ears distinctly heard a voice sighing:

"Knowledge, whither dost thou lead me? Thought, whither dost thou lure me?"

But entering the two rooms he saw nothing, and told himself that his ears must have deceived him.

CHAPTER VIII. WHICH SPEAKS OF LOVE, A SUBJECT WHICH ALWAYS GIVES PLEASURE, FOR A TALE WITHOUT LOVE IS LIKE BEEF WITHOUT MUSTARD: AN INSIPID DISH

NOTHING ever astonished Maurice. He never sought to know the causes of things and dwelt tranquilly in the world of appearances. Not denying the eternal truth, he nevertheless followed vain things as his fancy led him.

Less addicted to sport and violent exercise than most young people of his generation, he followed unconsciously the old erotic traditions of his race. The French were ever the most gallant of men, and it were a pity they should lose this advantage. Maurice preserved it. He was in love with no woman, but, as St. Augustine said, he loved to love. After paying the tribute that was rightly due to the imperishable beauty and secret arts of Madame de la Bertheliere, he had enjoyed the impetuous caresses of a young singer called Luciole. At present he was joylessly experiencing the primitive perversity of Odile, his mother's lady's-maid, and the tearful adoration of the beautiful Madame Boittier. And he felt a great void in his heart.

It chanced that one Wednesday, on entering the drawing-room where his mother entertained her friends -- who were, generally speaking, unattractive and austere ladies, with a sprinkling of old men and very young people he noticed, in this intimate circle, Madame des Aubels, the wife of the magistrate at the Law Courts, whom Monsieur d'Esparvieu had vainly consulted on the mysterious ransacking of his library. She was young, he found her pretty, and not without cause. Gilberte had been modelled by the Genius of the Race, and no other genius had had a part in the work.

Thus all her attributes inspired desire, and nothing in her shape or her being aroused any other sentiment.

The law of attraction which draws world to world moved young Maurice to approach this delicious creature, and under its influence he offered to escort her to the tea-table. And when Gilberte was served with tea, he said:

"We should hit it off quite well together, you and I, don't you think?"

He spoke in this way, according to modern usage, so as to avoid inane compliments and to spare a woman the boredom of listening to one of those old declarations of love which, containing nothing but what is vague and undefined, require neither a truthful nor an exact reply.

And profiting by the fact that he had an opportunity of conversing secretly with Madame des Aubels for a few minutes, he spoke urgently an to the point. Gilberte, so far as one could judge was made rather to awaken desire than to feel it. Nevertheless, she well knew that her fate was to love, and she followed it willingly and with pleasure. Maurice did not particularly displease her. She would have preferred him to be an orphan, for experience had taught her how disappointing it sometimes is to love the son of the house.

"Will you?" he said by way of conclusion.

She pretended not to understand, and with her little foie-gras sandwich raised half-way to her mouth she looked at Maurice with wondering eyes.

"Will I what?" she asked.

"You know quite well."

Madame des Aubels lowered her eyes, and sipped her tea, for her prudishness was not quite vanquished. Meanwhile Maurice, taking her empty cup from her hand, murmured:

"Saturday, five o'clock, 126 Rue de Rome, on the ground-floor, the door on the right, under the arch. Knock three times."

Madame des Aubels glanced severely and imperturbably at the son of the house, and with a self-possessed air rejoined the circle of highly respectable women to whom the Senator Monsieur Le Fol was explaining how artificial incubators were employed at the agricultural colony at St. Julienne.

The following Saturday, Maurice, in his groundfloor flat, awaited Madame des Aubels. He waited her in vain. No light hand came to knock three times on the door under the arch. And Maurice gave way to imprecation, inwardly calling the absent one a jade and a hussy. His fruitless wait, his frustrated desires, rendered him unjust. For Madame des Aubels in not coming where she had never promised to go hardly deserved these names; but we judge human actions by the pleasure or pain they cause us.

Maurice did not put in an appearance in his mother's drawing-room until a fortnight after the conversation at the tea-table. He came late. Madame des Aubels had been there for half an hour. He bowed coldly to her, took a seat some way off, and affected to be listening to the talk.

"Worthily matched," a rich male voice was saying; "the two antagonists were well calculated to render the struggle a terrible and uncertain one. General Bol, with unprecedented tenacity, maintained his position as though he were rooted in the very soil. General Milpertuis, with an agility truly superhuman, kept carrying out movements of the most dazzling rapidity around his immovable adversary. The battle continued to be waged with terrible stubbornness. We were all in an agony of suspense...."

It was General d'Esparvieu describing the autumn manoeuvres to a company of breathlessly interested ladies. He was talking well and his audience were delighted. Proceeding to draw a comparison between the French and German methods, he defined their distinguishing characteristics and brought out the conspicuous merits of both with a lofty impartiality. He did not hesitate to affirm that each system had its advantages, and at first made it appear to his circle of wondering, disappointed, and anxious dames, whose countenances were growing increasingly gloomy, that France and Germany were practically in a position of equality. But little by little, as the strategist went on to give a clearer definition of the two methods, that of the French began to appear flexible, elegant, vigorous, full of grace, cleverness, and verve; that of the Germans heavy, clumsy, and undecided. And slowly and surely the faces of the ladies began to clear and to light up with joyous smiles. In order to dissipate any lingering shadows of misgiving from the minds of these wives, sisters, and sweethearts, the General gave them to understand that we were in a position to make use of the German method when it suited us, but that the Germans could not avail themselves of the French method. No sooner had he delivered himself of these sentiments than he was button-holed by Monsieur le Truc de Ruffec, who was engaged in founding a patriotic society known as "Swordsmen All," of which the object was to regenerate France and ensure her superiority over all her adversaries. Even children in the cradle were to be enrolled, and Monsieur le Truc de Ruffec offered the honorary presidency to General d'Esparvieu.

Meanwhile Maurice was appearing to be interested in a conversation that was taking place between a very gentle old lady and the Abbé Lapetite, Chaplain to the Dames du Saint Sang. The old lady, severely tried of late by illness and the loss of friends, wanted to know how it was that people were unhappy in this world.

"How," she asked Abbé Lapetite, "do you explain the scourges that afflict mankind? Why are there plagues, famines, floods, and earthquakes?"

"It is surely necessary that God should sometimes remind us of his existence," replied Abbé Lapetite, with a heavenly smile.

Maurice appeared keenly interested in this conversation. Then he seemed fascinated by Madame Fillot-Grandin, quite a personable young woman, whose simple innocence, however, detracted all piquancy from her beauty, all savour from her bodily charms. A very sour, shrill-voiced old lady, who, affecting the dowdy, woollen weeds of poverty, displayed the pride of a great lady in the world of Christian finance, exclaimed in a squeaky voice:

"Well, my dear Madame d'Esparvieu, so you have had trouble here. The papers speak darkly of robbery, of thefts committed in Monsieur d'Esparvieu's valuable library, of stolen letters...."

"Oh," said Madame d'Esparvieu, "if we are to believe all the newspapers say..."

"Oh, so, dear Madame, you have got your treasures back. All's well that ends well."

"The library is in perfect order," asserted Madame d'Esparvieu. "There is nothing missing."

"The library is on the floor above this, is it not?" asked young Madame des Aubels, showing an unexpected interest in the books.

Madame d'Esparvieu replied that the library occupied the whole of the second floor, and that they had put the least valuable books in the attics.

"Could I not go and look at it?"

The mistress of the house declared that nothing could be easier. She called to her son:

"Maurice, go and do the honours of the library to Madame des Aubels."

Maurice rose, and without uttering a word, mounted to the second floor in the wake of Madame des Aubels.

He appeared indifferent, but inwardly he rejoiced, for he had no doubt that Gilberte had feigned her ardent desire to inspect the library simply to see him in secret. And, while affecting indifference, he promised himself to renew those offers which, this time, would not be refused.

Under the romantic bust of Alexandre d'Esparvieu, they were met by the silent shadow of a little wan, hollow-eyed old man, who wore a settled expression of mute terror.

"Do not let us disturb you, Monsieur Sariette," said Maurice. "I am showing Madame des Aubels round the library."

Maurice and Madame des Aubels passed on into the great room where against the four walls rose presses filled with books and surmounted by bronze busts of poets, philosophers, and orators of antiquity. All was in perfect order, an order which seemed never to have been disturbed from the beginning of things.

Only, a black void was to be seen in the place which, only the evening before, had been filled by an unpublished manuscript of Richard Simon. Meanwhile, by the side of the young couple walked Monsieur Sariette, pale, faded, and silent.

"Really and truly, you have not been nice," said Maurice, with a look of reproach at Madame des Aubels.

She signed to him that the librarian might overhear. But he reassured her.

"Take no notice. It is old Sariette. He has become a complete idiot." And he repeated:

"No, you have not been at all nice. I awaited you. You did not come. You have made me unhappy."

After a moment's silence, while one heard the low melancholy whistling of asthma in poor Sariette's bronchial tubes, young Maurice continued insistently:

"You are wrong."

"Why wrong?"

"Wrong not to do as I ask you."

"Do you still think so?"

"Certainly."

"You meant it seriously?"

"As seriously as can be."

Touched by his assurance of sincere and constant feeling, and thinking she had resisted sufficiently, Gilberte granted to Maurice what she had refused him a fortnight ago.

They slipped into an embrasure of the window, behind an enormous celestial globe whereon were graven the Signs of the Zodiac and the figures of the stars, and there, their gaze fixed on the Lion, the Virgin, and the Scales, in the presence of a multitude of Bibles, before the works of the Fathers, both Greek and Latin, beneath the casts of Homer, Eschylus, Sophocles, Euripides, Herodotus, Thucydides, Socrates, Plato, Aristotle, Demosthenes, Cicero, Virgil, Horace, Seneca, and Epictetus, they exchanged vows of love and a long kiss on the mouth.

Almost immediately Madame des Aubels bethought herself that she still had some calls to pay, and that she must make her escape quickly, for love had not made her lose all sense of her own importance. But she had barely crossed the landing with Maurice when they heard a hoarse cry and saw Monsieur Sariette plunge madly downstairs, exclaiming as he went:

"Stop it, stop it; I saw it fly away! It escaped from the shelf by itself. It crossed the room... there it is -- there! It's going downstairs. Stop it! It has gone out of the door on the ground floor!"

"What?" asked Maurice.

Monsieur Sariette looked out of the landing window, murmuring horror-struck:

"It's crossing the garden! It's going into the summer-house. Stop it, stop it!"

"But--what is it?" repeated Maurice "in God's name, what is it?"

"My Flavius Josephus," exclaimed Monsieur Sariette. "Stop it!"

And he fell down unconscious.

"You see he is quite mad," said Maurice to Madame des Aubels, as he lifted up the unfortunate librarian.

Gilberte, a little pale, said she also thought she had seen, something in the direction indicated by the unhappy man, something flying.

Maurice had seen nothing, but he had felt what seemed like a gust of wind.

He left Monsieur Sariette in the arms of Hippolyte and the housekeeper, who had both hastened to the spot on hearing the noise.

The old gentleman had a wound in his head.

"All the better," said the housekeeper; "this wound may save him from having a fit."

Madame des Aubels gave her handkerchief to stop the blood, and recommended an arnica compress.

CHAPTER IX. WHEREIN IT IS SHOWN THAT, AS AN ANCIENT GREEK POET SAID, "NOTHING IS SWEETER THAN APHRODITE THE GOLDEN"

ALTHOUGH he had enjoyed Madame des Aubel's favours for six whole months, Maurice still loved her. True they had had to separate during the summer. For lack of funds of his own he had had to go to Switzerland with his mother, and then to stop with the whole family at the Château d'Esparvieu. She had spent the summer with her mother at Niort, and the autumn with her husband at a little Normandy seaside place, so that they had hardly seen each other four or five times. But since the winter, kindly to lovers, had brought them back to town again, Maurice had been receiving her twice a week in his little flat in the Rue de Rome, and received no one else. No other woman had inspired him with feelings of such constancy and fidelity. What augmented his pleasure was that he believed himself loved, and indeed he was not unpleasing.

He thought that she did not deceive him, not that he had any reason to think so, but it appeared right and fitting that she should be content with him alone. What annoyed him was that she always kept him waiting, and was unpunctual in coming to their meeting-place; she was invariably late, -- at times very late.

Now on Saturday, January 30th, since four o'clock in the afternoon, Maurice had been awaiting Madame des Aubels in the little pink room where a bright fire was burning. He was gaily clad in a suit of flowered pyjamas, smoking Turkish cigarettes. At first he dreamt of receiving her with long kisses, with hitherto unknown caresses. A quarter of an hour having passed, he meditated serious and affectionate reproaches, then after an hour of disappointed waiting he vowed he would meet her with cold disdain.

At length she appeared, fresh and fragrant.

"It was scarcely worth while coming," he said bitterly, as she laid her muff and her little bag on the table and untied her veil before the wardrobe mirror.

Never, she told her beloved, had she had such trouble to get away. She was full of excuses, which he obstinately rejected. But no sooner had she the good sense to hold her tongue than he ceased his reproaches, and then nothing detracted him from the longing with which she inspired him.

The curtains were drawn, the room was bathed in warm shadows lit by the dancing gleams of the fire. The mirrors in the wardrobe and on the chimney-piece shone with mysterious lights. Gilberte, leaning on her elbow, head on hand, was lost in thought. A little jeweller, a trustworthy and intelligent man, had shown her a wonderfully pretty pearl and sapphire bracelet; it was worth a great deal, and was to be had for a mere nothing. He had got it from a cocotte down on her luck, who was in a hurry to dispose of it. It was a rare chance; it would be a huge pity to let it slip.

"Would you like to see it, darling? I will ask the little man to let me have it to show you."

Maurice did not actually decline the proposal. But it was clear that he took no interest in the wonderful bracelet. "When small jewellers come across a great bargain, they keep it to themselves, and do not allow their customers to profit by it. Moreover, jewellery means nothing just now. Wellbred women have given up wearing it. Everyone goes in for sport, and jewellery does not go with sport."

Maurice spoke thus, contrary to truth, because having given his mistress a fur coat, he was in no hurry to give her anything more. He was not stingy, but he was careful with his money. His people did not give him a very large allowance, and his debts grew bigger every day. By satisfying the wishes of his inamorata too promptly he feared to arouse others still more pressing. The bargain seemed less wonderful to him than to Gilberte; besides, he liked to take the initiative in choosing his gifts. Above all, he thought that if he gave her too many presents he would be no longer sure of being loved for himself.

Madame des Aubels felt neither contempt nor surprise at this attitude; she was gentle and temperate, she knew men, and judged that one must take them as one found them, that for the most part they do not give very willingly, and that a woman should know how to make them give.

Suddenly a gas lamp was lighted in the street, and shone through the gaps in the curtains.

"Half-past six," she said. "We must be on the move."

Pricked by the touch of Time's fleeting wing, Maurice was conscious of reawakened desires and reanimated powers. A white and radiant offering, Gilberte, with her head thrown back, her eyes half closed, her lips apart, sunk in dreamy languor, was breathing slowly and placidly, when suddenly she started up with a cry of terror.

"Whatever is that?"

"Stay still," said Maurice, holding her back in his arms.

In his present mood, had the sky fallen it would not have troubled him. But in one bound she escaped from him. Crouching down, her eyes filled with terror, she was pointing with her finger at a figure which appeared in a corner of the room, between the fire-place and the wardrobe with the mirror. Then, unable to bear the sight, and nearly fainting, she hid her face in her hands.

CHAPTER X. WHICH FAR SURPASSES IN AUDACITY THE IMAGINATIVE FLIGHTS OF DANTE AND MILTON

MAURICE at length turned his head, saw the figure, and perceiving that it moved, was also frightened. Meanwhile, Gilberte was regaining her senses. She imagined that what she had seen was some mistress whom her lover had hidden in the room. Inflamed with anger and disgust at the idea of such treachery, boiling with indignation, and glaring at her supposed rival, she exclaimed:

"A woman... a naked woman too! You bring me into a room where you allow your women to come, and when I arrive they have not had time to dress. And you reproach me with arriving late! Your impudence is beyond belief! Come, send the creature packing. If you wanted us both here together, you might at least have asked me whether it suited me...."

Maurice, wide-eyed and groping for a revolver that had never been there, whispered in her ear:

"Be quiet... it is no woman. One can scarcely see, but it is more like a man."

She put her hands over her eyes again and screamed harder than ever.

"A man! Where does he come from? A thief. An assassin! Help! Help! Kill him.... Maurice, kill him! Turn on the light. No, don't turn on the light...."

She made a mental vow that should she escape from this danger she would burn a candle to the Blessed Virgin. Her teeth chattered.

The figure made a movement.

"Keep away!" cried Gilberte. "Keep away!"

She offered the burglar all the money and jewels she had on the table if he would consent not to stir. Amid her surprise and terror the idea assailed her that her husband, dissembling his suspicions, had caused her to be followed, had posted witnesses, and had had recourse to the Commissaire de Police. In a flash she distinctly saw before her the long painful future, the glaring scandal, the pretended disdain, the cowardly desertion of her friends, the just mockery of society, for it is indeed ridiculous to be found out. She saw the divorce; the loss of her position and of her rank. She saw the dreary and narrow existence with her mother, when no one would make love to her, for men avoid women who fail to give them the security of the married state. And all this, why? Why this ruin, this disaster? For a piece of folly, for a mere nothing. Thus in a lightning flash spoke the conscience a Gilberte des Aubels.

"Have no fear, Madame," said a very sweet voice.

Slightly reassured, she found strength to ask:

"Who are you?"

"I am an angel," replied the voice.

"What did you say?"

"I am an angel. I am Maurice's guardian angel."

"Say it again. I am going mad. I do not understand...."

Maurice, without understanding either, was indignant. He sprang forward and showed himself; with his right hand armed with a slipper he made a threatening gesture, and said in a rough voice:

"You are a low ruffian; oblige me by going the way you came."

"Maurice d'Esparvieu," continued the sweet voice, "He whom you adore as your Creator has stationed by the side of each of the faithful a good angel, whose mission it is to counsel and protect him; it is the invariable opinion of the Fathers it is founded on many passages in the Bible, the Church admits it unanimously, without, however, pronouncing anathema upon those who hold a contrary opinion. You see before you one of these angels, yours, Maurice. I was commanded to watch over your innocence and to guard your chastity."

"That may be," said Maurice; "but you are certainly no gentleman. A gentleman would not permit himself to enter a room at such a moment. To be plain, what the deuce are you doing here?"

"I have assumed this appearance, Maurice, because, having henceforth to move among mankind, I have to make myself like them. The celestial spirits possess the power of assuming a form which renders them apparent to the eye and to the touch. This shape is real, because it is apparent, and all the realities in the world are but appearances."

Gilberte, pacified at length, was arranging her hair on her forehead.

The Angel pursued:

"The celestial spirits adopt, according to their fancy, one sex or the other, or both at once. But they cannot disguise themselves at any moment, according to their caprice or fantasy. Their metamorphoses are subject to constant laws, which you would not understand. Thus I have neither desire nor power to transform myself under your eyes, for your amusement or my own, into a lion, a tiger, a fly, or into a sycamore-shaving like the young Egyptian whose story was found in a tomb. I cannot change myself into an ass as did Lucius with the pomade of the youthful Photis. For in my wisdom I had fixed beforehand the hour of my apparition to mankind, nothing could hasten or delay it."

Impatient for enlightenment, Maurice asked for the second time:

"Still, what are you up to here?"

Joining her voice to his, Madame des Aubels asked: "Yes, indeed, what are you doing here?'

The Angel replied:

"Man, lend your ear. Woman, hear my voice. I am about to reveal to you a secret on which hangs the fate of the Universe. In rebellion against Him whom you hold to be the Creator of all things visible and invisible, I am preparing the Revolt of the Angels."

"Do not jest," said Maurice, who had faith and did not allow holy things to be played with.

But the Angel answered reproachfully: "What makes you think, Maurice, that I am frivolous and given to vain words?"

"Come, come," said Maurice, shrugging his shoulders. "You are not going to revolt against----"

He pointed to the ceiling -- not daring to finish.

But the Angel continued:

"Do you not know that the sons of God have already revolted and that a great battle took place in the heavens?"

"That was a long time ago." said Maurice, putting on his socks.

Then the Angel replied:

"It was before the creation of the world. But nothing has changed since then in the heavens. The nature of the Angels is no different now from what it was originally. What they did then they could do again now."

"No! It is not possible. It is contrary to faith. If you were an angel, a good angel as you make out you are, it would never occur to you to disobey your Creator."

"You are in error, Maurice, and the authority of the Fathers condemns you. Origen lays it down in his homilies that good angels are fallible, that they sin every day and fall from Heaven like flies. Possibly you may be tempted to reject the authority of this Father, despite his knowledge of the Scriptures, because he is excluded from the Canon of the Saints. If this be so, I would remind you of the second chapter of Revelation, in which the Angels of Ephesus and Pergamos are rebuked for that they kept not ward over their church. You will doubtless contend that the angels to whom the Apostle here refers are, properly speaking, the Bishops of the two cities in question, and that he calls them angels on account of their ministry. It may be so, and I cede the point. But with what arguments, Maurice, would you counter the opinion of all those Doctors and Pontiffs whose unanimous teaching it is that angels may fall from good into evil? Such is the statement made by Saint Jerome in his Epistle to Damasus...."

"Monsieur," said Madame des Aubels, "go away, I beg you."

But the Angel hearkened not, and continued:

"Saint Augustine, in his True Religion, Chapter XIII; Saint Gregory, in his Morals, Chapter XXIV; Isidore----"

"Monsieur, let me get my things on; I am in a hurry."

"In his treatise on The Greatest Good, Book I, Chapter XII; Bede on Job---
-"

"Oh, please, Monsieur..."

"Chapter VIII; John of Damascus on Faith, Book II, Chapter III. Those, I think, are sufficiently weighty authorities, and there is nothing for it, Maurice, but to admit your error. What has led you astray is that you have not duly considered my nature, which is free, active, and mobile, like that of all the angels, and that you have merely observed the grace and felicity with which you deem me so richly endowed. Lucifer possessed no less, yet he rebelled."

"But what on earth are you rebelling for?" asked Maurice.

"Isaiah," answered the child of light, "Isaiah has already asked, before you: 'Quomodo cecidisti de coelo, Lucifer, qui mane oriebaris?' Hearken, Maurice. Before Time was, the Angels rose up to win dominion over Heaven, the most beautiful of the Seraphim revolted through pride. As for me, it is science that has inspired me with the generous desire for freedom. Finding myself near you, Maurice, in a house containing one of the vastest libraries in the world, I acquired a taste for reading and a love of study. While, fordone with the toils of a sensual life, you lay sunk in heavy slumber, I surrounded myself with books, I studied, I pondered over their pages, sometimes in one of the rooms of the library, under the busts of the great men of antiquity, sometimes at the far end of the garden, in the room in the summer-house next to your own."

On hearing these words, young d'Esparvieu exploded with laughter and beat the pillow with his fist, an infallible sign of uncontrollable mirth.

"Ah... ah... ah! It was you who pillaged papa's library and drove poor old Sariette off his head. You know, he has become completely idiotic."

"Busily engaged," continued the Angel, "in cultivating for myself a sovereign intelligence, I paid no heed to that inferior being, and when he thought to offer obstacles to my researches and to disturb my work I punished him for his importunity.

"One particular winter's night in the abode of the philosophers and globes I let fall a volume of great weight on his head, which he tried to tear from my invisible hand. Then more recently raising, with a vigorous arm composed of a column of condensed air, a precious manuscript of Flavius Josephus, I gave the imbecile such a fright, that he rushed out screaming on to the landing and (to borrow a striking expression from Dante Alighieri) fell even as a dead body falls. He was well rewarded, for you gave him, Madame, to staunch the blood from his wound, your little scented handkerchief. It was the day, you may remember, when behind a celestial globe you exchanged a kiss on the mouth with Maurice."

"Monsieur," said Madame des Aubels, with a frown, "I cannot allow you..."

But she stopped short, deeming it was an inopportune moment to appear over-exacting on a matter of decorum.

"I had made up my mind," continued the Angel impassively, "to examine the foundations of belief. I first attacked the monuments of Judaism, and I read all the Hebrew texts."

"You know Hebrew, then?" exclaimed Maurice.

"Hebrew is my native tongue: in Paradise for a long time we have spoken nothing else."

"Ah, you are a Jew. I might have deduced it from your want of tact."

The Angel, not deigning to hear, continued in his melodious voice: "I have delved deep into Oriental antiquities and also into those of Greece and Rome. I have devoured the works of theologians, philosophers, physicists, geologists, and naturalists. I have learnt. I have thought. I have lost my faith."

"What? You no longer believe in God?"

"I believe in Him, since my existence depends on His, and if He should fail to exist, I myself should fall into nothingness. I believe in Him, even as the Satyrs and the Mænads believed in Dionysus and for the same reason. I believe in the God of the Jews and the Christians. But I deny that He created the world; at the most He organised but an inferior part of it, and all that He touched bears the mark of His rough and unforeseeing touch. I do not think He is either eternal or infinite, for it is absurd to conceive of a being who is not bounded by space or time. I think Him limited, even very limited. I no longer believe Him to be the only God. For a long time He did not believe it Himself; in the beginning He was a polytheist; later, His pride and the flattery of His worshippers made Him a monotheist. His ideas have little connection; He is less powerful than He is thought to be. And, to speak candidly, He is not so much a god as a vain and ignorant demiurge. Those who, like myself, know His true nature, call Him Ialdabaoth."

"What's that you say?"

"Ialdabaoth."

"Ialdabaoth. What's that?"

"I have already told you. It is the demiurge whom, in your blindness, you adore as the one and only God."

"You're mad. I don't advise you to go and talk rubbish like that to Abbé Patouille."

"I am not in the least sanguine, my dear Maurice, of piercing the dense night of your intellect. I merely tell you that I am going to engage Ialdabaoth in conflict with some hopes of victory."

"Mark my words, you won't succeed."

"Lucifer shook His throne, and the issue was for a moment in doubt."

"What is your name?"

"Abdiel for the angels and saints, Arcade for mankind."

"Well, my poor Arcade, I regret to see you going to the bad. But confess that you are jesting with us. I could at a pinch understand your leaving Heaven for a woman. Love makes us commit the greatest follies. But you will never make me believe that you, who have seen God face to face, ultimately found the truth in old Sariette's musty books. No, you will never get me to believe that!"

"My dear Maurice, Lucifer was face to face with God, yet he refused to serve Him. As to the kind of truth one finds in books, it is a truth that enables us sometimes to discern what things are not, without ever enabling us to discover what they are. And this poor little truth has sufficed to prove to me that He in whom I blindly believed is not believable, and that men and angels have been deceived by the lies of Ialdabaoth."

"There is no Ialdabaoth. There is God. Come, Arcade, do the right thing. Renounce these follies, these impieties, dis-incarnate yourself, become once more a pure Spirit, and resume your office of guardian angel. Return to duty. I forgive you, but do not let us see you again."

"I should like to please you, Maurice. I feel a certain affection for you, for my heart is soft. But fate henceforth calls me elsewhere towards beings capable of thought and action."

"Monsieur Arcade," said Madame des Aubels, "withdraw, I implore you. It makes me horribly shy to be in this position before two men. I assure you I am not accustomed to it."

CHAPTER XI. RECOUNTS IN WHAT MANNER THE ANGEL, ATTIRED IN THE CAST-OFF GARMENTS OF A SUICIDE, LEAVES THE YOUTHFUL MAURICE WITHOUT A HEAVENLY GUARDIAN

REASSURE yourself, Madame," replied the apparition, "your position is not as risky as you say. You are not confronted with two men, but with one man and an angel."

She examined the stranger with an eye which, piercing the gloom, was anxiously surveying a vague but by no means negligible indication, and asked:

"Monsieur, is it quite certain that you are an angel?"

The apparition prayed her to have no doubt about it, and gave some precise information as to his origin.

"There are three hierarchies of celestial spirits, each composed of nine choirs; the first comprises the Seraphim, Cherubim, and the Thrones; the second, the Dominations, the Virtues, and the Powers; the third, the Principalities, the Archangels, and the Angels properly so called. I belong to the ninth choir of the third hierarchy."

Madame des Aubels, who had her reasons for doubting this, expressed at least one:

"You have no wings."

"Why should I, Madame? Am I bound to resemble the angels on your holy-water stoups? Those feathery oars that beat the waves of the air in rhythmic cadences are not always worn by the heavenly messengers on their shoulders. Cherubim may be apterous. That all too beautiful angelic pair who spent an anxious night in the house of Lot compassed about by an Oriental horde -- they had no wings! No, they appeared just like men, and the dust of the road covered their feet, which the patriarch washed with pious hand. I would beg you to observe, Madame, that according to the Science of Organic Metamorphosis created by Lamarck and Darwin, the wings of birds have been successively transformed into fore-feet in the case of quadrupeds and into arms in the case of the Linnæan primates. And you may remember, Maurice, that by a rather annoying reversion to type, Miss Kate, your English nurse, who used to be so fond of giving you a whipping, had arms very like the pinions of a plucked fowl. One may say, then, that a being possessing both arms and wings is a monster and belongs to the department of Teratology. In Paradise we have Cherubim and Kerûbs in the shape of winged bulls, but those are the clumsy inventions of an inartistic god. It is nevertheless true, quite true, that the Victories of the Temple of Athena Nike on the Athenian Acropolis are beautiful, and possess both arms and wings; it is also true that the Victory of Brescia is beautiful, with her outstretched arms and her long wings folded on her mighty loins. It is one of the miracles of Greek genius to have known how to create harmonious monsters. The Greeks never err. The Moderns always."

"Yet on the whole," said Madame des Aubels, "you have not the look of a pure Spirit."

"Nevertheless, I am one, Madame, if ever there was one. And it ill becomes you, who have been baptised, to doubt it. Several of the Fathers, such as St. Justin, Tertullian, Origen, and Clement of Alexandria thought that the Angels were not purely spiritual, but possessed a body formed of some subtle material. This opinion has been rejected by the Church; hence I am merely Spirit. But what is spirit and what is matter? Formerly they were contrasted as being two opposites, and now your human science tends to reunite them as two aspects of the same thing. It teaches that everything proceeds from ether and everything returns to it, that the same movement transforms the waves of air into stones and minerals, and that the atoms scattered throughout illimitable space, form, by the varying speed of their orbits, all the substance of this material world."

But Madame des Aubels was not listening. She had something on her mind, and to put an end to her suspense, she asked:

"How long have you been here?"

"I came with Maurice."

"Well -- that's a nice thing!" said she, shaking her head. But the Angel continued with heavenly serenity:

"Everything in the Universe is circular, elliptical, or hyperbolic, and the same laws which rule the stars govern this grain of dust. In the original and native movement of its substance, my body is spiritual, but it may affect, as you perceive, this material state, by changing the rhythm of its elements."

Having thus spoken he sat down in a chair on Madame des Aubels' black stockings.

A clock struck outside.

"Good heavens, seven o'clock!" exclaimed Gilberte. "What am I to say to my husband? He thinks I am at that tea-party in the Rue de Rivoli. We are dining with the La Verdelières to-night. Go away immediately, Monsieur Arcade. I must get ready to go. I have not a second to lose."

The Angel replied that he would have willingly obeyed Madame des Aubels had he been in a state to show himself decently in public, but that he could not dream of appearing out of doors without any clothes. "Were I to walk naked in the street," he added, "I should offend a nation attached to its ancient habits, habits which it has never examined. They are the basis of all moral systems. Formerly," he added, "the angels, in revolt like myself, manifested themselves to Christians under grotesque and ridiculous appearances, black, horned, hairy, and cloven-footed. Pure stupidity! They were the laughing-stock of people of taste. They merely frightened old women and children and met with no success."

"It is true he cannot go out as he is," said Madame des Aubels with justice.

Maurice tossed his pyjamas and his slippers to the celestial messenger. Regarded as outdoor habiliments they were not adequate. Gilberte pressed her lover to run at once in quest of other clothes. He proposed to go and get some from the concierge. She was violently opposed to this. It would, she said, be madly imprudent to drag the concierge into such an affair.

"Do you want them to know that..." she exclaimed. She pointed to the Angel and was silent.

Young d'Esparvieu went out to see a clothes-shop.

Meanwhile, Gilberte, who could not delay any longer for fear of causing a horrible society scandal, turned on the light and dressed before the Angel. She did it without any awkwardness, for she knew how to adapt herself to circumstances; and she took it that in such an unheard-of encounter in which heaven and earth were mingled in unutterable confusion it was permissible to retrench in modesty.

Moreover, she knew that she possessed a good figure and had garments as dainty as the fashion demanded. As the apparition's sense of delicacy would not permit him to don Maurice's pyjamas, Gilberte could not help observing by the lamplight that her suspicions were well-founded, and that angels have the same appearance as men. Curious to know if the appearance were real or imaginary she asked the child of light if Angels were like monkeys, who, to win women, merely lack money.

"Yes, Gilberte," replied Arcade, "Angels are capable of loving mortals. It is the teaching of the Scriptures. It is said in the Seventh Book of Genesis, 'When men became numerous on the face of the earth, and daughters were born to them, the sons of God saw that the daughters of men were beautiful, and they took as wives all those which pleased them.'"

"Good heavens," cried Gilberte all at once, "I shall never be able to fasten my dress; it hooks down the back."

When Maurice entered the room he found the Angel on his knees tying the shoes of the woman taken in flagrante delicto.

Taking her muff and her bag off the table she said:

"I have not forgotten anything? No. Goodnight, Monsieur Arcade. Good-night, Maurice. I shall not forget to-day." And she vanished like a dream.

"Here," said Maurice, throwing the Angel a bundle of clothes.

The young man, having seen some dismal rags lying among clarionettes and clyster-pipes in the window of a second-hand shop, had bought for nineteen francs the cast-off suit of some wretched sable-clad mortal who had committed suicide The Angel, with native majesty, took the garments and put them on. Worn by him, they took on an unexpected elegance. He took a step to the door.

"So you are leaving me," said Maurice. "It's settled, then? I very much fear that, some day, you will bitterly regret this hasty action."

"I must not look back. Adieu, Maurice."

Maurice timidly slipped five louis into his hand.

"Adieu, Arcade."

But when the Angel had passed through the door, and all that was to be seen of him in the doorway was his uplifted heel, Maurice called him back.

"Arcade! I never thought of it! I have no guardian angel now!"

"Quite true, Maurice, you have one no longer."

"Then what will become of me? One must have a guardian angel. Tell me, -- are there not grave drawbacks, -- is there no danger in not having one?"

"Before replying, Maurice, I must ask you if you wish me to speak to you according to your belief, which formerly was my own, according to the teaching of the Church and the Catholic faith, or according to natural philosophy."

"I don't care a straw for your natural philosophy. Answer me according to the religion I believe in, and which I profess, and in which I wish to live and die."

"Very well, my dear Maurice. The loss of your guardian angel will probably deprive you of certain spiritual succour, of certain celestial grace. I am expressing to you the unvarying opinion of the Church on the matter. You will lack an assistance, a support, a consolation which would have guided and confirmed you in the way of salvation. You will have less strength to avoid sin, and as it was you hadn't much. In fact, in spiritual matters, you will be without strength and without joy. Adieu, Maurice; when you see Madame des Aubels, please remember me to her."

"You are going?"

"Farewell."

Arcade disappeared, and Maurice in the depths of an arm-chair sat for a long time with his head in his hands.

CHAPTER XII. WHEREIN IT IS SET FORTH HOW THE ANGEL
MIRAR, WHEN BEARING GRACE AND CONSOLATION TO THOSE
DWELLING IN THE NEIGHBOURHOOD OF THE CHAMPS ÉLYSÉES
IN PARIS, BEHELD A MUSICHALL SINGER NAMED BOUCHOTTE
AND FELL IN LOVE WITH HER

THROUGH streets filled with brown fog, pierced with white and yellow lights, where horses exhaled their smoking breath and motors radiated their rapid search-lights, the angel made his way, and, mingling with the black flood of foot-passengers which rolled unceasingly along, proceeded across the town from north to south till he came to the lonely boulevards on the left bank of the river. Not far from the old walls of Port Royal, a small restaurant flings night by night athwart the pavement the clouded rays of its streaming windows. Coming to a halt there, Arcade entered a room full of warm, savoury odours, pleasing to the unfortunate beings faint with cold and hunger. Glancing round him he beheld Russian Nihilists, Italian Anarchists, refugees, conspirators, revolutionaries from every quarter of the globe, picturesque old faces with tumbled masses of hair and beard that swept downwards even as the torrent and the waterfall sweep over their rocky bed. There were young faces of virginal coldness, expressions sombre and wild, pale eyes of infinite sweetness, drawn faces, and, in a corner, there were two Russian women, one extremely lovely, the other hideous, but both resembling each other in their indifference to ugliness and to beauty. But failing to find the face he sought, for there were no angels in the room, he sat down at a small vacant marble table.

Angels, when driven by hunger, eat as do the animals of this earth, and their food, transformed by digestive heat, becomes one with their celestial substance. Seeing three angels under the oaks of Mamre, Abraham offered them cakes, kneaded by Sarah, an whole calf, butter and milk, and they ate. Lot, on receiving two angels in his house, ordered unleavened bread to be baked, and they did eat. Arcade was given a tough beef-steak by a seedy waiter, and he did eat. Nevertheless, his dreams were of the sweet leisure, of the repose, of the delightful studies he had quitted, of the heavy task he had undertaken, of the toil, the weariness, the perils which he would have to endure, and his soul was sad and his heart troubled.

As he was finishing his modest repast, a young man of poor appearance and thinly clad entered the room, and rapidly surveying the tables approached the angel and greeted him by the name of Abdiel, because he himself was a celestial spirit.

"I knew you would answer my call, Mirar," replied Arcade, addressing his angelic brother in his turn by the name he formerly bore in heaven. But Mirar was remembered no more in heaven since he, an Archangel, had left the service of God. He was called Théophile Belais on earth, and to earn his bread gave music lessons to small children in the day-time and at night played the violin in dancing saloons."

"It is you, dear Abdiel?" replied Théophile. "So here we are reunited in this sad world. I am pleased to see you again. All the same I pity you, for we lead a hard life here."

But Arcade answered:

"Friend, your exile draws to an end. I have great plans. I will confide them to you and associate you with them."

And Maurice's guardian angel, having ordered two coffees, revealed his ideas and his projects to his companion: he told how, during his visit on earth, he had abandoned himself to researches little practised by celestial spirits and had studied theologies, cosmogonies, the system of the Universe, theories of matter, modern essays on the transformation and loss of energy. Having, he explained, studied Nature, he had found her in perpetual conflict with the teachings of the Master he served. This Master, greedy of praise, whom he had for a long time adored, appeared to him now as an ignorant, stupid, and cruel tyrant. He had denied Him, blasphemed Him, and was burning to combat Him. His plan was to recommence the revolt of the angels. He wished for war, and hoped for victory.

"But," he added, "it is necessary above all to know our strength and that of our adversary." And he asked if the enemies of Ialdabaoth were numerous and powerful on earth.

Théophile looked wonderingly at his brother. He appeared not to understand the questions addressed him.

"Dear compatriot," he said, "I came at your invitation because it was the invitation of an old comrade. But I do not know what you expect of me, and I fear I shall be unable to help you in anything. I take no hand in politics, neither do stand forth as a reformer. I am not like you, spirit in revolt, a free-thinker, a revolutionary. I remain faithful, in the depths of my soul, to the Celestial Creator. I still adore the Master I no longer serve, and I lament the days when shrouding myself with my wings I formed with the multitude of the children of light a wheel of flame around His throne of glory. Love, profane love has alone separated me from God. I quitted heaven to follow a daughter of men. She was beautiful and sang in music-halls."

They rose. Arcade accompanied Théophile, who was living at the other end of the town, at the corner of the Boulevard Rochechouart and the Rue de

Steinkerque. While walking through the deserted streets he who loved the singer told his brother of his love and his sorrows.

His fall, which dated from two years back, had been sudden. Belonging to the eighth choir of the third hierarchy he was a bearer of grace to the faithful who are still to be found in large numbers in France, especially among the higher ranks of the officers of the army and navy.

"One summer night," he said, "as I was descending from Heaven, to distribute consolations, the grace of perseverance and of good deaths to divers pious persons in the neighbourhood of the Etoile, my eyes, although well accustomed to immortal light, were dazzled by the fiery flowers with which the Champs Élysées were sown. Great candelabra, under the trees, marking the entrances to cafes and restaurants, gave the foliage the precious glitter of an emerald. Long garlands of luminous pearl surrounded the open-air enclosures where a crowd of men and women sat closely packed listening to the sounds of a lively orchestra, whose strains reached my ears confusedly.

"The night was warm, my wings were beginning to grow tired. I descended into one of the concerts and sat down, invisible, among the audience. At this moment, a woman appeared on the stage, clad in a short spangled frock. Owing to the reflection of the footlights and the paint on her face all that was visible of the latter was the expression and the smile. Her body was supple and voluptuous.

"She sang and danced.... Arcade, I have always loved dancing and music, but this creature's thrilling voice and insidious movements created in me an uneasiness I had never known before. My colour came and went. My eyelids drooped, my tongue clove to my mouth. I could not leave the spot."

And Théophile related, groaning, how, possessed by desire for this woman, he did not return to Heaven again, but, taking the shape of a man, lived an earthly life, for it is written: "In those days the sons of God saw that the daughters of men were beautiful."

A fallen angel, having lost his innocence along with the vision of God, Théophile at heart still retained his simplicity of soul. Clad in rags, filched from the stall of a Jewish hawker, he went to seek the woman he loved. She was called Bouchotte and lodged in a small house in Montmartre. He flung himself at her feet and told her she was adorable, that she sang delightfully, that he loved her madly, that, for her, he would renounce his family and his country, that he was a musician and had nothing to eat. Touched by such youthful ingenuousness, candour, poverty, and love, she fed, clothed, and loved him.

However, after long and painful struggles, he procured employment as a music-teacher, and made some money, which he brought to his mistress, keeping nothing for himself. From that time forward she loved him no longer. She despised him for earning so little and did not conceal her indifference, weariness, and disgust. She overwhelmed him with reproaches, irony, and abuse, in spite of which she kept him, for she had had experience of worse partners and was used to domestic quarrels. For the rest, she led a busy, serious, and rather hard life as artist and woman. Théophile loved her as he had loved her the first night, and he suffered.

"She overworks herself," he told his celestial brother, "that is what makes her so hard to please, but I am certain she loves me. I hope soon to give her more comfort."

And he spoke at length of an operetta at which he was working and which he hoped to have brought out at a Paris theatre. A young poet had given him the libretto. It was the story of Aline, queen of Golconda, after an eighteenth-century tale.

"I am strewing it profusely with melodies," said Théophile; "my music comes from my heart. My heart is an inexhaustible source of melody. Unfortunately nowadays people like recondite arrangements, difficult scoring. They accuse me of being too fluid, too limpid, of not imparting enough colour to my style, not aiming at stronger effects in harmony and more vigorous contrasts. Harmony, harmony!... No doubt it has given its merits, but it does not appeal to the heart. It is melody which carries us away and ravishes us and brings smiles and tears to our eyes." At these words he smiled and wept to himself. Then he continued with emotion:

"I am a fountain of melody. But the orchestration! there's the rub! In Paradise, you know, Arcade, in the matter of instruments, we only possess the harp, the psaltery, and the hydraulic organ."

Arcade was only listening to him with half an ear. He was meditating plans which filled his soul and swelled his heart.

"Do you know any angels in revolt?" he asked his companion. "As for me, I know only one, Prince Istar, with whom I have exchanged a few letters and who offered to share his attic with me while I was finding a lodging in this town, where I believe rents are very high."

Of angels in revolt Théophile knew none. When he met a fallen spirit who had formerly been one of his comrades he shook him by the hand, for he was a faithful friend. Sometimes he saw Prince Istar. But he avoided all those bad angels who shocked him by the violence of their opinions and whose conversations plagued him to death.

"Then you don't approve of me?" asked the impulsive Arcade.

"Friend, I neither approve of you nor blame you. I understand nothing of the ideas which trouble you. Neither do I think it good for an artist to concern himself with politics. One has quite sufficient to occupy oneself with one's art."

He loved his profession, and had hopes of "arriving" one day, but theatrical ways disgusted him. The only chance he saw of having his piece played was to take one or two -- perhaps three -- collaborators, who, without having done any work, would sign their names and share the profits. Soon Bouchotte would fail to find engagements. When she offered her services in some small hall the manager began by asking her how many shares she was taking in the business. Such customs, thought Théophile, were deplorable.

CHAPTER XIII. WHEREIN WE HEAR THE BEAUTIFUL ARCHANGEL ZITA UNFOLD HER LOFTY DESIGNS AND ARE SHOWN THE WINGS OF MIRAR, ALL MOTH-EATEN, IN A CUPBOARD

THUS talking, the two archangels had reached the Boulevard Rochechouart. As his eye lighted on a tavern, whence, through the mist, the light fell golden on the pavement, Théophile suddenly bethought himself of the Archangel Ithuriel who, in the guise of a poor but beautiful woman, was living in wretched lodgings on La Butte and came every evening to read the papers at this tavern. The musician often met her there. Her name was Zita. Théophile had never been curious enough to enquire into the opinions entertained by this archangel, but it was generally supposed that she was a Russian nihilist, and he took her to be, like Arcade, an atheist and a revolutionary. He had heard remarkable tales about her. People said she was an hermaphrodite, and that as the active and passive principles were united within her in a condition of stable equilibrium, she was an example of a perfect being, finding in herself complete and continuous satisfaction, contented yet unfortunate in that she knew not desire.

"But," added Théophile, "I have my doubts about it. I believe she's a woman and subject to love, like everything else that has life and breath in the Universe. Besides, someone caught her one day kissing her hand to a strapping peasant fellow."

He offered to introduce his companion to her.

The two angels found her alone, reading. As they drew near she lifted her great eyes in whose deeps of molten gold little sparks of light were forever a-dance. Her brows were contracted into that austere fold which we see on the forehead of the Pythian Apollo; her nose was perfect and descended without a curve; her lips were compressed and imparted a disdainful and supercilious air to her whole countenance. Her tawny hair, with its gleaming lights, was carelessly adorned with the tattered remnants of a huge bird of prey, her garments lay about her in dark and shapeless folds. She was leaning her chin on a small ill-tended hand.

Arcade, who had but recently heard references made to this powerful archangel, showed her marked esteem, and placed entire confidence in her. He immediately proceeded to tell of the progress his mind had made towards knowledge and liberty, of his lucubrations in the d'Esparvieu library, of his philosophical reading, his studies of nature, his works on exegesis, his anger and his contempt when he recognised the deception of the demiurge, his voluntary exile among mankind, and, finally, of his project to stir up rebellion in Heaven.

Ready to dare all against and odious master, whom he pursued with inextinguishable hatred, he expressed his profound happiness at finding in Ithuriel a mind capable of counselling and helping him in his great undertaking.

"You are not a very old hand at revolutions," said Zita, smiling.

Nevertheless, she doubted neither his sincerity nor the firmness of his declared resolve, and she congratulated him on his intellectual audacity.

"That is what is most lacking in our people," she said, "they do not think."

And she added almost immediately: "But on what can intelligence sharpen its wits, in a country where the climate is soft and existence made easy? Even here, where necessity calls for intellectual activity, nothing is rarer than a person who thinks."

"Nevertheless," replied Maurice's guardian angel, "man has created science. The important thing is to introduce it into Heaven. When the angels possess some notions of physics, chemistry, astronomy, and physiology; when the study of matter shows them worlds in an atom, and an atom in the myriads of planets; when they see themselves lost between these two infinities; when they weigh and measure the stars, analyse their composition, and calculate their orbits, they will recognise that these monsters work in obedience to forces which no intelligence can define, or that each star has its particular divinity, or indigenous god; and they will realise that the gods of Aldebaran, Betelgeuse, and Sirius are greater than Ialdabaoth. When at length they come to scrutinise with care the little world in which their lot is cast, and, piercing the crust of the earth, note the gradual evolution of its flora and fauna and the rude origin of man, who, under the shelter of rocks and in cave dwellings, had no God but himself; when they discover that, united by the bonds of universal kinship to plants, beasts, and men, they have successively indued all forms of organic life, from the simplest and the most primitive, until they became at length the most beautiful of the children of light, they will perceive that Ialdabaoth, the obscure demon of an insignificant world lost in space, is imposing on their credulity when he pretends that they issued from nothingness at his bidding; they will perceive that he lies in calling himself the Infinite, the Eternal, the Almighty, and that, so far from having created worlds, he knows neither their number nor their laws. They will perceive that he is like unto one of them; they will despise him, and, shaking off his tyranny, will fling him into the Gehenna where he has hurled those more worthy than himself."

"Do you think so?" murmured Zita, puffing out the smoke of her cigarette.... "Nevertheless, this knowledge by virtue of which you reckon to enfranchise Heaven, has not destroyed religious sentiment on earth. In countries where they have set up and taught this science of physics, of chemistry, astronomy, and geology, which you think capable of delivering the world, Christianity has retained almost all its sway. If the positive sciences have had such a feeble influence on the beliefs of mankind, it is not likely they will exercise a greater one on the opinions of the angels, and nothing is of such dubious efficacy as scientific propaganda."

"What!" exclaimed Arcade, "you deny that Science has given the Church its death-blow? Is it possible? The Church, at any rate, judges otherwise. Science, which you believe has no power over her, is redoubtable to her, since she proscribes it. From Galileo's dialogues to Monsieur Aulard's little manuals she has condemned all its discoveries. And not without reason.

"In former days, when she gathered within her fold all that was great in human thought, the Church held sway over the bodies as well as over the souls of men, and imposed unity of obedience by fire and sword. To-day her power is but a shadow and the elect among the great minds have withdrawn from her. That is the state to which Science has reduced her."

"Possibly," replied the beautiful archangel, "but how slowly, with what vicissitudes, at the price of what efforts, of what sacrifices!"

Zita did not absolutely condemn scientific propaganda, but she anticipated no prompt or certain results from it. For her it was not so much a question of enlightening the angels; the important thing was to enfranchise them. In her opinion one only exerted a strong influence on individuals, whoever they might be, by rousing their passions, and appealing to their interests.

"Persuade the angels that they will cover themselves with glory by overthrowing the tyrant, and that they will be happier once they are free; that is the most practical policy to attempt, and, for my own part, I am devoting all my energies to its fulfilment. It is certainly no light task, because the Kingdom of Heaven is a military autocracy and there is no public opinion in it. Nevertheless, I do not despair of starting an intellectual movement. I do not wish to boast, but no one is more closely acquainted than I with the different classes of angelic society."

Throwing away her cigarette, Zita pondered for a moment, then, amid the click of ivory balls on the billiard table, the clinking of glasses, the curt voices of the players announcing their points, the monotonous answers of the waiters to their customers, the Archangel enumerated the entire population of the spirits of light.

"We must not count on the Dominations, the Virtues, nor the Powers, which compose the celestial lower middle class. I have no need to tell you for you know it as well as I, how selfish, base, and cowardly the middle classes are. As to the great dignitaries, the Ministers, the Generals, Thrones, Cherubim, and Seraphim, you know what they are; they will take no action. Let us, however, once prove ourselves the stronger, and we shall have them with us. For if autocrats do not readily acquiesce in their own downfall, once overthrown, all their forces recoil upon themselves. It will be well to work the Army. Entirely loyal as the Army is, it will allow itself to be influenced by a clever anarchist propaganda. But our greatest and most constant efforts ought to be brought to bear upon the angels of your own category, Arcade; the guardian angels, who dwell upon earth in such great numbers. They fill the lowest ranks of the hierarchy, are for the most part discontented with their lot, and more or less imbued with the ideas of the present century."

She had already conferred with the guardian angels of Montmartre, Clignancourt, and Filles-du-Calvaire. She had devised the plan of a vast association of Spirits on Earth with the view of conquering Heaven.

"To accomplish this task," she said, "I have established myself in France. But not because I had the folly to believe myself freer in a republic than in a monarchy. Quite the contrary, for there is no country where the liberty of the individual is less respected than in France. But the people are indifferent to everything connected with religion; nowhere else, therefore, should I enjoy such tranquillity."

She invited Arcade to unite his efforts to hers, and when they separated at the door of the brasserie the steel shutter was already making its groaning descent.

"Above all," said Zita, "you must meet the gardener. I will take you to his rustic home one day."

Théophile, who had slumbered during all this talk, begged his friend to come home with him and smoke a cigarette. He lived quite near in the small street opposite, leading to the Boulevard. Arcade would see Bouchotte, she would please him.

They climbed up five flights of stairs. Bouchotte had not yet returned. A tin of sardines lay open on the piano. Red stockings coiled about the arm-chairs.

"It's a little place, but it's comfortable," said Théophile.

And gazing out of the window which looked out on the russet-coloured night, with its myriad lights, he added, "One can see the Sacre Coeur." His hand on Arcade's shoulder, he repeated several times, "I am glad to see you."

Then, dragging his former companion in glory into the kitchen passage, he put down his candle stick, drew a key from his pocket, opened a cupboard and, raising a linen covering, disclosed two large white wings.

"You see," he said, "I have preserved them. From time to time, when I am alone, I go and look at them; it does me good."

And he dabbed his reddened eyes. He stood awhile, overcome by silent emotion. Then, holding the candle near the long pinions which were moulting their down in places, he murmured, "They are eaten away."

"You must put some pepper on them," said Arcade.

"I have done so," replied the angelic musician sighing. "I have put pepper, camphor, and powder on them. But nothing does any good."

CHAPTER XIV. WHICH REVEALS THE CHERUB TOILING FOR
THE WELFARE OF HUMANITY AND CONCLUDES IN AN
ENTIRELY NOVEL MANNER WITH THE MIRACLE OF THE FLUTE

THE first night of his incarnation Arcade slept at the angel Istar's, in a
garret in that narrow, gloomy Rue Mazarine which wallows along beneath the
shadow of the old Institute of France. Istar, who had been expecting him, had
pushed against the wall the shattered retorts, cracked pots, broken bottles, and
odds and ends of iron stoves, which made up the furniture of his room, and
spread his clothes on the floor to lie on, leaving his guest his folding-bed with it
straw mattress.

The celestial spirits differ from one another in appearance according to the
hierarchy and the choir to which they belong, and according to their own
particular nature. They are all beautiful; but in different fashion, and they do not
all offer to the eye the soft contours and dimpling smiles of childhood with its
rosy lights and pearly tints. Nor do they all adorn themselves with eternal youth,
that indefinable beauty that Greek art in its decline has imparted to its most
lovingly handled marbles, and whereof Christian painters have so often timidly
essayed to give us veiled and softened imitations. In some of them the chin glows
with tufts of hair, and the limbs are furnished with such vigorous muscles that
it seems as if serpents were writhing beneath the skin. Some have no wings,
others possess two, four, or six; others again are formed entirely of conjoined
pinions. Many, and these not the least illustrious, take the form of superb
monsters, such as the Centaurs of fable; nay, one may even see some who are
living chariots, and wheels of fire. A member of the highest celestial hierarchy,
Istar belonged to the choir of Cherubim or Kerûbs who see above them the
Seraphim alone. In common with all the angelic spirits of his rank he had
formerly borne in Heaven the bodily shape of a winged bull surmounted by the
head of a horned and bearded man, and carrying between his loins the attributes
of generous fecundity. He as vaster and more vigorous than any animal on earth,
and when he stood erect with outspread wings he covered in his shadow sixty
archangels.

Such was Istar in his native home. There he radiated strength and
sweetness. His heart was full of courage and his soul benevolent. Moreover, in
those days he loved his lord. He believed him to be good and yielded him faithful
service. But even while guarding the portals of his Master, he used to ponder
unceasingly on the punishment of the rebellious angels and the curse of Eve. His
mind worked slowly but profoundly. When, after a long course of centuries, he

persuaded himself that Ialdabaoth in creating the world had created evil and death, he ceased to adore and to serve him. His love changed to hatred, his veneration to contempt. He shouted his execrations in his face, and fled to earth.

Embodied in human form and reduced to the stature of the sons of Adam, he still retained some characteristics of his former nature. His big protruding eyes, his beaked nose, his thick lips framed in a black beard which descended in curls on to his chest recalled those Cherubs of the tabernacle of Iahveh, of which the bulls of Nineveh afford us a pretty accurate representation. He bore the name of Istar on earth as well as in Heaven, and although exempt from vanity and free from all social prejudice, he was immensely desirous of showing himself sincere and truthful in all things. He therefore proclaimed the illustrious rank in which his birth had placed him in the celestial hierarchy and translated into French his title of Cherub by the equivalent one of Prince, calling himself Prince Istar. Seeking shelter among mankind he had developed an ardent love for them. While awaiting the coming of the hour when he should deliver Heaven from bondage, he dreamed of the salvation of regenerate humanity and was eager to consummate the destruction of this wicked world, in order to raise upon its ashes, to the sound of the lyre, a city radiant with happiness and love. A chemist in the pay of a dealer in nitrates, he lived very frugally. He wrote for newspapers with advanced views on liberty, spoke at public meetings, and had got himself sentenced several times to several months' imprisonment for anti-militarism.

Istar greeted his brother Arcade cordially, approved of his rupture with the party of crime, and informed him of the descent of fifty of the children of light who, at the present moment, formed a colony near Val de Grace, imbued with a really excellent spirit.

"It is simply raining angels in Paris," he said, laughing. "Every day some dignitary of the sacred palace falls on one's head, and soon the Sultan of the Cherubs will have no one to make into Vizirs or guards but the little unbreeched vagabonds of his pigeon coops."

Soothed by the good news, Arcade fell asleep, full of happiness and hope.

He awoke in the early dawn and saw Prince Istar bending over his furnaces, his retorts, and his testtubes. Prince Istar was working for the good of humanity.

Every morning when Arcade woke he saw Prince Istar fulfilling his work of tenderness and love. Sometimes the Kerûb, huddled up with his head in his hands, would softly murmur a few chemical formulæ; at others, drawing himself up to his full height, like a dark naked column, with his head, his arms, nay, his entire bust clean out of the skylight window, he would deposit his melting-pot on the roof, fearing the perquisition with which he was constantly menaced. Moved by an immense pity for the miseries of the world wherein he dwelt in exile, conscious perhaps of the rumours to which his name gave rise, inebriated with his own virtue, he played the part of apostle to the Human Race, ant neglecting the task he had undertaken in coming to earth, he forgot all about the emancipation of the angels. Arcade, who, on the contrary, dreamed of nothing else but of conquering Heaven and returning thither in triumph, reproached the Cherub with forgetting his native land.

Prince Istar, with a great frank, uncouth laugh, acknowledged that he had no preference for angels over men.

"If I am doing my best," he replied to his celestial brother, "if I am doing my best to stir up France and Europe, it is because the day is dawning which will behold the triumph of the social revolution. It is a pleasure to cast one's seed on ground so well prepared. The French having passed from feudalism to monarchy, and from monarchy to a financial oligarchy, will easily pass from a financial oligarchy to anarchy."

"How erroneous it is," retorted Arcade, "to believe in great and sudden changes in the social order in Europe! The old order is still young in strength and power. The means of defence at her disposal are formidable. On the other hand, the proletariat's plan of defensive organisation is of the vaguest description and brings merely weakness and confusion to the struggle. In our celestial country all goes quite otherwise. Beneath an apparently unchangeable exterior all is rotten within. A mere push would suffice to overturn an edifice which has not been touched for millions of centuries. Out-worn administration, out-worn army, out-worn finance, the whole thing is more worm-eaten than either the Russian or Persian autocracy."

And the kindly Arcade adjured the Cherub to fly first to the aid of his brethren who, though dwelling amid the soft clouds with the sound of citterns and their cups of paradisal wine around them, were in more wretched plight than mankind bowed over the grudging earth. For the latter have a conception of justice, while the angels rejoice in iniquity. He exhorted him to deliver the Prince of Light and his stricken companions and to re-establish them in their ancient honours.

Prince Istar allowed himself to be convinced.

He promised to put the sweet persuasiveness of his words and the excellent formulæ of his explosives at the service of the celestial revolution. He gave his promise.

"To-morrow," he said.

And when the morrow came he continued is anti-militarist propaganda at Issy-les-Moulineaux. Like the Titan Prometheus, Istar loved mankind.

Arcade, suffering from all the desires to which the sons of Adam are subjected, found himself lacking in resources to satisfy them. Istar gave him a start in a printing house in the Rue de Vaugirard where he knew the foreman.

Arcade, thanks to his celestial intelligence, soon knew how to set up type and became, in a short time, a good compositor.

After standing all day in the whirring workroom, holding the composing-stick in his left hand, and swiftly drawing the little leaden signs from the case in the order required by the copy fixed in the visorium, he would go and wash his hands at the pump and dine at the corner bar, a newspaper propped up before him on the marble table. Being now no longer invisible, he could not make his way into the d'Esparvieu library, and was thus debarred from allaying his ardent thirst for Knowledge at that inexhaustible source. He went, of an evening, to read at the library of Ste. Genevieve on the famous hill of learning, but there were only ordinary books to be had there; greasy things, covered its ridiculous annotations, and lacking many pages.

The sight of women troubled and unsettled him. He would remember Madame des Aubels and her charm, and, although he was handsome, he was not loved, because of his poverty and his workaday clothes. He saw much of Zita, and took a certain pleasure in going for walks with her on Sundays along the dusty roads which edge the grass-grown trenches of the fortifications. They wandered, the pair of them, by wayside inns, market-gardens and green retreats, propounding and discussing the vastest plans that ever stirred the world, and, occasionally, as they passed along by some travelling circus, the steam organ of the merry-go-round would furnish an accompaniment to their words as they breathed fire and fury against Heaven.

Zita used often to say:

"Istar means well, but he's a simple fellow. He believes in the goodness of men and things. He undertakes the destruction of the old world and imagines that anarchy of itself will create order and harmony. You, Arcade, you believe in Science; you deem that men and angels are capable of understanding, whereas, in point of fact, they are only creatures of sentiment. You may be quite sure that nothing is to be obtained from them by appealing to their intelligence; one must rouse their interests and their passions."

Arcade, Istar, Zita, and three or four other angelic conspirators occasionally foregathered in Théophile Belais' little flat, where Bouchotte gave them tea. Though she did not know that they were rebellious angels, she hated them instinctively, and feared them, for she had had a Christian education, albeit she had sadly failed to keep it up.

Prince Istar alone pleased her; she thought there was something kind-hearted and an air of natural distinction about him. He stove in the sofa, broke down the arm-chairs, and tore covers off sheets of music to make notes, which he thrust into pockets invariably crammed with pamphlets and bottles. The musician used to gaze sorrowfully at the manuscript of his operetta, Aline, Queen of Golconda, with its covers all torn off. The prince also had a habit of giving Théophile Belais all sorts of things to take care of -- mechanical contrivances, chemicals, bits of old iron, powders, and liquids which gave off noisome smells. Théophile Belais put them cautiously away in the cupboard where he kept his wings, and the responsibility weighed heavily upon him.

Arcade was much pained at the disdain of those of his fellows who had remained faithful. When they met him a they went on their sacred errands they regarded him as they passed by with looks of cruel hatred or of pity that was crueller still.

He used to visit the rebel angels whom Prince Istar pointed out to him, and usually met with a good reception, but as soon as he began to speak of conquering Heaven, they did not conceal the embarrassment and displeasure he caused them. Arcade perceived that they had no desire to be disturbed in their tastes, their affairs, and their habits. The falsity of their judgment, the narrowness of their minds, shocked him; and the rivalry, the jealousy they displayed towards one another deprived him of all hope of uniting them in a common cause. Perceiving how exile debases the character and warps the intellect, he felt his courage fail him.

One evening, when he had confessed his weariness of spirit to Zita, the beautiful archangel said:

"Let us go and see Nectaire; Nectaire has remedies of his own for sadness and fatigue."

She led him into the woods of Montmorency and stopped at the threshold of a small white house, adjoining a kitchen garden, laid waste by winter, where far back in the shadows the light shone on forcing-frames and cracked glass melon shades.

Nectaire opened the door to his visitors, and, after quieting the growls of a big mastiff which protected the garden, led them into a low room warmed by an earthenware stove.

Against the whitewashed wall, on a deal board, among the onions and seeds, lay a flute ready to be put to the lips. A round walnut table bore a stone tobacco-jar, a pipe, a bottle of wine and some glasses. The gardener offered each of his guests a cane-seated chair, and himself sat down on a stool by the table.

He was a sturdy old man; thick grey hair stood up on his head, he had a furrowed brow, a snub-nose, a red face, and a forked beard.

The big mastiff stretched himself at his master's feet, rested his short black muzzle on his paws, and closed his eyes. The gardener poured out some wine for his guests, and when they had drunk and talked a little, Zita said to Nectaire:

"Please play your flute to us, you will give pleasure to my friend whom I have brought to see you."

The old man immediately consented. He put the boxwood pipe to his lips, -- so clumsy was it that it looked as if the gardener had fashioned it himself, --

and preluded with a few strange runs. Then he developed rich melodies in which the thrills sparkled like diamonds and pearls on a velvet ground. Touched by cunning fingers, animated with creative breath, the rustic pipe sang like a silver flute. There were no over-shrill notes and the tone was always even and pure. One seemed to be listening to the nightingale and the Muses singing together, the soul of Nature and the soul of Man. And the old man ordered and developed his thoughts in a musical language full of race and daring. He told of love, of fear, of vain quarrels, of all-conquering laughter, of the calm light of the intellect, of the arrows of the mind piercing with their golden shafts the monsters of Ignorance and Hate. He told also of Joy and Sorrow bending their twin heads over the earth and of Desire which brings worlds into being.

The whole night listened to the flute of Nectaire. Already the evening star was rising above the paling horizon.

There they sat; Zita with hands clasped about her knees, Arcade, his head leaning on his hand, his lips apart. Motionless they listened. A lark, which had awakened hard by in a sandy field, lured by these novel sounds, rose swiftly in the air, hovered a few seconds, then dropped at one swoop into the musician's orchard. The neighbouring sparrows, forsaking the crannies of the mouldering walls, came and sat in a row on the window-ledge whence notes came welling forth that gave them more delight than oats or grains of barley. A jay, coming for the first time out of his wood, folded his sapphire wings on a leafless cherry tree. Beside the drain-head, a large black rat, glistening with the greasy water of the sewers, sitting on his hind legs, raised his short arms and slender fingers in amazement. A field-mouse, that dwelt in the orchard, was seated near him. Down from the tiles came the old tom-cat, who retained the grey fur, the ringed tail, the powerful loins, the courage, and the pride of his ancestors. He pushed against the half-open door with his nose and approaching the flute-player with silent tread, sat gravely down, pricking his ears that had been torn in many a nocturnal combat; the grocer's white cat followed him, sniffing the vibrant air and then, arching her back and closing her blue eyes, listened in ravishment. Mice, swarming in crowds from under the boards, surrounded them, and fearing neither tooth nor claw, sat motionless, their pink hands folded voluptuously on their bosoms. Spiders that had strayed far from their webs, with waving legs, gathered in a charmed circle on the ceiling. A small grey lizard, that had glided on to the doorstep, stayed there, fascinated, and, in the loft, the bat might have been seen hanging by her nails, head down, now half-awakened from her winter sleep, swaying to the rhythm of the marvellous flute.

CHAPTER XV. WHEREIN WE SEE YOUNG MAURICE BEWAILING THE LOSS OF HIS GUARDIAN ANGEL, EVEN IN HIS MISTRESS'S ARMS, AND WHEREIN WE HEAR THE ABBÉ PATOUILLE REJECT AS VAIN AND ILLUSORY ALL NOTIONS OF A NEW REBELLION OF THE ANGELS

A FORTNIGHT had elapsed since the angel's apparition in the flat. For the first time Gilberte arrived before Maurice at the rendezvous. Maurice was gloomy, Gilberte sulky. So far as they were concerned Nature had resumed her drab monotony. They eyed each other languidly, and kept glancing towards the angle between the wardrobe with the mirror and the window, where recently the pale shade of Arcade had taken shape, and where now the blue cretonne of the hangings was the only thing visible. Without giving him a name (it was unnecessary) Madame des Aubels asked:

"You have not seen him since?"

Slowly, sadly, Maurice turned his head from right to left, and from left to right.

"You look as if you missed him," continued Madame des Aubels. "But come, confess that he gave you a terrible fright, and that you were shocked at his unconventionality."

"Certainly he was unconventional," said Maurice without any resentment.

"Tell me, Maurice, is it nothing to you now to be with me alone?... You need an angel to inspire you. That is sad, for a young man like you!"

Maurice appeared not to hear, and asked gravely:

"Gilberte, do you feel that your guardian angel is watching over you?"

"I, not at all. I have never thought of him, and yet I am not without religion. In the first place, people who have none are like animals. And then one cannot go straight without religion. It is impossible."

"Exactly, that's just it," said Maurice, his eyes on the violet stripes of his flowerless pyjamas; "when one has one's guardian angel one does not even think about him, and when one has lost him one feels very lonely."

"So you miss this..."

"Well, the fact is..."

"Oh, yes, yes, you miss him. Well, my dear, the loss of such a guardian angel as that is no great matter. No, no! he is not worth much, that Arcade of yours. On that famous day, while you were out getting him some clothes, he was ever so long fastening my dress, and I certainly felt his hand... Well, at any rate, don't trust him."

Maurice dreamily lit a cigarette. They spoke of the six days' bicycle race at the winter velodrome, and of the aviation show at the motor exhibition at Brussels, without experiencing the slightest amusement. Then they tried love-making as a sort of convenient pastime, and succeeded in becoming moderately absorbed in it; but at the very moment when she might have been expected to play a part more in accordance with a mutual sentiment, she exclaimed with a sudden start:

"Good Heavens! Maurice, how stupid of you to tell me that my guardian angel can see me. You cannot imagine how uncomfortable the idea makes me."

Maurice, somewhat taken aback, recalled, a little roughly, his mistress's wandering thoughts.

She declared that her principles forbade her to think of playing a round game with angels.

Maurice was longing to see Arcade again and had no other thought. He reproached himself for suffering him to depart without discovering where he was going, and he cudgelled his brains night and day thinking how to find him again.

On the bare chance, he put a notice in the personal column of one of the big papers, running thus:

"Arcade. Come back to your Maurice."

Day after day went by, and Arcade did not return.

One morning, at seven o'clock, Maurice went to St. Sulpice to hear Abbé Patouille say Mass, then, as the priest was leaving the sacristy, he went up to him and asked to be heard for a moment.

They descended the steps of the church together and in the bright morning light walked round the fountain of the Quatre Évêques. In spite of his troubled conscience and the difficulty of presenting so extraordinary a case with any degree of credibility, Maurice related how the angel Arcade had appeared to him and had announced his unhappy resolve to separate from him and to stir up a new revolt of the spirits of glory. And young d'Esparvieu asked the worthy ecclesiastic how to find his celestial guardian again, since he could not bear his absence, and how to lead his angel back to the Christian faith. Abbé Patouille replied in a tone of affectionate sorrow that his dear child had been dreaming, that he took a morbid hallucination for reality, and that it was not permissible to believe that good angels may revolt.

"People have a notion," he added, "that they can lead a life of dissipation and disorder with impunity. They are wrong. The abuse of pleasure corrupts the intelligence and impairs the understanding. The devil takes possession of the sinner's senses, penetrating even to his soul. He has deceived you, Maurice, by a clumsy artifice."

Maurice objected that he was not in any way a victim of hallucinations, that he had not been dreaming, that he had seen his guardian angel with his eyes and heard him with his ears.

"Monsieur l'Abbé," he insisted, "a lady who happened to be with me at the time, -- I need not mention her name, -- also saw and heard him. And, moreover, she felt the angel's fingers straying... well, anyhow, she felt them.... Believe me, Monsieur l'Abbé, nothing could be more real, more positively certain than this apparition. The angel was fair, young, very handsome. His clear skin seemed, in the shadow, as if bathed in milky light. He spoke in a pure, sweet voice."

"That, alone, my child," the Abbé interrupted quickly, "proves you were dreaming. According to all the demonologies, bad angels have a hoarse voice, which grates like a rusty lock, and even if they did contrive to give a certain look of beauty to their faces, they cannot succeed in imitating the pure voice of the good spirits. This fact, attested by numerous witnesses, is established beyond all doubt."

"But, Monsieur l'Abbé, I saw him. I saw him sit down, stark naked, in an arm-chair on a pair of black stockings. What else do you want me to tell you?"

The Abbé Patouille appeared in no way disturbed by this announcement.

"I say once more, my son," he replied, "that these unhappy illusions, these dreams of a deeply troubled soul, are to be ascribed to the deplorable state of your conscience. I believe, moreover, that I can detect the particular circumstance that has caused your unstable mind thus to come to grief. During the winter in company with Monsieur Sariette and your Uncle Gaétan, you came, in an evil frame of mind, to see the Chapel of the Holy Angels in this church, then undergoing repair. As I observed on that occasion, it is impossible to keep artists too closely to the rules of Christian art; they cannot be too strongly enjoined to respect Holy Writ and its authorized interpreters. Monsieur Eugène Delacroix did not suffer his fiery genius to be controlled by tradition. He brooked no guidance and, here, in this chapel he has painted pictures which in common parlance we call lurid, compositions of a violent, terrible nature which, far from inspiring the soul with peace, quietude, and calm, plunge it into a state of agitation. In them the angels are depicted with wrathful countenances, their features are sombre and uncouth. One might take them to be Lucifer and his companions meditating their revolt. Well, my son, it was these pictures, acting upon a mind already weakened and undermined by every kind of dissipation, that have filled it with the trouble to which it is at present a prey."

But Maurice would have none of it.

"Oh, no! Monsieur l'Abbé," he cried, "it is not Eugène Delacroix's pictures that have been troubling me. I didn't so much as look at them. I am completely indifferent to that kind of art."

"Well, then, my son, believe me: there is no truth, no reality, in any of the story you have just related to me. Your guardian angel has certainly not appeared to you."

"But, Abbé," replied Maurice, who had the most absolute confidence in the evidence of the senses, "I saw him tying up a woman's shoe-laces and putting on the trousers of a suicide."

And stamping his feet on the asphalt, Maurice called as witnesses to the truth of his words the sky, the earth, all nature, the towers of St. Sulpice, the walls of the great seminary, the Fountain of the Quatre Évêques, the public lavatory, the cabmen's shelter, the taxis and motor 'buses' shelter, the trees, the passers-by, the dogs, the sparrows, the flower-seller and her flowers.

The Abbé made haste to end the interview.

"All this is error, falsehood, and illusion, my child," said he. "You are a Christian: think as a Christian, -- a Christian does not allow himself to be seduced by empty shadows. Faith protects him against the seduction of the marvellous, he leaves credulity to freethinkers. There are credulous people for you -- freethinkers! There is no humbug they will not swallow. But the Christian carries a weapon which dissipates diabolical illusions, -- the sign of the Cross. Reassure yourself, Maurice, -- you have not lost your guardian angel. He still watches over you. It lies with you not to make this task too difficult nor too painful for him. Goodbye, Maurice. The weather is going to change, for I feel a burning in my big toe."

And Abbé Patouille went of with his breviary under his arm, hobbling along with a dignity that seemed to foretell a mitre.

That very day, Arcade and Zita were leaning over the parapet of La Butte, gazing down on the mist and smoke that lay floating over the vast city.

"Is it possible," said Arcade, "for the mind to conceive all the pain and suffering that lie pent within a great city? It is my belief that if a man succeeded in realising it, the weight of it would crush him to the earth."

"And yet," answered Zita, "every living being in that place of torment is enamoured of life. It is a great enigma!

"Unhappy, ill-fated, while they live, the idea of ceasing to be is, nevertheless, a horror to them. They look not for solace in annihilation, it does not even bring them the promise of rest. In their madness they even look upon nothingness with terror: they have peopled it with phantoms. Look you at these pediments, these towers and domes and spires that pierce the mist and rear on high their glittering crosses. Men bow in adoration before the demiurge who has given them a life that is worse than death, and a death that is worse than life."

Zita was for a long time lost in thought. At length she broke silence, saying:

"There is something, Arcade, that I must confess to you. It was no desire for a purer justice or wiser laws that hurried Ithuriel earthward. Ambition, a taste for intrigue, the love of wealth and honour, all these things made Heaven, with its calm, unbearable to me, and I longed to mingle with the restless race of men. I came, and by an art unknown to nearly all the angels, I learned how to fashion myself a body which, since I could change it as the fancy seized me, to whatsoever age and sex I would, has permitted me to experience the most diverse and amazing of human destinies. A hundred times I took a position of renown among the leaders of the day, the lords of wealth and princes of nations. I will not reveal to you, Arcade, the famous names I bore; know only that I was pre-eminent in learning, in the fine arts, in power, wealth, and beauty, among all the nations of the world. At last, it was but a few years since, as I was journeying in France, under the outward semblance of a distinguished foreigner, I chanced to be roaming at evening through the forest of Montmorency, when I heard a lute unfolding all the sorrows of Heaven. The purity and sadness of its notes rent my very soul. Never before had I hearkened to aught so lovely. My eyes were wet with tears, my bosom full of sobs, as I drew near and beheld, on the skirts of a glade, an old man like to a faun, blowing on a rustic pipe. It was Nectaire. I cast myself at his feet, imprinted kisses on his hands and on his lips divine, and fled away....

"From that day forth, conscious of the littleness of human achievements, weary of the tumult and the vanity of earthly things, ashamed of my vast and profitless endeavours, and deciding to seek out a loftier aim for my ambition, I looked upwards towards my skiey home and vowed I would return to it as a Deliverer. I rid myself of titles, name, wealth, friends, the horde of sycophants and flatterers and, as Zita the obscure, set to work in indigence and solitude, to bring freedom into Heaven."

"And I," said Arcade, "I too have heard the flute of Nectaire. But who is this old gardener who can thus woo from a rude wooden pipe notes that are so moving and so beautiful?"

"You will soon know," answered Zita.

CHAPTER XVI. WHEREIN MIRA THE SEERESS, ZÉPHYRINE AND THE FATAL AMÉDÉE ARE SUCCESSIVELY BROUGHT UPON THE SCENE, AND WHEREIN THE NOTION OF EURIPIDES THAT THOSE WHOM ZEUS WISHES TO CRUSH HE FIRST MAKES MAD, IS ILLUSTRATED BY THE TERRIBLE EXAMPLE OF MONSIEUR SARIETTE

DISAPPOINTED at his failure to enlighten an ecclesiastic renowned for his clarity of mind, and frustrated in the hope of finding his angel again on the high road of orthodoxy, Maurice took it into his head to resort to occultism and resolved to go and consult a seer. He would have undoubtedly applied to Madame de Thèbes, but he had already questioned her on the occasion of his early love troubles, and her replies showed such wisdom that he no longer believed her to be a soothsayer. He therefore had recourse to a fashionable medium, Madame Mira. He had heard many examples quoted of the extraordinary insight of this seeress, but it was necessary to present Madame Mira with some object which the absent one had either touched or worn and to which her translucent gaze had to be attracted. Maurice, trying to remember what the angel had touched since his ill-fated incarnation, recollected that in his celestial nudity he had sat down in an armchair on Madame des Aubels' black stockings and that he had afterwards helped that lady to dress.

Maurice asked Gilberte for one of the talismans required by the clairvoyante. But Gilberte could not give him a single one, unless, as she said, she herself were to play the part of the talisman. For the angel had, in her case, displayed the greatest indiscretion, and such agility that it was impossible always to forestall his enterprise. On hearing this confession, which nevertheless told him nothing new, Maurice lost his temper with the angel, calling him by the names of the lowest animals and swearing he would give him a good kick when he got him within reach of his foot. But his fury soon turned against Madame des Aubels; he accused her of having provoked the insolence she now denounced, and in his wrath he referred to her by all the zoological symbols of immodesty and perversity. His love for Arcade was rekindled in his heart, and burned with a more ardent flame than ever, and the deserted youth, with outstretched arms and bended knees, invoked his angel with sobs and lamentations.

During his sleepless nights it occurred to him that perhaps the books the angel had turned over before his incarnation might serve as a talisman. One morning, therefore, Maurice went up to the library and greeted Monsieur

Sariette, who was cataloguing under the romantic gaze of Alexandre d'Esparvieu. Monsieur Sariette smiled, but his face was deathly pale. Now that an invisible hand no longer upset the books placed under his charge, now that tranquillity and order once more reigned in the library, Monsieur Sariette was happy, but his strength diminished day by day. There was little left of him but a frail and contented shadow.

"One dies, in full content, of sorrow past." "Monsieur Sariette," said Maurice, "you remember that time when your books were disarranged every night, how armfuls disappeared, how they were dragged about, turned over, ruined, and sent rolling helter-skelter as far as the gutter in the Rue Palatine. Those were great days! Point out to me, Monsieur Sariette, the books which suffered most."

This proposition threw Monsieur Sariette into a melancholy stupor, and Maurice had to repeat his request three times before he could make the aged librarian understand. At length he pointed to a very ancient Talmud from Jerusalem as having been frequently touched by those unseen hands. An apocryphal Gospel of the third century, consisting of twenty papyrus sheets, had also quitted its place time after time. Gassendi's Correspondence too seemed to have been well thumbed.

"But," added Monsieur Sariette, "the book to which the mysterious visitant devoted the most particular attention was undoubtedly a little copy of Lucretius adorned with the arms of Philippe de Vendôme, Grand Prieur de France, with autograph annotations by Voltaire, who, as is well known, frequently visited the Temple in his younger days. The fearsome reader who caused me such terrible anxiety never grew weary of this Lucretius and made it his bedside book, as it were. His taste was sound, for it's a gem of a thing. Alas! the monster made a blot of ink on page 137 which perhaps the chemists with all the science at their disposal will be powerless to erase."

And Monsieur Sariette heaved a profound sigh. He repented having said all this when young d'Esparvieu asked him for the loan of the precious Lucretius. Vainly did the jealous custodian affirm that the book was being repaired at the binder's and was not available. Maurice made it clear that he wasn't to be taken in like that. He strode resolutely into the abode of the philosophers and the globes and seating himself in an arm-chair said:

"I am waiting."

Monsieur Sariette suggested his having another edition. There were some that, textually, were more correct, and were, therefore, preferable from the student's point of view. He offered him Barbou's edition, or Coustelier's, or, better still, a French translation. He could have the Baron des Coutures' version -- which was perhaps a little oldfashioned -- or La Grange's, or those in the Nisard and Panckouke series; or, again, there were two versions of striking elegance, one in verse and the other in prose, both from the pen of Monsieur de Pongerville of the French Academy.

"I don't need a translation," said Maurice proudly. "Give me the Prior de Vendôme's copy."

Monsieur Sariette went slowly up to the cupboard in which the jewel in question was contained. The keys were rattling in his trembling hand. He raised them to the lock and withdrew them again immediately and suggested that Maurice should have the common Lucretius published by Garnier.

"It's very handy," said he with an engaging smile.

But the silence with which this proposal was received made it clear that resistance was useless. He slowly drew forth the volume from its place, and having taken the precaution to see that there wasn't a speck of dust on the table-cloth, he laid it tremblingly thereon before the great-grandson of Alexandre d'Esparvieu.

Maurice began to turn the leaves, and when he got to page 137 he saw the stain which had been made with violet ink. It was about the size of a pea.

"Ay, that's it," said old Sariette, who had his eye on the Lucretius the whole time; "that's the trace those invisible monsters left behind them."

"What, there were several of them, Monsieur Sariette?" exclaimed Maurice.

"I cannot tell. But I don't know whether I have a right to have this blot removed since, like the blot Paul Louis Courier made on the Florentine manuscript, it constitutes a literary document, so to speak."

Scarcely were the words out of the old fellow's mouth when the front door bell rang and there was a confused noise of voices and footsteps in the next room. Sariette ran forward at the sound and collided with Père Guinardon's mistress, old Zéphyrine, who, with her tousled hair sticking up like a nest of vipers, her face aflame, her bosom heaving, her abdominal part like an eiderdown quilt puffed out by a terrific gale, was choking with grief and rage. And amid sobs and sighs and groans and all the innumerable sounds which, on earth, make up the mighty uproar to which the emotions of living beings and the tumult of nature give rise, she cried:

"He's gone, the monster! He's gone off with her. He's cleared out the whole shanty and left me to shift for myself with eighteenpence in my purse."

And she proceeded to give a long and incoherent nt of how Michel Guinardon had abandoned her and gone to live with Octavie, the bread-woman's daughter, and she let loose a torrent of abuse against the traitor.

"A man whom I've kept going with my own money for fifty years and more. For I've had plenty of the needful and known plenty of the upper ten and all. I dragged him out of the gutter and now this is what I get for it. He's a bright beauty, that friend of yours. The lazy scoundrel. Why, he had to be dressed like a child, the drunken contemptible brute. You don't know him yet, Monsieur Sariette. He's a forger. He turns out Giottos, Giottos, I tell you, and Fra Angelicos and Grecos, as hard as he can and sells them to art-dealers -- yes, and Fragonards too, and Baudouins. He's a debauchee, and doesn't believe in God! That's the worst of the lot, Monsieur Sariette, for without the fear of God..."

Long did Zéphyrine continue to pour forth vituperations. When at last her breath failed her, Monsieur Sariette availed himself of the opportunity to exhort her to be calm and bring herself to look on the bright side of things. Guinardon would come back. A man doesn't forget anyone he's lived and got on well with for fifty years --

These two observations only goaded her to a fresh outburst, and Zéphyrine swore she would never forget the slight that had been put on her; she swore she would never have the monster back with her any more. And if he came to ask her to forgive him on his knees, she would let him grovel at her feet.

"Don't you understand, Monsieur Sariette, that I despise and hate him, that he makes me sick?"

Sixty times she voiced these lofty sentiments; sixty times she vowed she would never have Guinardon back with her again, that she couldn't bear he sight of him, even in a picture.

Monsieur Sariette made no attempt to oppose a resolve which, after protestations such as these, he regarded as unshakable. He did not blame Zéphyrine in the least. He even supported her. Unfolding to the deserted one a purer future, he told her of he frailty of human sentiment, exhorted her to display a spirit of renunciation and enjoined her to show a pious resignation to the will of God.

"Seeing, in truth, that your friend is so little worthy of affection..."

He was not suffered to continue. Zéphyrine flew at him, and shaking him furiously by the collar of his frock-coat, she yelled, half choking with rage: "So little worthy of affection! Michel! Ah! my boy, you find another more kind, more gay, more witty, you find another like him, always young, yes, always. Not worthy of affection! Anyone can see you don't know anything about love, you old duffer."

Taking advantage of the fact that Père Sariette was thus deeply engaged, young d'Esparvieu slipped the little Lucretius into his pocket, and strolled deliberately past the crouching librarian, bidding him adieu with a little wave of the hand.

Armed with his talisman, he hastened to the Place des Ternes, to interview Madame Mira. She received him in a red drawing-room where neither owl nor frog nor any of the paraphernalia of ancient magic were to be found. Madame Mira, in a prune-coloured dress, her hair powdered, though already past her prime, was of very good appearance. She spoke with a certain elegance and prided herself on discovering hidden things by the help alone of Science, Philosophy, and Religion. She felt the morocco binding, feigning to close her eyes, and looking meanwhile through the narrow slit between her lids at the Latin title and the coat of arms which conveyed nothing to her.

Accustomed to receive as tokens such things as rings, handkerchiefs, letters, and locks of hair, she could not conceive to what sort of individual this singular book could belong. By habitual and mechanical cunning she disguised her real surprise under a feigned surprise.

"Strange!" she murmured, "strange! I do not see quite clearly... I perceive a woman...."

As she let fall this magic word, she glanced furtively to see what sort of an effect it had and beheld on her questioner's face an unexpected look of disappointment. Perceiving that she was off the track, she immediately changed her oracle:

"But she fades away immediately. It is strange, strange! I have a confused impression of some vague form, a being that I cannot define," and having assured herself by a hurried glance that, this time, her words were going down, she expatiated on the vagueness of the person and on the mist that enveloped him.

However, the vision grew clearer to Madame Mira, who was following a clue step by step.

"A wide street... a square with a statue... a deserted street, -- stairs. He is there in a bluish room -- he is a young man, with pale and careworn face. There are things he seems to regret, and which he would not do again did they still remain undone."

But the effort at divination had been too great. Fatigue prevented the clairvoyante from continuing her transcendental researches. She spent her remaining strength in impressively recommending him who consulted her to remain in intimate union with God if he wished to regain what he had lost and succeed in his attempts.

On leaving Maurice placed a louis on the mantelpiece and went away moved and troubled, persuaded that Madame Mira possessed supernatural faculties, but unfortunately insufficient ones.

At the bottom of the stairs he remembered he had left the little Lucretius on the table of the pythoness, and, thinking that the old maniac Sariette would never get over its loss, went up to recover possession of it.

On re-entering the paternal abode his gaze lighted upon a shadowy and grief-stricken figure. It was old Sariette, who in tones as plaintive as the wail of the November wind began to beg for his Lucretius. Maurice pulled it carelessly out of his great-coat pocket.

"Don't flurry yourself, Monsieur Sariette," said he. "There the thing is."

Clasping the jewel to his bosom the old librarian bore it away and laid it gently down on the blue table-cloth, thinking all the while where he might safely hide his precious treasure, and turning over all sorts of schemes in his mind as became a zealous curator. But who among us shall boast of his wisdom? The foresight of man is short, and his prudence is for ever being baffled. The blows of fate are ineluctable; no man shall evade his doom. There is no counsel, no caution that avails against destiny. Hapless as we are, the same blind force which regulates the courses of atom and of star fashions universal order from our vicissitudes. Our ill-fortune is necessary to the harmony of the Universe. It was the day for the binder, a day which the revolving seasons brought round twice a year, beneath the sign of the Ram and the sign of the Scales. That day, ever since morning, Monsieur Sariette had been making things ready for the binder. He had laid out on the table as many of the newly purchased paper-bound volumes as were deemed worthy of a permanent binding or of being put in boards, and also those books whose binding was in need of repair, and of all these he had drawn up a detailed and accurate list. Punctually at five o'clock, old Amédée, the man from Léger-Massieu's, the binder in the Rue de l'Abbaye, presented himself at the d'Esparvieu library and, after a double check had been carried out by Monsieur Sariette, thrust the books he was to take back to his master into a piece of cloth which he fastened into knots at the four corners and hoisted on to his shoulder. He then saluted the librarian with the following words, "Good night, all!" and went downstairs.

Everything went off on this occasion as usual. But Amédée, seeing the Lucretius on the table, innocently put it into the bag with the others, and took it away without Monsieur Sariette's perceiving it. The librarian quitted the home of the Philosophers and Globes in entire forgetfulness of the book whose absence had been causing him such horrible anxiety all day long. Some people may take a stern view of the matter and call this a lapse, a defection of his better nature. But would it not be more accurate to say that fate had decided that things should come to pass in this manner, and that what is called chance, and is in fact but the regular order of nature, had accomplished this imperceptible deed which was to have such awful consequences in the sight of man? Monsieur Sariette went of to his dinner at the Quatre Évêques, and read his paper La Croix. He was tranquil and serene. It was only the next morning when he entered the abode of the Philosophers and Globes that he remembered the Lucretius. Failing to see it on the table he looked for it everywhere, but without success. It never entered his head that Amédée might have taken it away by mistake. What he did think was that the invisible visitant had returned, and he was mightily disturbed.

The unhappy curator, hearing a noise on the landing, opened the door and found it was little Léon, who, with a gold-braided képi stuck on his head, was shouting "Vive la France" and hurling dusters and feather-brooms and

Hippolyte's floor polish at imaginary foes. The child preferred this landing for playing soldiers to any other part of the house, and sometimes he would stray into the library. Monsieur Sariette was seized with the sudden suspicion that it was he who had taken the Lucretius to use as a missile and he ordered him, in threatening tones, to give it back. The child denied that he had taken it, and Monsieur Sariette had recourse to cajolery.

"Léon, if you bring me back the little red book, I will give you some chocolates."

The child grew thoughtful; and in the evening, as Monsieur Sariette was going downstairs, he met Léon, who said:

"There's the book!"

And, holding out a much-torn picture-book called The Story of Gribouille, demanded his chocolates.

A few days later the post brought Maurice the prospectus of an enquiry agency managed by an ex-employee at the Prefecture of Police; it promised celerity and discretion. He found at the address indicated a moustached gentleman morose and careworn, who demanded a deposit and promised to find the individual.

The ex-police official soon wrote to inform him that very onerous investigations had been commenced and asked for fresh funds. Maurice gave him no more and resolved to carry on the search himself. Imagining, not without some likelihood, that the angel would associate with the wretched, seeing that he had no money, and with the exiled of all nations -- like himself, revolutionaries -- he visited the lodging-houses at St. Ouen, at la Chapelle, Montmartre, and the Barrière d'Italie. He sought him in the doss-houses, public-houses where they give you plates of tripe, and others where you can get a sausage for three sous; he searched for him in the cellars at the Market and at Père Momie's.

Maurice visited the restaurants where nihilists and anarchists take their meals. There he came across men dressed as women, gloomy and wild-looking youths, and blue-eyed octogenarians who laughed like little children. He observed, asked questions, was taken for a spy, had a knife thrust into him by a very beautiful woman, and the very next day continued his search in beer-houses, lodging-houses, houses of ill-fame, gambling-hells down by the fortifications, at the receivers of stolen goods, and among the "apaches."

Seeing him thus pale, harassed, and silent, his mother grew worried.

"We must find him a wife," she said. "It is a pity that Mademoiselle de la Verdelière has not a bigger fortune."

Abbé Patouille did not hide his anxiety.

"This child," he said, "is passing through a moral crisis."

"I am more inclined to think," replied Monsieur René d'Esparvieu, "that he is under the influence of some bad woman. We must find him an occupation which will absorb him and flatter his vanity. I might get him appointed Secretary to the Committee for the Preservation of Country Churches, or Consulting Counsel to the Syndicate of Catholic Plumbers."

CHAPTER XVII. WHEREIN WE LEARN THAT SOPHAR NO LESS
EAGER FOR GOLD THAN MAMMON, LOOKED UPON HIS
HEAVENLY HOME LESS FAVOURABLY THAN UPON FRANCE, A
COUNTRY BLESSED WITH A SAVINGS BANK AND LOAN
DEPARTMENTS AND WHEREIN WE SEE, YET ONCE AGAIN THAT
WHOSO IS POSSESSED OF THIS WORLD'S GOODS FEARS THE
EVIL EFFECTS OF ANY CHANGE

MEANWHILE Arcade led a life of obscure toil. He worked at a printer's
in the Rue St. Benoit, and lived in an attic in the Rue Mouffetard. His comrades
having gone on strike, he left the workroom and devoted his day to his
propaganda. So successful was he that he won over to the side of revolt fifty
thousand of those guardian angels who, as Zita had surmised, were discontented
with their condition and imbued with the spirit of the times. But lacking money,
he lacked liberty, and could not employ his time as he wished in instructing the
sons of Heaven. So, too, Prince Istar, hampered by want of funds, manufactured
fewer bombs than were needed, and these less fine. Of course he prepared a
good many small pocket machines. He had filled Théophile's rooms with them,
and not a day passed but he forgot some and left them lying about on the seats
in various cafes. But a nice bomb, easily handled and capable of destroying
many big mansions, cost him from twenty to twenty-five thousand francs; and
Prince Istar only possessed two of this kind. Equally bent on procuring funds,
Arcade and Istar both went to make a request for money from a celebrated
financier named Max Everdingen, who, as everyone knows, is the managing
director of the biggest banking concern in France and indeed in the whole world.
What is not so well known is that Max Everdingen was not born of woman, but
is a fallen angel. Nevertheless, such is the truth. In Heaven he was named
Sophar, and guarded the treasures of Ialdabaoth, a great collector of gold and
precious stones. In the exercise of this function Sophar contracted a love of
riches which could not be satisfied in a state of society in which banks and stock
exchanges are alike unknown. His heart flamed with an ardent love for the god
of the Hebrews to whom he remained faithful during a long course of centuries.
But at the commencement of the twentieth century of the Christian era, casting
his eyes down from the height of the firmament upon France, he saw that this
country, under the name of a Republic, was constituted as a plutocracy and that,
under the appearance of a democratic government, high finance exercised
sovereign sway, untrammelled and unchecked.

Henceforth life in the Empyrean became intolerable to him. He longed for
France as for the promised land, and one day, bearing with him all the precious

stones he could carry, he descended to earth and established himself in Paris. This angel of cupidity did good business there. Since his materialisation his face had lost its celestial aspect; it reproduced the Semitic type in all its purity, and one could admire the lines and the puckers which wrinkle the faces of bankers and which are to be seen in the money-changers of Quintin Matsys.

His beginnings were humble and his success amazing. He married an ugly woman and they saw themselves reflected in their children as in a mirror. Baron Max Everdingen's large mansion, which rears itself on the heights of the Trocadero, is crammed with the spoils of Christian Europe.

The Baron received Arcade and Prince Istar in his study, -- one of the most modest rooms in his mansion. The ceiling is decorated with a fresco of Tiepolo, taken from a Venetian palace. The bureau of the Regent, Philip of Orleans, is in this room, which is full of cabinets, show-cases, pictures, and statues.

Arcade allowed his gaze to wander over the walls.

"How comes it, my brother Sophar," said he, "that you, in spite of your Jewish heart, obey so ill the commandment of the Lord your God who said: 'Thou shalt have no graven images'? for here I see an Apollo of Houdon's and a Hebe of Lemoine's, and several busts by Caffieri. And, like Solomon in his old age, O son of God, you set up in your dwelling-place the idols of strange nations: for such are this Venus of Boucher, this Jupiter of Rubens, and those nymphs that are indebted to Fragonard's brush for the gooseberry jam which smears their gleaming limbs. And here in this single show-case, Sophar, you keep the sceptre of St. Louis, six hundred pearls of Marie Antoinette's broken necklace, the imperial mantle of Charles V, the tiara wrought by Ghiberti for Pope Martin V, the Colonna, Bonaparte's sword -- and I know not what besides."

"Mere trifles," said Max Everdingen.

"My dear Baron," said Prince Istar, "you even possess the ring which Charlemagne placed on a fairy's finger and which was thought to be lost. But let us discuss the business on which we have come. My friend and I have come to ask you for money."

"I can well believe it," replied Max Everdingen. "Everyone wants money, but for different reasons. What do you want money for"

Prince Istar replied simply:

"To stir up a revolution in France."

"In France!" repeated the Baron, "in France? Well, I shall give you no money for that, you may be quite sure."

Arcade did not disguise the fact that he had expected greater liberality and more generous help from a celestial brother.

"Our project," he said, "is a vast one. It embraces both Heaven and Earth. It is settled in every detail. We shall first bring about a social revolution in

France, in Europe, on the whole planet; then we shall carry war into the heavens, where we shall establish a peaceful democracy. And to reduce the citadels of Heaven, to overturn the mountain of God, to storm celestial Jerusalem, a vast army is needful, enormous resources, formidable machines, and electrophores of a strength yet unknown. It is our intention to commence with France."

"You are madmen!" exclaimed Baron Everdingen; "madmen and fools! Listen to me. There is not one single reform to carry out in France. All is perfect, finally settled, unchangeable. You hear? -- unchangeable." And to add force to his statement, Baron Everdingen banged his fist three times on the Regent's bureau.

"Our points of view differ," said Arcade sweetly. "I think, as does Prince Istar, that everything should be changed in this country. But what boots it to dispute the matter? Moreover, it is too late. We have come to speak to you, O my brother Sophar, in the name of five hundred thousand celestial spirits, all resolved to commence the universal revolution to-morrow."

Baron Everdingen exclaimed that they were crazy, that he would not give a sou, that it was both criminal and mad to attack the most admirable thing in the world, the thing which renders earth more beautiful than heaven -- Finance. He was a poet and a prophet. His heart thrilled with holy enthusiasm; he drew attention to the French Savings Bank, the virtuous Savings Bank, that chaste and pure Savings Bank like unto the Virgin of the Canticle who, issuing from the depths of the country in rustic petticoat, bears to the robust and splendid Bank -- her bridegroom, who awaits her -- the treasures of her love; and drew a picture of the Bank, enriched with the gifts of its spouse, pouring on all the nations of the world torrents of gold, which, of themselves, by a thousand invisible channels return in still greater abundance to the blessed land from which they sprung.

"By Deposit and Loan," he went on, "France has become the New Jerusalem, shedding her glory over all the nations of Europe, and the Kings of the Earth come to kiss her rosy feet. And that is what you would fain destroy? You are both impious and sacrilegious."

Thus spoke the angel of finance. An invisible harp accompanied his voice, and his eyes darted lightning.

Meanwhile Arcade, leaning carelessly against the Regent's bureau, spread out under the Banker's eyes various ground-plans, underground-plans, and sky-plans of Paris with red crosses indicating the points where bombs should be simultaneously placed in cellars and catacombs, thrown on public ways, and flung by a flotilla of æroplanes. All the financial establishments, and notably the Everdingen Bank and its branches, were marked with red crosses.

The financier shrugged his shoulders.

"Nonsense! you are but wretches and vagabonds, shadowed by all the police of the world. You are penniless. How can you manufacture all the machines?"

By way of reply, Prince Istar drew from his pocket a small copper cylinder, which he gracefully presented to Baron Everdingen.

"You see," said he, "this ordinary-looking box. It is only necessary to let it fall on the ground immediately to reduce this mansion with its inmates to a mass of smoking ashes, and to set a fire going which would devour all the Trocadero quarter. I have ten thousand like that, and I make three dozen a day."

The financier asked the Cherub to replace the machine in his pocket, and continued in a conciliatory tone:

"Listen to me, my friends. Go and start a revolution at once in Heaven, and leave things alone in this country. I will sign a cheque for you. You can procure all the material you need to attack celestial Jerusalem."

And Baron Everdingen was already working up in his imagination a magnificent deal in electrophores and war-material.

CHAPTER XVIII. WHEREIN IS BEGUN THE GARDENER'S STORY, IN THE COURSE OF WHICH WE SHALL SEE THE DESTINY OF THE WORLD UNFOLDED IN A DISCOURSE AS BROAD AND MAGNIFICENT IN ITS VIEWS AS BOSSUET'S DISCOURSE ON THE HISTORY OF THE UNIVERSE IS NARROW AND DISMAL

THE gardener bade Arcade and Zita sit down in an arbour walled with wild bryony, at the far end of the orchard.

"Arcade," said the beautiful Archangel, "Nectaire will perhaps reveal to you to-day the things you are burning to know. Ask him to speak."

Arcade did so and old Nectaire, laying down his pipe, began as follows:--

"I knew him. He was the most beautiful of all the Seraphim. He shone with intelligence and daring. His great heart was big with all the virtues born of pride: frankness, courage, constancy in trial, indomitable hope. Long, long ago, ere Time was, in the boreal sky where gleam the seven magnetic stars, he dwelt in a palace of diamond and gold, where the air was ever tremulous with the beating of wings and with songs of triumph. Iahveh, on his mountain, was jealous of Lucifer. You both know it: angels like unto men feel love and hatred quicken within them. Capable, at times, of generous resolves, they too often follow their own interests and yield to fear. Then, as now, they showed themselves, for the most part, incapable of lofty thoughts, and in the fear of the Lord lay their sole virtue. Lucifer, who held vile things in proud disdain, despised this rabble of commonplace spirits for ever wallowing in a life of feasts and pleasure. But to those who were possessed of a daring spirit, a restless soul, to those fired with a wild love of liberty, he proffered friendship, which was returned with adoration. These latter deserted in a mass the mountain of God and yielded to the Seraph the homage which That Other would fain have kept for himself alone.

"I ranked among the Dominations, and my name, Alaciel, was not unknown to fame. To satisfy my mind -- that was ever tormented with an insatiable thirst for knowledge and understanding -- I observed the nature of things, I studied the properties of minerals, air, and water. I sought out the laws which govern nature, solid or ethereal, and after much pondering I perceived that the Universe had not been formed as its pretended Creator would have us believe; I knew that all that exists, exists of itself and not by the caprice of Iahveh; that the world is itself its own creator and the spirit its own God. Henceforth I despised Iahveh for his imposture, and I hated him because he showed himself to be opposed to all that I found desirable and good: liberty, curiosity, doubt. These feelings drew me towards the Seraph. I admired him, I loved him. I dwelt in his light. When at length it appeared that a choice had to be made between him and That Other I ranged myself on the side of Lucifer and knew no other aim than to serve him, no other desire than to share his lot.

"War having become inevitable, he prepared for it with indefatigable vigilance and all the resourcefulness of a far-seeing mind. Making the Thrones and Dominations into Chalybes and Cyclopes, he drew forth iron from the mountains bordering his domain; iron, which he valued more than gold, and forged weapons in the caverns of Heaven. Then in the desert plain of the North he assembled myriads of Spirits, armed them, taught them, and drilled them. Although prepared in secret, the enterprise was too vast for his adversary not to be soon aware of it. It might in truth be said that he had always foreseen and dreaded it, for he had made a citadel of his abode and a warlike host of his angels, and he gave himself the name of the God of Hosts. He made ready his thunderbolts. More than half of the children of Heaven remained faithful to him; thronging round him he beheld obedient souls and patient hearts. The Archangel Michael, who knew not fear, took command of these docile troops. Lucifer, as soon as he saw that his army could gain no more in numbers or in warlike skill, moved it swiftly against the foe, and promising his angels riches and glory marched at their head towards the mountain upon whose summit stands the Throne of the Universe. For three days our host swept onward over the ethereal plains. Above our heads streamed the black standards of revolt. And now, behold, the Mountain of God shone rosy in the orient sky and our chief scanned with his eyes the glittering ramparts. Beneath the sapphire walls the foe was drawn up in battle array, and, while we marched clad in our iron and bronze, they shone resplendent in gold and precious stones.

"Their gonfalons of red and blue floated in the breeze, and lightning flashed from the points of their lances. In a little while the armies were only sundered one from the other by a narrow strip of level and deserted ground, and at this sight even the bravest shuddered as they thought that there in bloody conflict their fate would soon be sealed.

"Angels, as you know, never die. But when bronze and iron, diamond point or flaming sword tear their ethereal substance, the pain they feel is more acute than men may suffer. for their flesh is more exquisitely delicate; and should some essential organ be destroyed, they fall inert and, slowly decomposing, are resolved into clouds and during long æons float insensible in the cold ether. And when at length they resume spirit and form they fail to recover full memory of their past life. Therefore it is but natural that angels shrink from suffering, and the bravest among them is troubled at the thought of being reft of light and sweet remembrance. Were it otherwise the angelic race would know neither the delight of battle nor the glory of sacrifice. Those who, before the beginning of Time, fought in the Empyrean for or against the God of Armies, would have taken part without honour in mock battles, and it would not now become me to say to you, my children, with rightful pride:

"'Lo, I was there!'

"Lucifer gave the signal for the onset and led the assault. We fell upon the enemy, thinking to destroy him then and there and carry the sacred citadel at the first onslaught. The soldiers of the jealous God, less fiery, but no whit less firm than ours, remained immovable. The Archangel Michael commanded them with the calmness and resolution of a mighty spirit. Thrice we strove to break through their lines, thrice they opposed to our ironclad breast the flaming points of their lances, swift to pierce the stoutest cuirass. In millions the glorious bodies fell. At length our right wing pierced the enemy's left and we beheld the Principalities, the Powers, the Virtues, the Dominations, and the Thrones turn and flee in full career; while the Angels of the Third Choir, flying distractedly above them, covered them with a snow of feathers mingled with a rain of blood. We sped in pursuit of them amid the debris of chariots and broken weapons, and we spurred their nimble flight. Suddenly a storm of cries amazed us. It grew louder and nearer. With desperate shrieks and triumphal clamour the right wing of the enemy, the giant archangels of the Most High, had flung themselves upon our left flank and broken it. Thus we were forced to abandon the pursuit of the fugitives and hasten to the rescue of our own shattered troops. Our prince flew to rally them, and re-established the conflict. But the left wing of the enemy, whose ruin he had not quite consummated, no longer pressed by lance or arrow, regained courage, returned, and faced us yet again. Night fell upon the dubious field. While under the shelter of darkness, in the still, silent air stirred ever and anon by the moans of the wounded, his forces were resting from their toils, Lucifer began to make ready for the next day's battle. Before dawn the trumpets sounded the reveille. Our warriors surprised the enemy at the hour of prayer, put them to rout, and long and fierce was the carnage that ensued. When all had either fallen or fled, the Archangel Michael, none with him save a few companions with four wings of flame, still resisted the onslaughts of a countless host. They fell back ceaselessly opposing their breasts to us, and Michael still displayed an impassible countenance. The sun had run a third of its course when we commenced to scale the Mountain of God. An arduous ascent it was: sweat ran from our brows, a dazzling light blinded us. Weighed down with steel, our feathery wings could not sustain us, but hope gave us wings that bore us up. The beautiful Seraph, pointing with glittering hand, mounting ever higher and higher, showed us the way. All day long we slowly climb the lofty heights which at evening were robed in azure, rose, and violet. The starry host appearing in the sky seemed as the reflection of our own arms. Infinite silence reigned above us. We went on, intoxicated with hope; all at once from the darkened sky lightning darted forth, the thunder muttered, and from the cloudy mountain-top fell fire from Heaven. Our helmets, our breastplates were running with flames, and our bucklers broke under bolts sped by invisible hands. Lucifer, in the storm of fire, retained his haughty mien. In vain the lightning smote him; mightier than ever he stood erect, and still defied the foe. At length, the thunder, making the mountain totter, flung us down pell-mell, huge fragments of sapphire and ruby crashing down with us as we fell, and we rolled inert, swooning, for a period whose duration none could measure.

"I awoke in a darkness filled with lamentations. And when my eyes had grown accustomed to the dense shadows I saw round me my companions in arms, scattered in thousands on the sulphurous ground, lit by fitful gleams of livid light. My eyes perceived but fields of lava, smoking craters, and poisonous swamps.

"Mountains of ice and shadowy seas shut in the horizon. A brazen sky hung heavy on our brows. And the horror of the place was such that we wept as we sat, crouched elbow on knee, our cheeks resting on our clenched hands.

"But soon, raising my eyes, I beheld the Seraph standing before me like a tower. Over his pristine splendour sorrow had cast its mantle of sombre majesty.

"'Comrades,' said he, 'we must be happy and rejoice, for behold we are delivered from celestial servitude. Here we are free, and it were better to be free in Hell than serve in Heaven. We are not conquered, since the will to conquer is still ours. We have caused the Throne of the jealous God to totter; by our hands it shall fall. Arise, therefore, and be of good heart.'

"Thereupon, at his command, we piled mountain upon mountain and on the topmost peak we reared engines which flung molten rocks against the divine habitations. The celestial host was taken unaware and from the abodes of glory there issued groans and cries of terror. And even then we thought to re-enter in triumph on our high estate, but the Mountain of God was wreathed with lightnings, and thunderbolts, falling on our fortress, crushed it to dust. After this fresh disaster, the Seraph remained awhile in meditation, his head buried in his hands. At length he raised his darkened visage. Now he was Satan, greater than Lucifer. Steadfast and loyal the angels thronged about him.

"'Friends,' he said, 'if victory is denied us now, it is because we are neither worthy nor capable of victory. Let us determine wherein we have failed. Nature shall not be ruled, the sceptre of the Universe shall not be grasped, Godhead shall not be won, save by knowledge alone. We must conquer the thunder; to that task we must apply ourselves unwearyingly. It is not blind courage (no one this day has shown more courage than have you) which will win us the courts of Heaven; but rather study and reflection. In these silent realms where we are fallen, let us meditate, seeking the hidden causes of things; let us observe the course of Nature; let us pursue her with compelling ardour and all-conquering desire; let us strive to penetrate her infinite grandeur, her infinite minuteness. Let us seek to know when she is barren and when she brings forth fruit; how she makes cold and heat, joy and sorrow, life and death; how she assembles and disperses her elements, how she produces both the light air we breathe and the rocks of diamond and sapphire whence we have been precipitated, the divine fire wherewith we have been scarred and the soaring thought which stirs our minds. Torn with dire wounds, scorched by flame and by ice, let us render thanks to Fate which has sedulously opened our eyes, and let us rejoice at our lot. It is through pain that, suffering a first experience of Nature, we have been roused to know her and to subdue her. When she obeys us we shall be as gods. But even though she hide her mysteries for ever from us, deny us arms and keep the secret of the thunder, we still must needs congratulate ourselves on having known pain, for pain has revealed to us new feelings, more precious and more sweet than those experienced in eternal bliss, and inspired us with love and pity unknown to Heaven.'

"These words of the Seraph changed our hearts and opened up fresh hope to us. Our hearts were filled with a great longing for knowledge and love.

"Meanwhile the Earth was coming into being. Its immense and nebulous orb took on hourly more shape and more certainty of outline. The waters which fed the seaweed, the madrepores and shell fish, and bore the light flotilla of the nautilus upon their bosom, no longer covered it in its entirety; they began to sink into beds, and already continents appeared, where, on the warm slime, amphibious monsters crawled. Then the mountains were overspread with forests, and divers races of animals commenced to feed on the grass, the moss, the berries on the trees, and on the acorns. Then there took possession of cavernous shelters under the rocks, a being who was cunning to wound with a sharpened stone the savage beasts, and by his ruses to overcome the ancient denizens of forest, plain, and mountain.

"Man entered painfully on his kingdom. He was defenceless and naked. His scanty hair afforded him but little protection from the cold. His hands ended in nails too frail to do battle with the claws of wild beasts, but the position of his thumb, in opposition to the rest of his fingers, allowed him easily to grasp the most diverse objects and endowed him with skill in default of strength. Without differing essentially from the rest of the animals, he was more capable than any others of observing and comparing. As he drew from his throat various sounds, it occurred to him to designate by a particular inflexion of the voice whatever impinged upon his mind, and by this sequence of different sounds he was enabled to fix and communicate his ideas. His miserable lot and his painstaking spirit aroused the sympathy of the vanquished angels, who discerned in him an audacity equalling their own, and the germ of the pride that was at once their glory and their bane. They came in large numbers to be near him, to dwell on this young earth whither their wings wafted them in effortless flight. And they took pleasure in sharpening his talents and fostering his genius. They taught him to clothe himself in the skins of wild beasts, to roll stones before the mouths of caves to keep out the tigers and bears. They taught him how to make the flame burst forth by twirling a stick among the dried leaves and to foster the sacred fire upon the hearth. Inspired by the ingenious spirits he dared to cross the rivers in the hollowed trunks of cleft trees, he invented the wheel, the grinding-mill, and the plough; the share tore up the earth and the wound brought forth fruit, and the grain offered to him who ground it divine nourishment. He moulded vessels in clay, and out of the flint he fashioned various tools.

"In fine, taking up our abode among mankind, we consoled them and taught them. We were not always visible to them, but of an evening, at the turn of the road, we would appear to them under forms often strange and weird, at times dignified and charming, and we adopted at will the appearance of a monster of the woods and waters, of a venerable old man, of a beautiful child, or of a woman with broad hips. Sometimes we would mock them in our songs or test their intelligence by some cunning prank. There were certain of us of a rather turbulent humour who loved to tease their women and children, but though lowly folk, they were our brothers, and we were never loath to come to their aid. Through our care their intelligence developed sufficiently to attain to mistaken ideas, and to acquire erroneous notions of the relations of cause and effect. As they supposed that some magic bond existed between the reality and its counterfeit presentment, they covered the walls of their caves with figures of animals and carved in ivory images of the reindeer and the mammoth in order to secure as prey the creatures they represented. Centuries passed by with infinite slowness while their genius was coming to birth. We sent them happy thoughts in dreams, inspired them to tame the horse, to castrate the bull, to teach the dog to guard the sheep. They created the family and the tribe. It came to pass one day that one of their wandering tribes was assailed by ferocious hunters. Forthwith the young men of the tribe formed an enclosed ring with their chariots, and in it they shut their women, children, old people, cattle, and treasures, and from the platform of their chariots they hurled murderous stones at their assailants. Thus was formed the first city. Born in misery and condemned to do murder by the law of Iahveh, man put his whole heart into doing battle, and to war he was indebted for his noblest virtues. He hallowed with his blood that sacred love of country which should (if man fulfils his destiny to the very end) enfold the whole earth in peace. One of us, Dædalus, brought him the axe, the plumb-line, and the sail. Thus we rendered the existence of mortals less hard and difficult. By the shores of the lakes they built dwellings of osier, where they might enjoy a meditative quiet unknown to the other inhabitants of the earth, and when they had learned to appease their hunger without too painful efforts we breathed into their hearts the love of beauty.

"They raised up pyramids, obelisks, towers, colossal statues which smiled stiff and uncouth, and genetic symbols. Having learnt to know us or trying at least to divine what manner of beings we were, they felt both friendship and fear for us. The wisest among them watched us with sacred awe and pondered our teaching. In their gratitude the people of Greece and of Asia consecrated to us stones, trees, shadowy woods; offered us victims, and sang us hymns; in fact we became gods in their sight, and they called us Horus, Isis, Astarte, Zeus, Cybele, Demeter, and Triptolemus. Satan was worshipped under the names of Evan, Dionysus, Bacchus, and Lenæus. He showed in his various manifestations all the strength and beauty which it is given to mortals to conceive. His eyes had the sweetness of the wood-violet, his lips were brilliant with the ruby-red of the pomegranate, a down finer than the velvet of the peach covered his cheeks and his chin: his fair hair, wound like a diadem and knotted loosely on the crown of his head, was encircled with ivy. He charmed the wild beasts, and penetrating into the deep forests drew to him all wild spirits, every thing that climbed in trees and peered through the branches with wild and timid gaze. On all these creatures fierce and fearful, that lived on bitter berries and beneath whose hairy breasts a wild heart beat, half-human creatures of the woods -- on all he bestowed loving-kindness and grace, and they followed him drunk with joy and beauty. He planted the vine and showed mortals how to crush the grapes underfoot to make the wine flow. Magnificent and benign, he fared across the world, a long procession following in his train. To bear him company I took the form of a satyr; from my brow sprang two budding horns. My nose was flat and my ears were pointed. Glands, like those of the goat, hung on my neck, a goat's tail moved with my moving loins, and my hairy legs ended in a black cloven hoof which beat the ground in cadence.

"Dionysus fared on his triumphal march over the world. In his company I passed through Lydia, the Phrygian fields, the scorching plains of Persia, Media bristling with hoar-frost, Arabia Felix, and rich Asia where flourishing cities were laved by the waves of the sea. He proceeded on a car drawn by lions and lynxes, to the sound of flutes, cymbals, and drums, invented for his mysteries. Bacchantes, Thyades, and Menads, girt with the dappled fawnskin, waved the thyrsus encircled with ivy. He bore in his train the Satyrs, whose joyous troop I led, Sileni, Pans, and Centaurs. Under his feet flowers and fruit sprang to life, and striking the rocks with his wand he made limpid streams gush forth. In the month of the Vintage he visited Greece, and the villagers ran forth to meet him, stained with the green and ruddy juices of the plants, they wore masks of wood, or bark, or leaves; in their hands they bore earthen cups, and danced wanton dances. Their womenfolk, imitating the companions of the God, their heads wreathed with green smilax, fastened round their supple loins skins of fawn or goat. The virgins twined about their throats garlands of fig leaves, they kneaded cakes of flour, and bore the Phallus in the mystic basket. And the vine-dressers, all daubed with lees of wine, standing up in their wains and bandying mockery or abuse with the passers-by, invented Tragedy.

"Truly, it was not in dreaming beside a fountain, but by dint of strenuous toil that Dionysus taught them to grow plants and to make them bring forth succulent fruits. And while he pondered the art of transforming the rough woodlanders into a race that should love music and submit to just laws, more than once over his brow, burning with the fire of enthusiasm, did melancholy and gloomy fever pass. But his profound knowledge and his friendship for mankind enabled him to triumph over every obstacle. O days divine! Beautiful dawn of life We led the Bacchanals on the leafy summits of the mountains and on the yellow shores of the seas. The Naiads and the Oreads mingled with us at our play. Aphrodite at our coming rose from the foam of the sea to smile upon us."

WHEN men had learned to cultivate the earth, to herd cattle, to enclose their holy places within walls, and to recognise the gods by their beauty, I withdrew to that smiling land girdled with dark woods and watered by the Stymphalos, the Olbios, the Erymanthus, and the proud Crathis, swollen with the icy waters of the Styx, and there, in a green valley at the foot of a hill planted with arbutus, olive, and pine, beneath a cluster of white poplars and plane trees, by the side of a stream flowing with soft murmur amid tufted mastic trees, I sang to the shepherds and the nymphs of the birth of the world, the origin of fire, of the tenuous air, of water and of earth. I told them how primeval men had lived wretched and naked in the woods, before the ingenious spirits had taught them the arts; of God, too, I sang to them, and why they gave Dionysus Semele to mother, because his desire to befriend mankind was born amid the thunder.

"It was not without effort that this people, more pleasing than all the others in the eyes of the gods, these happy Greeks, achieved good government and a knowledge of the arts. Their first temple was a hut composed of laurel branches; their first image of the gods, a tree; their first altar, a rough stone stained with the blood of Iphigenia. But in a short time they brought wisdom and beauty to a point that no nation had attained before them, that no nation has since approached. Whence comes it, Arcade, this solitary marvel on the earth? Wherefore did the sacred soil of Ionia and of Attica bring forth this incomparable flower? Because nor priesthood, nor dogma, nor revelation ever found a place there, because the Greeks never knew the jealous God.

"It was his own grace, his own genius that the Greek enthroned and deified as his God, and when he raised his eyes to the heavens it was his own image that he saw reflected there. He conceived everything in due measure; and to his temples he gave perfect proportion. All therein was grace, harmony, symmetry, and wisdom; all were worthy of the immortals who dwelt within them and who under names of happy choice, in realised shapes, figured forth the genius of man. The columns which bore the marble architrave, the frieze and the cornice were touched with something human, which made them venerable; and sometimes one might see, as at Athens and at Delphi, beautiful young girls strong-limbed and radiant upstaying the entablature of treasure house and sanctuary. O days of splendour, harmony, and wisdom!

"Dionysus resolved to repair to Italy, whither he was summoned under the name of Bacchus by a people eager to celebrate his mysteries. I took passage in his ship decked with tendrils of the vine, and landed under the eyes of the two brothers of Helen at the mouth of the yellow Tiber. Already under the teaching of the god, the inhabitants of Latium had learned to wed the vine to the young stripling elm. It was my pleasure to dwell at the foot of the Sabine hills in a valley crowned with trees and watered with pure springs. I gathered the verbena and the mallow in the meadows. The pale olive-trees twisting their perforated trunks on the slope of the hill gave me of their unctuous fruit. There I taught a race of men with square heads, who had not, like the Greeks, a fertile mind, but whose hearts were true, whose souls were patient, and who reverenced the gods. My neighbour, a rustic soldier, who for fifteen years had bowed under the burden of his haversack, had followed the Roman eagle over land and sea, and had seen the enemies of the sovereign people flee before him. Now he drove his furrow with his two red oxen, starred with white between their spreading horns, while beneath the cabin's thatch his spouse, chaste and sedate of mien, pounded garlic in a bronze mortar and cooked the beans upon the sacred hearth. And I, his friend, seated near by under an oak, used to lighten his labours with the sound of my flute, and smile on his little children, when the sun, already low in the sky, was lengthening the shadows, and they returned from the wood all laden with branches. At the garden gate where the pears and pumpkins ripened, and where the lily and the evergreen acanthus bloomed, a figure of Priapus carved out of the trunk of a fig tree menaced thieves with his formidable emblem, and the reeds swaying with the wind over his head scared away the plundering birds. At new moon the pious husbandman made offering of a handful of salt and barley to his household gods crowned with myrtle and with rosemary.

"I saw his children grow up, and his children's children, who kept in their hearts their early piety and did not forget to offer sacrifice to Bacchus, to Diana, and to Venus, nor omit to pour fresh wines and scatter flowers into the fountains. But slowly they fell away from their old habits of patient toil and simplicity.

"I heard them complain when the torrent, swollen with many rains, compelled them to construct a dyke to protect the paternal fields, and the rough Sabine wine grew unpleasing to their delicate palate. They went to drink the wines of Greece at the neighbouring tavern; and the hours slipped unheeded by, while within the arbour shade they watched the dance of the flute player, practised at swaying her supple limbs to the sound of the castanets.

"Lulled by murmuring leaves and whispering streams, the tillers of the soil took sweet repose, but between the poplars we saw along borders of the sacred way vast tombs, statues, and altars arise, and the rolling of the chariot wheels grew more frequent over the worn stones. A cherry sapling brought home by a veteran told us of the far-distant conquests of a Consul, and odes sung to the lyre related the victories of Rome, mistress of the world.

"All the countries where the great Dionysus had journeyed, changing wild beasts into men, and making the fruit and grain bloom and ripen beneath the passing of his Menads, now breathed the Pax Romana. The nursling of the she-wolf, soldier and labourer, friend of conquered nations, laid out roads from the margin of the misty sea to the rocky slopes of the Caucasus; in every town rose the temple of Augustus and of Rome, and such was the universal faith in Latin justice that in the gorges of Thessaly or on the wooded borders of the Rhine, the slave, ready to succumb under his iniquitous burden, called aloud on the name of Cæsar.

"But why must it be that on this ill-starred globe of land and water, all should perish and die and the fairest things be ever the most fleeting? O adorable daughters of Greece! O Science! O Wisdom! O Beauty! kindly divinities, you were wrapt in heavy slumber ere you submitted to the outrages of the barbarians, who already in the marshy wastes of the North and on the lonely steppes, ready to assail you, bestrode bare-backed their little shaggy horses.

"While, dear Arcade, the patient legionary camped by the borders of the Phasis and the Tanais, the women and the priests of Asia and of monstrous Africa invaded the Eternal City and troubled the sons of Remus with their magic spells. Until now, Iahveh, the persecutor of the laborious demons, was unknown to the world that he pretended to have created, save to certain miserable Syrian tribes, ferocious like himself, and perpetually dragged from servitude to servitude. Profiting by the Roman peace which assured free travel and traffic everywhere, and favoured the exchange of ideas and merchandise, this old God insolently made ready to conquer the Universe. He was not the only one, for the matter of that, to attempt such an undertaking. At the same time a crowd of gods, demiurges, and demons, such as Mithra, Thammuz, the good Isis, and Eubulus, meditated taking possession of the peace-enfolded world. Of all the spirits, Iahveh appeared the least prepared for victory. His ignorance, his cruelty, his ostentation, his Asiatic luxury, his disdain of laws, his affectation of rendering himself invisible, all these things were calculated to offend those Greeks and Latins who had absorbed the teaching of Dionysus and the Muses. He himself felt he was incapable of winning the allegiance of free men and of cultivated minds, and he employed cunning. To seduce their souls he invented a fable which, although not so ingenious as the myths wherewith we have surrounded the spirits of our disciples of old, could, nevertheless, influence those feebler intellects which are to be found everywhere in great masses. He declared that men having committed a crime against him, an hereditary crime, should pay the penalty for it in their present life and in the life to come (for mortals vainly imagine that their existence is prolonged in hell); and the astute Iahveh gave out that he had sent his own son to earth to redeem with his blood the debt of mankind. It is not credible that a penalty should redress a fault, and it is still less credible that the innocent should pay for the guilty. The sufferings of the innocent atone for nothing, and do but add one evil to another. Nevertheless, unhappy creatures were found to adore Iahveh and his son, the expiator, and to announce their mysteries as good tidings. We should not be surprised at this folly. Have we not seen many times indeed human beings who, poor and naked, prostrate themselves before all the phantoms of fear, and rather than follow the teaching of well-disposed demons, obey the commandments of cruel demiurges? Iahveh, by his cunning, took souls as in a net. But he did not gain therefrom, for his glorification, all that he expected. It was not he, but his son, who received the homage of mankind, and who gave his name to the new cult. He himself remained almost unknown upon earth."

CHAPTER XX. THE GARDENER'S STORY, CONTINUED

THE new superstition spread at first over Syria and Africa; it won over the seaports where the filthy rabble swarm, and, penetrating into Italy, infected at first the courtesans and the slaves, and then made rapid progress among the middle classes of the towns. But for a long while the country-side remained undisturbed. As in the past, the villagers consecrated a pine tree to Diana, and sprinkled it every year with the blood of a young boar; they propitiated their Lares with the sacrifice of a sow, and offered to Bacchus -- benefactor of mankind -- a kid of dazzling whiteness, or if they were too poor for this, at least they had a little wine and a little flour from the vineyard and from the fields for their household gods. We had taught them that it sufficed to approach the altar with clean hands, and that the gods rejoiced over a modest offering.

"Nevertheless, the reign of Iahveh proclaimed its advent in a hundred places by its extravagances. The Christians burnt books, overthrew temples, set fire to the towns, and carried on their ravages as far as the deserts. There, thousands of unhappy beings, turning their fury against themselves, lacerated their sides with points of steel. And from the whole earth the sighs of voluntary victims rose up to God like songs of praise.

"My shadowy retreat could not escape for long from the fury of their madness.

"On the summit of the hill which overlooked the olive woods, brightened daily with the sounds of my flute, had stood since the earliest days of the Pax Romana, a small marble temple, round as the huts of our forefathers. It had no walls, but on a base of seven steps, sixteen columns rose in a circle with the acanthus on the capitals, bearing a cupola of white tiles. This cupola sheltered a statue of Love fashioning his bow, the work of an Athenian sculptor. The child seemed to breathe, joy was welling from his lips, all his limbs were harmonious and polished. I honoured this image of the most powerful of all the gods, and I taught the villagers to bear to him as an offering a cup crowned with verbena and filled with wine two summers old.

"One day, when seated as my custom was at the feet of the god, pondering precepts and songs, an unknown man, wild-looking, with unkempt hair, approached the temple, sprang at one bound up the marble steps, and with savage glee exclaimed:

"'Die, poisoner of souls, and joy and beauty perish with you.' He spoke thus, and drawing an axe from his girdle raised it against the god. I stayed his arm, I threw him down, and trampled him under my feet.

"'Demon,' he cried desperately, 'suffer me to overturn this idol, and you may slay me afterwards.'

"I heeded not his atrocious plea, but leaned with all my might on his chest, which cracked under my knee, and, squeezing his throat with my two hands, I strangled the impious one.

"While he lay there, with purple face and lolling tongue, at the feet of the smiling god, I went to purify myself at the sacred stream. Then leaving this land, now the prey of the Christian, I passed through Gaul and gained the banks of the Saone, whither Dionysus had, in days gone by, carried the ine. The god of the Christians had not yet been proclaimed to this happy people. They worshipped for its beauty a leafy beech-tree, whose honoured branches swept the ground, and they hung fillets of wool thereon. They also worshipped a sacred stream and set up images of clay in a dripping grotto. They made offering of little cheeses and a bowl of milk to the Nymphs of the woods and mountains.

"But soon an apostle of sorrow was sent to them by the new God. He was drier than a smoked fish. Although attenuated with fasting and watching, he taught with unabated ardour all manner of gloomy mysteries. He loved suffering, and thought it good; his anger fell upon all that was beautiful, comely, and joyous. The sacred tree fell beneath his hatchet. He hated the Nymphs, because they were beautiful, and he flung imprecations at them when their shining limbs gleamed among the leaves at evening, and he held my melodious flute in aversion. The poor wretch thought that there were certain forms of words wherewith to put to flight the deathless spirits that dwell in the cool groves, and in the depths of the woods and on the tops of the mountains. He thought to conquer us with a few drops of water over which he had pronounced certain words and made certain gestures. The Nymphs, to avenge themselves, appeared to him at nightfall and inflamed him with desire which he foolish knave thought animal; then they fled, their laughter scattered like grain over the fields, while their victim lay tossing with burning limbs on his couch of leaves. Thus do the divine nymphs laugh at exorcisers, and mock the wicked and their sordid chastity.

"The apostle did not do as much harm as he wished, because his teaching was given to the simple souls living in obedience to Nature, and because the mediocrity of most of mankind is such that they gain but little from the principles inculcated in them. The little wood in which I dwelt belonged to a Gaul of senatorial family, who retained some traces of Latin elegance. He loved his young freed-woman and shared with her his bed of broidered purple. His slaves cultivated his garden and his vineyard; he was a poet and sang, in imitation of Ausonius, Venus whipping her son with roses. Although a Christian, he offered me milk, fruit, and vegetables as if I were the genius of the place. In return I charmed his idle moments with the music of my flute, and I gave him happy dreams. In fact, these peaceful Gauls knew very little of Iahveh and his son.

"But now behold fires looming on the horizon, and ashes driven by the wind fall within our forest glades. Peasants come driving a long file of waggons along the roads or urging their flocks before them. Cries of terror rise from the villages, 'The Burgundians are upon us!'

"Now one horseman is seen, lance in hand, clad in shining bronze, his long red hair falling in two plaits on his shoulders. Then come two, then twenty, then thousands, wild and blood-stained; old men and children they put to the sword, ay, even aged grandams whose grey hairs cleave to the soles of the slaughterer's boots, mingled with the brains of babes new-born. My young Gaul and his young freed-woman stain with their blood the couch broidered with narcissi. The barbarians burn the basilicas to roast their oxen whole, shatter the amphoræ, and drain the wine in the mud of the flooded cellars. Their women accompany them, huddled, half naked, in their war chariots. When the Senate, the dwellers in the cities, and the leaders of the churches had perished in the flames, the Burgundians, soddened with wine, lay down to slumber beneath the arcades of the Forum. Two weeks later one of them might have been seen smiling in his shaggy beard at the little child whom, on the threshold of their dwelling, his fair-haired spouse gathers in her arms; while another, kindling the fire of his forge, hammers out his iron with measured stroke; another sings beneath the oak tree to his assembled comrades of the gods and heroes of his race; and yet others spread out for sale stones fallen from Heaven, aurochs' horns, and amulets. And the former inhabitants of the country, regaining courage little by little, crept from the woods where they had fled for refuge, and returned to rebuild their burnt-down cabins, plough their fields, and prune their vines.

"Once more life resumed its normal course; but those times were the most wretched that mankind had yet experienced. The barbarians swarmed over the whole Empire. Their ways were uncouth, and as they nurtured feelings of vengeance and greed, they firmly believed in the ransom of sin.

"The fable of Iahveh and his son pleased them, and they believed it all the more easily in that it was taught them by the Romans whom they knew to be wiser than themselves, and to whose arts and mode of life they yielded secret admiration. Alas! the heritage of Greece and Rome had fallen into the hands of fools. All knowledge was lost. In those days it was held to be a great merit to sing among the choir, and those who remembered a few sentences from the Bible passed for prodigious geniuses. There were still poets as there were birds, but their verse went lame in every foot. The ancient demons, the good genii of mankind, shorn of their honours, driven forth, pursued, hunted down, remained hidden in the woods. There, if they still showed themselves to men, they adopted, to hold them in awe, a terrible face, a red, green, or black skin, baleful eyes, an enormous mouth fringed with boars' teeth, horns, a tail, and sometimes a human face on their bellies. The nymphs remained fair, and the barbarians, ignorant of the winsome names they bore in other days, called them fairies, and, imputing to them a capricious character and puerile tastes, both feared and loved them.

"We had suffered a grievous fall, and our ranks were sadly thinned; nevertheless we did not lose courage and, maintaining a laughing aspect and a benevolent spirit, we were in those direful days the real friends of mankind. Perceiving that the barbarians grew daily less sombre and less ferocious, we lent ourselves to the task of conversing with them under all sorts of disguises. We incited them, with a thousand precautions, and by prudent circumlocutions, not to acknowledge the old Iahveh as an infallible master, not blindly to obey his orders, and not to fear his menaces. When need was, we had recourse to magic. We exhorted them unceasingly to study nature and to strive to discover the traces of ancient wisdom.

"These warriors from the North -- rude though they were -- were acquainted with some mechanical arts. They thought they saw combats in the heavens; the sound of the harp drew tears from their eyes; and perchance they had souls capable of greater things than the degenerate Gauls and Romans whose lands they had invaded. They knew not how to hew stone or to polish marble; but they caused porphyry and columns to be brought from Rome and from Ravenna; their chief men took for their seal a gem engraved by a Greek in the days when Beauty reigned supreme. They raised walls with bricks, cunningly arranged like ears of corn, and succeeded in building quite pleasing-looking churches with cornices upheld by consoles depicting grim faces, and heavy capials whereon were represented monsters devouring one another.

"We taught them letters and sciences. A mouthpiece of their god, one Gerbert, took lessons in physics, arithmetic, and music with us, and it was said that he had sold us his soul. Centuries passed, and man's ways remained violent. It was a world given up to fire and blood. The successors of the studious Gerbert, not content with the possession of souls (the profits one gains thereby are lighter than air), wished to possess bodies also. They pretended that their universal and prescriptive monarchy was held from a fisherman on the lake of Tiberias. One of them thought for a moment to prevail over the loutish Germanus, successor to Augustus. But finally the spiritual had to come to terms with the temporal, and the nations were torn between two opposing masters.

"Nations tool shape amid horrible tumult. On every side were wars, famines, and internecine conflicts. Since they attributed the innumerable ills that fell upon them to their God, they called him the Most Good, not by way of irony, but because to them the best was he who smote the hardest. In those days of violence, to give myself leisure for study I adopted a rôle which may surprise you, but which was exceedingly wise.

"Between the Saone and the mountains of Charolais, where the cattle pasture, there lies a wooded hill sloping gently down to fields watered by a clear stream. There stood a monastery celebrated throughout the Christian world. I hid my cloven feet under a robe and became a monk in this Abbey, where I lived peacefully, sheltered from the men at arms who to friend or foe alike showed themselves equally exacting. Man, who had relapsed into childhood, had all his lessons to learn over again. Brother Luke, whose cell was next to mine, studied the habits of animals and taught us that the weasel conceives her young within her ear. I culled simples in the fields wherewith to soothe the sick, who until then were made by way of treatment to touch the relics of saints. In the Abbey were several demons similar to myself whom I recognised by their cloven feet and by their kindly speech. We joined forces in our endeavours to polish the rough mind of the monks.

"While the little children played at hop-scotch under the Abbey walls our friends the monks devoted themselves to another game equally unprofitable, at which, nevertheless, I joined them, for one must kill time, -- that, when one comes to think of it, is the sole business of life. Our game was a game of words which pleased our coarse yet subtle minds, set school fulminating against school, and put all Christendom in an uproar. We formed ourselves into two opposing camps. One camp maintained that before there were apples there was the Apple; that before there were popinjays there was the Popinjay; that before there were lewd and greedy monks there was the Monk, Lewdness and Greed; that before there were feet and before there were posteriors in this world the kick in the posterior must have had existence for all eternity in the bosom of God. The other camp replied that, on the contrary, apples gave man the idea of the apple; popinjays the idea of the popinjay; monks the idea of the monk, greed and lewdness, and that the kick in the posterior existed only after having been duly given and received. The players grew heated and came to fisticuffs. I was an adherent of the second party, which satisfied my reason better, and which was, in fact, condemned by the Council of Soissons.

"Meanwhile, not content with fighting among themselves, vassal against suzerain, suzerain against vassal, the great lords took it into their heads to go and fight in the East. They said, as well as I can remember, that they were going to deliver the tomb of the son of God.

"They said so, but their adventurous and covetous spirit excited them to go forth and seek lands, women, slaves, gold, myrrh, and incense. These expeditions, need it be said, proved disastrous; but our thick-headed compatriots brought back with them the knowledge of certain crafts and oriental arts and a taste for luxury. Henceforth we had less difficulty in making them work and in putting them in the way of inventions. We built wonderfully beautiful churches, with daringly pierced arches, lancet-shaped windows, high towers, thousands of pointed spires, which, rising in the sky towards Iahveh, bore at one and the same time the prayers of the humble and the threats of the proud, for it was all as much our doing as the work of men's hands; and it was a strange sight to see men and demons working together at a cathedral, each one sawing, polishing, collecting stones, graving, on capital and on cornice, nettles, thorns, thistles, wild parsley, and wild strawberry, -- carving faces of virgins and saints and weird figures of serpents, fishes with asses' heads, apes scratching their buttocks; each one, in fact, putting his own particular talent, -- mocking, sublime, grotesque, modest, or audacious, -- into the work and making of it all a harmonious cacophony, a rapturous anthem of joy and sorrow, a Babel of victory. At our instigation the carvers, the goldsmiths, the enamellers, accomplished marvels and all the sumptuary arts flourished at once; there were silks at Lyons, tapestries at Arras, linen at Rheims, cloth at Rouen. The good merchants rode on their palfreys to the fairs, bearing pieces of velvet and brocade, embroideries, orfrays, jewels, vessels of silver, and illuminated books. Strollers and players set up their trestles in the churches and in the public squares, and represented, according to their lights, simple chronicles of Heaven, Earth, and Hell. Women decked themselves in splendid raiment and lisped of love.

"In the spring when the sky was blue, nobles an peasants were possessed with the desire to make merry in the flower-strewn meadows. The fiddler tuned his instrument, and ladies, knights and demoiselles, townsfolk, villagers and maidens, holding hands, began the dance. But suddenly War, Pestilence, and Famine entered the circle, and Death, tearing the violin from the fiddler's hands, led the dance. Fire devoured village and monastery. The men-at-arms hanged the peasants on the sign-posts at the cross-roads when they were unable to pay ransom, and bound pregnant women to tree-trunks, where at night the wolves came and devoured the fruit within the womb. The poor people lost their senses. Sometimes, peace being re-established, and good times come again, they were seized with mad, unreasoning terror, abandoned their homes, and rushed hither and thither in troops, half naked, tearing themselves with iron hooks, and singing. I do not accuse Iahveh and his son of all this evil. Many ill things occurred without him and even in spite of him. But where I recognise the instigation of the All Good (as they called him) was in the custom instituted by his pastors, and established throughout Christendom, of burning, to the sound of bells and the singing of psalms, both men and women who, taught by the demons, professed, concerning this God, opinions of their own."

CHAPTER XXI. THE GARDENER'S STORY, CONCLUDED

IT seemed as if science and thought had perished for all eternity, and that the earth would never again know peace, joy, and beauty.

"But one day, under the walls of Rome, some workmen, excavating the earth on the borders of an ancient road, found a marble sarcophagus which bore carved on its sides simulacra of Love and the triumphs of Bacchus.

"The lid being raised, a maiden appeared whose face shone with dazzling freshness. Her long hair spread over her white shoulders, she was smiling in her sleep. A band of citizens, thrilled with enthusiasm, raised the funeral couch and bore it to the Capitol. The people came in crowds to contemplate the ineffable beauty of the Roman maiden and stood around in silence, watching for the awakening of the divine soul held within this form of adorable beauty.

"And it came to pass that the City was so greatly stirred by this spectacle that the Pope, fearing, not without reason, the birth of a pagan cult from this radiant body, caused it to be removed at night and secretly buried. The precaution was vain, the labour fruitless. After so many centuries of barbarism, the beauty of the antique world had appeared for a moment before the eyes of men; it was long enough for its image, graven on their hearts, to inspire them with an ardent desire to love and to know.

"Henceforth, the star of the God of the Christians paled and sloped to its decline. Bold navigators discovered worlds inhabited by numerous races who knew not old Iahveh, and it was suspected that he was no less ignorant of them, since he had given them no news of himself or of his son the expiator. A Polish Canon demonstrated the true motions of the earth, and it was seen that, far from having created the world, the old demiurge of Israel had not even an inkling of its structure. The writings of philosophers, orators, jurisconsults, and ancient poets were dragged from the dust of the cloisters and passing from hand to hand inspired men's minds with the love of wisdom. The Vicar of the jealous God, the Pope himself, no longer believed in Him whom he represented on earth. He loved the arts and had no other care than to collect ancient statues and to rear sumptuous buildings wherein were displayed the orders of Vitruvius reestablished by Bramante. We began to breathe anew. Already the old gods, recalled from their long exile, were returning to dwell upon earth. There they found once more their temples and their altars. Leo, placing at their feet the ring, the three crowns, and the keys, offered them in secret the incense of sacrifices. Already Polyhymnia, leaning on her elbow, had begun to resume the golden thread of her meditations; already, in the gardens, the comely Graces and the Nymphs and Satyrs were weaving their mazy dances, and at length the earth had joy once more within its grasp. But, O calamity, unlucky fate, -- most tragic circumstance! A German monk, all swollen with beer and theology, rose up against this renaissance of paganism, hurled menaces against it, shattered it, and prevailed single handed against the Princes of the Church. Inciting the nations, he called upon them to undertake a reform which saved that which was about to be destroyed. Vainly did the cleverest among us try to turn him from his work. A subtle demon, on earth called Beelzebub, marked him out for attack, now embarrassing him with learned controversial argument, now tormenting him with cruel mockery. The stubborn monk hurled his ink-pot at his head and went on with his dismal reformation. What ultimately happened? The sturdy mariner repaired, calked, and refloated the damaged ship of the Church. Jesus Christ owes it to this shaveling that his shipwreck was delayed for perhaps more than ten centuries. Henceforth things went from bad to worse. In the wake of this loutish monk, this beerswiller and brawler, came that tall, dry doctor from Geneva, who, filled with the spirit of the ancient Iahveh, strove to bring the world back again to the abominable days of Joshua and the Judges of Israel. A maniac was he, filled with cold fury, a heretic and a burner of heretics, the most ferocious enemy of the Graces.

"These mad apostles and their mad disciples made even demons like myself, even the horned devils, look back longingly on the time when the Son with his Virgin Mother reigned over the nations dazzled with splendours: cathedrals with their stone tracery delicate as lace, flaming roses of stained glass, frescoes painted in vivid colours telling countless wondrous tales, rich orfrays, glittering enamel of shrines and reliquaries, gold of crosses and of monstrances, waxen tapers gleaming like starry galaxies amid the gloom of vaulted arches, organs with their deep-toned harmonies. All this doubtless was not the Parthenon, nor yet the Panathenæa, but it gladdened eyes and hearts; it was, at all events, beauty. And these cursed reformers would not suffer anything either pleasing or lovable. You should have seen them climbing in black swarms over doorways, plinths, spires, and bell-towers, striking with senseless hammers those images in stone which the demons had carved working hand in hand with the master designers, those genial saints and dear, holy women, and the touching idols of Virgin Mothers pressing heir suckling to their heart. For, to be just, a little agreeable paganism had slipped into he cult of the jealous God. These monsters of heretics were for extirpating idolatry. We did our best, my companions and I, to hamper their horrible work, and I, for one, had the pleasure of flinging down some dozens from the top of the porches and galleries on to the Cathedral Square, where their detestable brains got knocked out. The worst of it was that the Catholic Church also reformed herself and grew more mischievous than ever. In the pleasant land of France, the seminarists and the monks were inflamed with unheard-of fury against the ingenious demons and the men of learning. My prior was one of the most violent opponents of sound knowledge. For some time past my studious lucubrations had caused him anxiety, and perhaps he had caught sight of my cloven foot. The scoundrel searched my cell and found paper, ink, some Greek books newly printed, and some Pan-pipes hanging on the wall. By these signs he knew me for an evil spirit and had me thrown into a dungeon where I should have eaten the bread of suffering and drunk the waters of bitterness, had I not promptly made my escape by the window and sought refuge in the wooded groves among the Nymphs and the Fauns.

"Far and wide the lighted pyres cast the odour of charred flesh. Everywhere there were tortures, executions, broken bones, and tongues cut out. Never before had the spirit of Iahveh breathed forth such atrocious fury. However, it was not altogether in vain that men had raised the lid of the ancient sarcophagus and gazed upon the Roman Virgin.

"During this time of great terror when Papists and Reformers rivalled one another in violence and cruelty, amidst all these scenes of torture, the mind of man was regaining strength and courage. It dared to look up to the heavens, and there it saw, not the old Jew drunk with vengeance, but Venus Urania, tranquil and resplendent. Then a new order of things was born, then the great centuries came into being. Without publicly denying the god of their ancestors, men of intellect submitted to his mortal enemies, Science and Reason, and Abbé Gassendi relegated him gently to the far-distant abyss of first causes. The kindly demons who teach and console unhappy mortals, inspired the great minds of those days with discourses of all kinds, with comedies and tales told in the most polished fashion. Women invented conversation, the art of intimate letter-writing, and politeness. Manners took on a sweetness and a nobility unknown to preceding ages. One of the finest minds of that age of reason, the amiable Bernier, wrote one day to St. Evremond: 'It is a great sin to deprive oneself of a pleasure.' And this pronouncement alone should suffice to show the progress of intelligence in Europe. Not that there had not always been Epicureans but, unlike Bernier, Chapelle, and Moliere, they had not the consciousness of their talent.

"Then even the very devotees understood Nature. And Racine, fierce bigot that he was, knew as well as such an atheistical physician as Guy Patin, how to attribute to divers states of the organs the passions which agitate mankind.

"Even in my abbey, whither I had returned after the turmoil, and which sheltered only the ignorant and the shallow thinker, a young monk, less of a dunce than the rest, confided to me that the Holy Spirit expresses itself in bad Greek to humiliate the learned.

"Nevertheless, theology and controversy were still raging in this society of thinkers. Not far from Paris in a shady valley there were to be seen solitary beings known as 'les Messieurs,' who called themselves disciples of St. Augustine, and argued with honest conviction that the God of the Scriptures strikes those who fear Him, spares those who confront Him, holds works of no account, and damns -- should He so wish it -- His most faithful servant; for His justice is not our justice, and His ways are incomprehensible.

"One evening I met one of these gentlemen in his garden, where he was pacing thoughtfully among the cabbage-plots and lettuce-beds. I bowed my horned head before him and murmured these friendly words: 'May old Jehovah protect you, sir. You know him well. Oh, how well you know him, and how perfectly you have understood his character.' The holy man thought he discerned in me a messenger from Hell, concluded he was eternally damned, and died suddenly of fright.

"The following century was the century of philosophy. The spirit of research was developed, reverence was lost; the pride of the flesh was diminished and the mind acquired fresh energy. Manners tool on an elegance until then unknown. On the other hand, the monks of my order grew more and more ignorant and dirty, and the monastery no longer offered me any advantage now that good manners reigned in the town. I could bear it no longer. Flinging my habit to the nettles, I put a powdered wig on my horned brow, hid my goat's legs under white stockings, and cane in hand, my pockets stuffed with gazettes, I frequented the fashionable world, visited the modish promenades, and showed myself assiduously in the cafes where men of letters were to be found. I was made welcome in salons where, as a happy novelty, there were arm-chairs that fitted the form, and where both men and women engaged in rational conversation.

"The very metaphysicians spoke intelligibly. I acquired great weight in the town as an authority on matters of exegesis, and, without boasting, I was largely responsible for the Testament of the cure Meslier and The Bible Explained, brought out by the chaplains to the King of Prussia.

"At this time a comic and cruel misadventure befel the ancient Iahveh. An American Quaker, by means of a kite, stole his thunderbolts.

"I was living in Paris, and was at the supper where they talked of strangling the last of the priests with the entrails of the last of the kings. France was in a ferment; a terrible revolution broke out. The ephemeral leaders o the disordered State carried on a Reign of Terror amidst unheard-of perils. They were, for the most part, less pitiless and less cruel than the princes and judges instituted by Iahveh in the kingdoms of the earth; nevertheless, they appeared more ferocious, because they gave judgment in the name of Humanity. Unhappily they were easily moved to pity and of great sensibility. Now men of sensibility are irritable and subject to fits of fury. They were virtuous; they had moral laws, that is to say they conceived certain narrowly defined moral obligations, and judged human actions not by their natural consequences but by abstract principles. Of all the vices which contribute to the undoing of a statesman, virtue is the most fatal; it leads to murder. To work effectively for the happiness of mankind, a man must be superior to all morals, like the divine Julius. God, so ill-used for some time past, did not, on the whole, suffer excessively harsh treatment from these new men. He found protectors among them, and was adored under the name of the Supreme Being. One might even go so far as to say that terror created a diversion from philosophy and was profitable to the old demiurge, in that he appeared to represent order, public tranquillity, and the security of person and property.

"While Liberty was coming to birth amid the storm, I lived at Auteuil, and visited Madame Helvetius, where freethinkers in every branch of intellectual activity were to be met with. Nothing could be rarer than a freethinker, even after Voltaire's day. A man who will face death without trembling dare not say anything out of the ordinary about morals. That very same respect for Humanity which prompts him to go forth to his death, makes him bow to public opinion. In those days I enjoyed listening to the talk of Volney, Cabanis, and Tracy. Disciples of the great Condillac, they regarded the senses as the origin of all our knowledge. They called themselves ideologists, were the most honourable people in the world, and grieved the vulgar minds by refusing them immortality. For the majority of people, though they do not know what to do with this life, long for another that shall have no end. During the turmoil, our small philosophical society was sometimes disturbed in the peaceful shades of Auteuil by patrols of patriots. Condorcet, our great man, was an outlaw. I myself was regarded as suspect by the friends of the people, who, in spite of my rustic appearance and my frieze coat, believed me to be an aristocrat, and I confess that independence of thought is the proudest of all aristocracies.

"One evening while I was stealthily watching the dryads of Boulogne, who gleamed amid the leaves like the moon rising above the horizon, I was arrested as a suspect, and put in prison. It was a pure misunderstanding; but the Jacobins of those days, like the monks whose place they had usurped, laid great stress on unity of obedience. After the death of Madame Helvetius our society gathered together in the salon of Madame de Condorcet. Bonaparte did not disdain to chat with us sometimes.

"Recognizing him to be a great man, we thought him an ideologist like ourselves. Our influence in the land was considerable. We used it in his favour, and urged him towards the Imperial throne, thinking to display to the world a second Marcus Aurelius. We counted on him to establish universal peace; he did not fulfil our expectations, and we were wrongheaded enough to be wroth with him for our own mistake.

"Without any doubt he greatly surpassed all other men in quickness of intelligence, depth of dissimulation, and capacity for action. What made him an accomplished ruler was that he lived entirely in the present moment, and had no thoughts for anything beyond the immediate and actual reality. His genius was far-reaching and agile; his intelligence, vast in extent but common and vulgar in character, embraced humanity, but did not rise above it. He thought what every grenadier in the army thought; but he thought it with unprecedented force. He loved the game of chance, and it pleased him to tempt fortune by urging pigmies in their hundreds and thousands against each other. It was the game of a child as big as the world. He was too wily not to introduce old Iahveh into the game, -- Iahveh, who was still powerful on earth, and who resembled him in his spirit of violence and domination. He threatened him, flattered him, caressed him, and intimidated him. He imprisoned his Vicar, of whom he demanded, with the knife at his throat, that rite of unction which, since the days of Saul of old, has bestowed might upon kings; he restored the worship of the demiurge, sang Te Deums to him, and made himself known through him as God of the earth, in small catechisms scattered broadcast throughout the Empire. They united their thunders, and a fine uproar they made.

"While Napoleon's amusements were throwing Europe into a turmoil, we congratulated ourselves on our wisdom, a little sad, withal, at seeing the era of philosophy ushered in with massacre, torture, and war. The worst is that the children of the century, fallen into the most distressing disorder, formed the conception of a literary and picturesque Christianity, which betokens a degeneracy of mind really unbelievable, and finally fell into Romanticism. War and Romanticism, what terrible scourges! And how pitiful to see these same people nursing a childish and savage love for muskets and drums! They did not understand that war, which trained the courage and founded the cities of barbarous and ignorant men, brings to the victor himself but ruin and misery, and is nothing but a horrible and stupid crime when nations are united together by common bonds of art, science, and trade.

"Insane Europeans who plot to cut each others' throats, now that one and the same civilisation enfolds and unites them all!

"I renounced all converse with these madmen and withdrew to this village, where I devoted myself to gardening. The peaches in my orchard remind me of the sun-kissed skin of the Mænads. For mankind I have retained my old friendship, a little admiration, and much pity, and I await, while cultivating this enclosure, that still distant day when the great Dionysus shall come, followed by his Fauns and his Bacchantes, to restore beauty and gladness to the world, and bring back the Golden Age. I shall fare joyously behind his car. And who knows if in that day of triumph mankind will be there for us to see? Who knows whether their worn-out race will not have already fulfilled its destiny, and whether other beings will not rise upon the ashes and ruins of what once was man and his genius? Who knows if winged beings will not have taken possession of the terrestrial empire? Even then the work of the good demons will not be ended, -- they will teach a winged race arts and the joy of life."

CHAPTER XXII. WHEREIN WE ARE SHOWN THE INTERIOR OF A
BRIC-A-BRAC SHOP, AND SEE HOW PÈRE GUINARDON'S GUILTY
HAPPINESS IS MARRED BY THE JEALOUSY OF A LOVE-LORN
DAME.

PÈRE GUINARDON (as Zéphyrine had faithfully reported to Monsieur
Sariette) smuggled out the pictures, furniture, and curios stored in his attic in the
rue Princesse -- his studio he called it -- and used them to stock a shop he had
taken in the rue de Courcelles. Thither he went to take up his abode, leaving
Zéphyrine, with whom he had lived for fifty years, without a bed or a saucepan
or a penny to call her own, except eighteen pence the poor creature had in her
purse. Père Guinardon opened an old picture and curiosity shop, and in it he
installed the fair Octavie.

The shop-front presented an attractive appearance: there were Flemish
angels in green copes, after the manner of Gerard David, a Salome of the Luini
school, a Saint Barbara in painted wood of French workmanship, Limoges
enamel-work, Bohemian and Venetian glass, dishes from Urbino. There were
specimens of English pointlace which, if her tale was true, had been presented
to Zéphyrine, in the days of her radiant girlhood, by the Emperor Napoleon III.
Within, there were golden articles that glinted in the shadows, while pictures of
Christ, the Apostles, high-bred dames, and nymphs also presented themselves
to the gaze. There was one canvas that was turned face to the wall so that it
should only be looked at by connoisseurs; and connoisseurs are scarce. It was
a replica of Fragonard's Gimblette, a brilliant painting that looked as if it had
barely had time to dry. Papa Guinardon himself remarked on the fact. At the far
end of the shop was a king-wood cabinet, the drawers of which were full of all
manner of treasures: water colours by Baudouin, eighteenth-century books of
illustrations, miniatures, and so forth.

But the real masterpiece, the marvel, the gem, the pearl of great price,
stood upon an easel veiled from public view. It was a Coronation of the Virgin
by Fra Angelico, an exquisitely delicate thing in gold and blue and pink. Père
Guinardon was asking a hundred thousand francs for it. Upon a Louis XV chair
beside an Empire work-table on which stood a vase of flowers, sat the fair
Octavie, broidery in hand. She, having left her glistering rags behind her in the
garret in the rue Princesse, no longer presented the appearance of a touched-up
Rembrandt, but shone, rather, with the soft radiance and limpidity of a Vermeer
of Delft, for the delectation of the connoisseurs who frequented the shop of Papa
Guinardon. Tranquil and demure, she remained alone in the shop all day, while
the old fellow himself was up aloft working away at the deuce knows what

picture. About five o'clock he used to come downstairs and have a chat with the habitues of the establishment.

The most regular caller was the Comte Desmaisons, a thin, cadaverous man. A strand of hair issued from the deep hollow under each cheekbone, and, broadening as it descended, shed upon his chin and chest torrents of snow in which he was for ever trailing his long, fleshless, gold-ringed fingers. For twenty years he had been mourning the loss of his wife, who had been carried off by consumption in the flower of her youth and beauty. Since then he had spent his whole life in endeavouring to hold converse with the dead and in filling his lonely mansion with second-rate paintings. His confidence in Guinardon knew no bounds. Another client who was a scarcely less frequent visitor to the shop was Monsieur Blancmesnil, a director of a large financial establishment. He was a florid, prosperous-looking man of fifty. He took no great interest in matters of art, and was perhaps an indifferent connoisseur, but, in his case, it was the fair Octavie, seated in the middle of the shop, like a son-bird in its cage, that offered the attraction.

Monsieur Blancmesnil soon established relation with her, a fact which Père Guinardon alone failed to perceive, for the old fellow was still young in his love-affair with Octavie. Monsieur Gaétan d'Esparvieu used to pay occasional visits to Père Guinardon's shop out of mere curiosity, for he strongly suspected the old man of being a first-rate "faker."

And then that doughty swordsman, Monsieu Le Truc de Ruffec, also came to see the old antiquary on one occasion, and acquainted him with a plan he had on foot. Monsieur Le Truc de Ruffec was getting up a little historical exhibition of small arms at the Petit Palais in aid of the fund for the education of the native children in Morocco and wanted Père Guinardon to lend him a few of the most valuable articles in his collection.

"Our first idea," he said, "was to organise an exhibition to be called 'The Cross and the Sword.' The juxtaposition of the two words will make the idea which has prompted our undertaking sufficiently clear to you. It was an idea pre-eminently patriotic and Christian which led us to associate the Sword, which is the symbol of Honour, with the Cross, which is the symbol of Salvation. It was hoped that our work would be graced by the distinguished patronage of the Minister of War and Monseigneur Cachepot. Unfortunately there were difficulties in the way, and the full realisation of the project had to be deferred. In the meantime we are limiting our exhibition to 'The Sword.' I have drawn up an explanatory note indicating the significance of the demonstration." Having delivered himself of these remarks, Monsieur Le Truc de Ruffec produced a pocket-case stuffed full of papers. Picking out from a medley of judgment summonses and other odds and ends a little piece of very crumpled paper, he exclaimed, "Ah, here it is," and proceeded to read as follows: "'The Sword is a fierce Virgin; it is par excellence the Frenchman's weapon. And now, when patriotic sentiment, after suffering an all too protracted eclipse, is beginning to shine forth again more ardently than ever...' and so forth; you see?"

And he repeated his request for some really fine specimen to be placed in the most conspicuous position in the exhibition to be held on behalf of the little native children of Morocco, of which General d'Esparvieu was to be honorary President.

Arms and armour were by no means Père Guinardon's strong point. He dealt principally in pictures, drawings, and books. But he was never to be taken unawares. He took down a rapier with a gilt colander-shaped hilt, a highly typical piece of workmanship of the Louis XIII-Napoleon III period, and presented it to the exhibition promoter, who, while contemplating it with respect, maintained a diplomatic silence.

"I have something better still in here," said the antiquary, and he produced from his inner shop -- where it had been lying among the walking-sticks and umbrellas -- a real demon of a sword, adorned with fleurs-de-lys, a genuine royal relic. It was the sword of Philippe-Auguste as worn by an actor at the Odéon when Agnès de Méranie was being performed in 1846. Guinardon held it point downwards, as though it were a cross, clasping his hands piously on the cross-bar. He looked as loyal as the sword itself.

"Have her for your exhibition," said he. "The damsel is well worth it. Bouvines is her name."

"If I find a buyer for it," said Monsieur Le Truc de Ruffec, twirling his enormous moustachios, "I suppose you will allow me a little commission?"

Some days later, Père Guinardon was mysteriously displaying a picture to the Comte Desmaisons and Monsieur Blancmesnil. It was a newly discovered work of El Greco, an amazingly fine example of the Master's later style. It represented a Saint Francis of Assisi standing erect upon Mont Alverno. He was mounting heavenward like a column of smoke, and was plunging into the regions of the clouds a monstrously narrow head that the distance rendered smaller still. In fine it was a real, very real, nay, too real El Greco. The two collectors were attentively scrutinizing the work, while Père Guinardon was belauding the depth of the shadows and the sublimity of the expression. He was raising his arms aloft to convey an idea of the greatness of Theotocopuli, who derived from Tintoretto, whom, however, he surpassed in loftiness by a hundred cubits.

"He was chaste and pure and strong; a mystic, a visionary."

Comte Desmaisons declared that El Greco was his favourite painter. In his inmost heart Blancmesnil was not so entirely struck with it.

The door opened, and Monsieur Gaétan quite unexpectedly appeared on the scene.

He gave a glance at the Saint Francis, and said:

"Bless my soul!"

Monsieur Blancmesnil, anxious to improve his knowledge, asked him what he thought of this artist who was now so much in vogue. Gaétan replied, glibly enough, that he did not regard El Greco as the eccentric, the madman that people used to take him for. It was rather his opinion that a defect of vision from which Theotocopuli suffered compelled him to deform his figures.

"Being afflicted with astigmatism and strabismus," Gaétan went on, "he painted the things he saw exactly as he used to see them."

Comte Desmaisons was not readily disposed to accept so natural an explanation, which, however, by its very simplicity, highly commended itself to Monsieur Blancmesnil.

Père Guinardon, quite beside himself, exclaimed:

"Are you going to tell me, Monsieur d'Esparvieu, that Saint John was astigmatic because he beheld a woman clothed with the sun, crowned with stars, with the moon about her feet; the Beast with seven heads and ten horns, and the seven angels robed in white linen that bore the seven cups filled with the wrath of the Living God"

"After all," said Monsieur Gaétan, by way of conclusion, "people are right in admiring El Greco if he had genius enough to impose his morbidity of vision upon them. By the same token, the contortions to which he subjects the human countenance may give satisfaction to those who love suffering, -- a class more numerous than is generally supposed."

"Monsieur," replied the Comte Desmaisons, stroking his luxuriant beard with his long, thin hand, "we must love those that love us. Suffering loves us and attaches itself to us. We must love it if life is to be supportable to us. In the knowledge of this truth lies the strength and value of Christianity. Alas! I do not possess the gift of Faith. It is that which drives me to despair."

The old man thought of her for whom he had been mourning twenty years, and forthwith his reason left him, and his thoughts abandoned themselves unresistingly to the morbid imaginings of gentle and melancholy madness.

Having, he said, made a study of psychic matters, and having, with the co-operation of a favourable medium, carried out experiments concerning the nature and duration of the soul, he had obtained some remarkable results, which, however, did not afford him complete satisfaction. He had succeeded in viewing the soul of his dead wife under the appearance of a transparent and gelatinous mass which bore not the slightest resemblance to his adored one. The most painful part about the whole experiment -- which he had repeated over and over again -- was that the gelatinous mass, which was furnished with a number of extremely slender tentacles, maintained them in constant motion in time to a rhythm apparently intended to make certain signs, but of what these movements were supposed to convey there was not the slightest clue.

During the whole of this narrative Monsieur Blancmesnil had been whispering in a corner with the youthful Octavie, who sat mute and still, with her eyes on the ground.

Now Zéphyrine had by no means made up her mind to resign her lover into the hands of an unworthy rival. She would often go round of a morning, with her shopping-basket on her arm, and prowl about outside the curio shop. Torn betwixt grief and rage, tormented by warring ideas, she sometimes thought she would empty a saucepanful of vitriol on the head of the faithless one at others that she would fling herself at his feet, and shower tears and kisses on his precious hands. One day, as she was thus eyeing her Micheh -- her beloved but guilty Michel -- she noticed through the window the fair and youthful Octavie, who was sitting with her embroidery at a table upon which, in a vase of crystal, a rose was swooning to death. Zéphyrine, in a transport of fury, brought down her umbrella on her rival's fair head, and called her a bitch and a trollop. Octavie fled in terror, and ran for the police, while Zéphyrine, beside herself with grief and love, kept digging away with her old gamp at the Gimblette of Fragonard, the fuliginous Saint Francis of El Greco, the virgins, the nymphs, and the apostles, and knocked the gilt off the Fra Angelico, shrieking all the while:

"All those pictures there, the El Greco, the Beato Angelico, the Fragonard, the Gerard David, and the Baudouins -- Guinardon painted the whole lot of them himself, the wretch, the scoundrel! That Fra Angelico there, why I saw him painting it on my ironing-board, and that Gerard David he executed on an old midwife's sign-board. You and that bitch of yours, why, I'll do for the pair of you just as I'm doing for these pictures."

And tugging away at the coat of an aged collector who, trembling all over, had hidden himself in the darkest corner of the shop, she called him to witness to the crimes of Guinardon, perjurer and impostor. The police had simply to tear her out of the ruined shop. As she was being taken off to the station, followed by a great crowd of people, she raised her fiery eyes to Heaven, crying in a voice choked with sobs:

"But don't you know Michel? If you knew him, you would understand that it is impossible to live without him. Michel! He is handsome and good and charming. He is a very god. He is Love itself. I love him! I love him! I love him! I have known men high up in the world -- Dukes, Ministers of State, and higher still. Not one of them was worthy to clean the mud off Michel's boots. My good, kind sirs, give him back to me again."

CHAPTER XXIII. WHEREIN WE ARE PERMITTED TO OBSERVE
THE ADMIRABLE CHARACTER OF BOUCHOTTE, WHO RESISTS
VIOLENCE BUT YIELDS TO LOVE. AFTER THAT LET NO ONE
CALL THE AUTHOR A MISOGYNIST

ON coming away from the Baron Everdingen's, Prince Istar went have a few oysters and a bottle white wine at an eating-house in the Market. Then, being prudent as well as powerful, he paid a visit to his friend, Théophile Belais, for his pockets were full of bombs, and he wanted to secrete them in the musician's cupboard. The composer of Aline, Queen of Golconda was not at home. However, the Kerûb found Bouchotte busily working up the role of Zigouille; for the young artiste was booked to play the principal part in Les Apaches, an operetta that was then being rehearsed in one of the big music halls. The part in question was that of a street-walker who by her obscene gestures lures a passer-by into a trap, and then, while her victim is being gagged and bound repeats with fiendish cruelty the lascivious motions by which he had been led astray. The part required that she should appear both as mime and singer, and she was in a state of high enthusiasm about it.

The accompanist had just left. Prince Istar seated himself at the piano, and Bouchotte resumed her task. Her movements were unseemly and delicious. Her tawny hair was flying in all directions in wild disordered curls; her skin was moist, it exhaled a scent of violets and alkaline salts which made the nostrils throb; even she herself felt the intoxication. Suddenly, inebriated with her intoxicating presence, Prince Istar arose, and with never a word or a look, caught her into his arms and drew her on to the couch, the little couch with the flowered tapestry which Théophile had procured at one of the big shops by promising to pay ten francs a month for a long term of years. Now Istar might have solicited Bouchotte's favours; he might have invited her to a rapid, and, withal, a mutual embrace, and, despite her preoccupation and excitement, she would not have refused him. But Bouchotte was a girl of spirit. The merest hint of coercion awoke all her untamable pride. She would consent of her own accord, yes; but be mastered, never! She would readily yield to love, curiosity, pity, to less than that even, but she would die rather than yield to force. Her surprise immediately gave place to fury. She fought her agressor with all her heart and soul. With nails, to which fury lent an added edge, she tore at the cheeks and eyelids of the Kerûb, and, though he held her as in a vice, she arched herself so stiffly and made such excellent play with knee and elbow, that the human-headed bull, blinded with blood and rage, was sent crashing into the piano which gave forth a prolonged groan, while the bombs, tumbling out of his pockets, fell on the floor with a noise like thunder. And Bouchotte, with dishevelled locks, and one breast bare, beautiful and terrible, stood brandishing the poker over the prostrate giant, crying:

"Be off with you, or I'll put your eyes out!"

Prince Istar went to wash himself in the kitchen, and plunged his gory visage into a basin where some haricot beans lay soaking; then he withdrew without anger or resentment, for he had a noble soul.

Scarcely had he gone when the door-bell rang. Bouchotte, calling upon the absent maid in vain, slipped on a dressing-gown and opened the door herself. A young man, very correct in appearance and rather good-looking, bowed politely, and apologising for having to introduce himself, gave his name. It was Maurice d'Esparvieu.

Maurice was still seeking his guardian angel. Upheld by a desperate hope, he sought him in the queerest places. He enquired for him at the houses of sorcerers, magicians, and thaumaturgists, who in filthy hovels lay bare the ineffable secrets of the future, and who, though masters of all the treasures of the earth, wear trousers without any seats to them, and eat pigs' brains. That very day, having been to a back street in Montmartre to consult a priest of Satan, who practised black magic by piercing waxen images, Maurice had gone on to Bouchotte's, having been sent by Madame de la Verdelière, who, being about to give a fete in aid of the fund for the Preservation of Country Churches, was anxious to secure Bouchotte's services, since she had suddenly become -- no one knew why -- a fashionable artiste.

Bouchotte invited the visitor to sit down on the little flowered couch; at his request she seated herself beside him, and our young man of fashion explained to the singer what Madame de la Verdelière desired of her. The lady wished Bouchotte to sing one of those apache songs which were giving such delight in the fashionable world. Unfortunately Madame de la Verdelière could only offer a very modest fee, one out of all proportion to the merits of the artiste, but then it was for a good cause.

Bouchotte agreed to take part, and accepted the reduced fee with the accustomed liberality of the poor towards the rich and of artists towards society people. Bouchotte was not a selfish girl; the work for the preservation of country churches interested her. She remembered with sobs and tears her first communion, and she still retained her faith. When she passed by a church she wanted to enter it, especially in the evening. And so she did not love the Republic which had done its utmost to destroy both the Church and the Army. Her heart rejoiced to see the re-birth of national sentiment. France was lifting up her head. What was most applauded in the music halls were songs about the soldiers and the kind nuns. Meanwhile Maurice inhaled the odour of her tawny hair, the subtle bitter perfume of her body, all the odours of her person, and desire grew in him. He felt her near him on the little couch, very warm and very soft. He complimented the artiste on her great talent. She asked him what he liked best in all her repertory. He knew nothing about it, still he made replies that satisfied her. She had dictated them herself without knowing it. The vain creature spoke of her talent, of her success, as she wished others to speak of them. She never ceased talking of her triumphs, yet withal she was candour itself. Maurice in all sincerity praised Bouchotte's beauty, her fresh skin, her purity of line. She attributed this advantage to the fact that she never made up and never "put messes on her face." As to her figure, she admitted that there was enough everywhere and none too much, and to illustrate this assertion she passed her hand over all the contours of her charming body, rising lightly to follow the delightful curves on which she reposed.

Maurice was quite moved by it. It began to grow dark; she offered to light up. He begged her to do nothing of the sort.

Their talk, at first gay and full of laughter, grew more intimate and very sweet, with a certain languor in its tone. It seemed to Bouchotte that she had known Monsieur Maurice d'Esparvieu for a long time, and holding him for a man of delicacy, she gave him her confidence. She told him that she was by nature a good woman, but that she had had a grasping and unscrupulous mother. Maurice recalled her to the consideration of her own beauty, and exalted by subtle flattery the excellent opinion she had of herself. Patient and calculating, in spite of the burning desire growing in him, he aroused and increased in the desired one the longing to be still further admired. The dressing-gown opened and slipped down of its own accord, the living satin of her shoulders gleamed in the mysterious light of evening. He -- so prudent, so clever, so adroit, -- let her sink in his arms, ardent and half swooning before she had even perceived she had granted anything at all. Their breath and their murmurs intermingled. And the little flowery couch sighed in sympathy with them.

When they recovered the power to express their feelings in words, she whispered in his ear that his cheek was even softer than her own.

He answered, holding her embraced:

"It is charming to hold you like this. One would think you had no bones."

She replied, closing her eyes:

"It is because I love you. Love seems to dissolve my bones; it makes me as soft and melting as a pig's foot á la Ste. Menebould.

Hereupon Théophile came in, and Bouchotte called upon him to thank Monsieur Maurice d'Esparvieu, who had been amiable enough to be the bearer of a handsome offer from Madame la Comtesse de la Verdelière.

The musician was happy, feeling the quiet and peace of the house after a day of fruitless applications, of colourless lessons, of failure and humiliation. Three new collaborators had been thrust upon him who would add their signatures to his on his operetta, and receive their share of the author's rights, and he had been told to introduce the tango into the Court of Golconda. He pressed young d'Esparvieu's hand and dropped wearily on to the little couch, which, being now at the end of its strength, gave way at the four legs and suddenly collapsed.

And the angel, precipitated to the ground, rolled terror-struck on to the watch, match-box and cigarette-case that had fallen from Maurice's pocket, and on to the bombs Prince Istar had left behind him.

CHAPTER XXIV. CONTAINING AN ACCOUNT OF THE VICISSITUDES THAT BEFEL THE "LUCRETIUS" OF THE PRIOR DE VENDÔME.

LÉGER-MASSIEU, successor to Léger senior, the binder, whose establishment was in the rue de l'Abbaye, opposite the old Hôtel of the Abbés of Saint Germain-des-Près, in the hotbed of ancient schools and learned societies, employed an excellent but by no means numerous staff of workmen, and served with leisurely deliberation a clientèle who had learned to practise the virtue of patience. Six weeks had elapsed since he had received the parcel of books that had been despatched by Monsieur Sariette, but still Léger-Massieu had not yet put the work in hand. It was not until fifty-three days had come and gone, that, after calling over the books against he list that had been drawn up by Monsieur Sariette, the binder gave them out to his workmen. The little Lucretius with the Prior de Vendôme's arms not being mentioned on the list, it was assumed that it had been sent by another customer. And as it did not figure on any list of goods received it remained shut up in a cupboard, from which Léger-Massieu's son, the youthful Ernest, one day surreptitiously abstracted it, and slipped it into his pocket. Ernest was in love with a neighbouring seamstress whose name was Rose. Rose was fond of the country, and liked to hear the birds singing in the woods, and in order to procure the wherewithal to take her to Chatou one Sunday and give her a dinner, Ernest parted with the Lucretius for ten francs to old Moranger, a second-hand dealer in the rue Saint X----, who displayed no great curiosity regarding the origin of his acquisitions. Old Moranger handed over the volume, the very same day, to Monsieur Poussard, an expert in books, of the faubourg Saint Germain, for sixty francs. The latter removed the stamp which disclosed the ownership of the matchless copy, and sold it for five hundred francs to Monsieur Joseph Meyer, the well-known collector, who handed it straight away for three thousand francs to Monsieur Ardon, the bookseller, who immediately transferred it to Monsieur R----, the great Parisian bibliopolist, who gave six thousand for it, and sold it again a fortnight later at a handsome profit to Madame la Comtesse de Gorce. Well known in the higher ranks of Parisian society, the lady in question is what was called in the seventeenth century a "curieuse," that is to say, a lover of pictures, books, and china. In her mansion in the Avenue d'Jéna she possesses collections of works of art which bear witness to the diversity of her knowledge and the excellence of her taste. During the month of July, while the Comtesse de Gorce was away at her château at Sarville in Normandy, the house in the Avenue d'Jéna, being unoccupied, was visited one night by a thief said to belong to a gang known as "The Collectors," who made works of art the special objects of their raids.

The police enquiry elicited the fact that the marauder had reached the first floor by means of the waste-pipe, that he had then climbed over the balcony, forced a shutter with a jemmy, broken a pane of glass, turned the window-fastener, and made his way into the long gallery. There he broke open several cupboards and possessed himself of whatever took his fancy. His booty consisted for the most part of small but valuable articles, such as gold caskets, a few ivory carvings of the fourteenth century, two splendid fifteenth-century manuscripts, and a volume which the Countess's secretary briefly described as "a morocco-bound book with a coat of arms on it," and which was none other than the Lucretius from the d'Esparvieu library.

The malefactor, who was supposed to be an English cook, was never discovered. But, two months or so after the theft, a well-dressed, clean-shaven young man passed down the rue de Courcelles, in the dimness of twilight, and went to offer the Prior de Vendôme's Lucretius to Père Guinardon. The antiquary gave him four shillings for it, examined it carefully, recognised its interest and its beauty, and put it in the king-wood cabinet, where he kept his special treasures.

Such were the vicissitudes which, in the course of a single season, befel this thing of beauty.

CHAPTER XXV. WHEREIN MAURICE FINDS HIS ANGEL AGAIN

THE performance was over. Bouchotte in her dressing-room was taking off her make-up, when the door opened softly and old Monsieur Sandraque, her protector, came in, followed by a troop of her other admirers. Without so much as turning her head, she asked them what they meant by coming and staring at her like a pack of imbeciles, and whether they thought they were in a tent at the Neuilly Fair, looking at the freak woman.

"Now, then, ladies and gentlemen," she rattled on derisively, "just put a penny in the box for the young lady's marriage-portion, and she'll let you feel her legs, -- all made of marble!"

Then, with an angry glance at the admiring throng, she exclaimed: "Come, off you go! Look alive!"

She sent them all packing, her sweetheart Théophile among them, -- the pale-faced, long-haired, gentle, melancholy, short-sighted, and dreamy Théophile.

But recognizing her little Maurice, she gave him a smile. He approached her, and leaning over the back of the chair on which she was seated, congratulated her on her playing and singing, duly performing a kiss at the end of every compliment She did not let him escape thus, and with reiterated enquiries, pressing solicitations, feigned incredulity obliged him to repeat his stock panegyrics three or four times over, and when he stopped she seemed so disappointed that he was forced to take up the strain again immediately. He found it trying, for he was no connoisseur, but he had the pleasure of kissing her plump curved shoulders all golden in the light, and of catching glimpses of her pretty face in the mirror over the toilet-table.

"You were delicious."

"Really?... you think so?"

"Adorable... div----"

Suddenly he gave a loud cry. His eyes had seen in the mirror a face appear at the back of the dressingroom. He turned swiftly round, flung his arms about Arcade, and drew him into the corridor.

"What manners!" exclaimed Bouchotte, gasping.

But, pushing his way through a troop of performing dogs, and a family of American acrobats, young d'Esparvieu dragged his angel towards the exit.

He hurried him forth into the cool darkness of the boulevard, delirious with joy and wondering whether it was all too good to be true.

"Here you are!" he cried; "here you are! I have been looking for you a long time, Arcade, -- or Mirar if you like, -- and I have found you at last. Arcade, you have taken my guardian angel from me. Give him back to me. Arcade, do you love me still?"

Arcade replied that in accomplishing the super-angelic task he had set himself he had been forced to crush under foot friendship, pity, love, and all those feelings which tend to soften the soul; but that, on the other hand, his new state, by exposing him to suffering and privation, disposed him to love Humanity, and that he felt a certain mechanical friendship for his poor Maurice.

"Well, then," exclaimed Maurice, "if only you love me, come back to me, stay with me. I cannot do without you. While I had you with me I was not aware of your presence. But no sooner did you depart than I felt a horrible blank. Without you I am like a body without a soul. Do you know that in the little flat in the rue de Rome, with Gilberte by my side, I feel lonely, I miss you sorely, and long to see you and to hear you as I did that day when you made me so angry. Confess I was right, and that your behaviour on that occasion was not that of a gentleman. That you, you of so high an origin, so noble a mind, could commit such an indiscretion is extraordinary, when one comes to think about it. Madame des Aubels has not yet forgiven you. She blames you for having frightened her by appearing at such an inconvenient moment, and for being insolent and forward while hooking her dress and tying her shoes. I, I have forgotten everything. I only remember that you are my celestial brother, the saintly companion of my childhood. No, Arcade, you must not, you cannot leave me. You are my angel; you are my property."

Arcade explained to young d'Esparvieu that he could no longer be guiding angel to a Christian, having himself gone down into the pit. And he painted a horrible picture of himself; he described himself as breathing hatred and fury; in fact, an infernal spirit.

"All nonsense!" said Maurice, smiling, his eyes big with tears.

"Alas! our ideas, our destiny, everything tends to part us, Maurice. But I cannot stifle the tenderness I feel for you, and your candour forces me to love you."

"No," sighed Maurice. "You do not love me. You have never loved me. In a brother or a sister such indifference would be natural; in a friend it would be ordinary; in a guardian angel it is monstrous. Arcade, you are an abominable being. I hate you."

"I have loved you dearly, Maurice, and I still love you. You trouble my heart which I deemed encased in triple bronze. You show me my own weakness. When you were a little innocent boy I loved you as tenderly and purely as Miss Kate, your English governess, who caressed you with so much fervour. In the country, when the thin bark of the plane trees peels o in long strips and discloses the tender green trunk, after the rains which make the fine sand run on the sloping paths, I showed you how with that sand, those strips of bark, a few wild flowers, and a spray of maidenhair fern to make rustic bridges, rustic shelters, terraces, and those gardens of Adonis, which last but an hour. During the month of May in Paris we raised an altar to the Virgin, and we burnt incense before it, the scent of which, permeating all the house, reminded Marcelline, the cook, of her village church and her lost innocence, and drew from her floods of tears; it also gave your mother a headache, your mother who, with all her wealth, was crushed with the ennui that is common to the fortunate ones of this world. When you went to college I interested myself in your progress, I shared your work and your play, I pondered with you over arduous problems in arithmetic, I sought the impenetrable meaning of a phrase of Julius Cæsar's. What fine games of prisoners' base and football we had together! More than once did we know the intoxication of victory, and our young laurels were not soaked in blood or tears. Maurice, I did all I could to protect your innocence, but I could not prevent your losing it at the age of fourteen. Afterwards I regretfully saw you loving women of all sorts, of divers ages, by no means beautiful, at least in the eyes of an angel. Saddened at the sight, I devoted myself to study; a fine library offered me resources rarely met with. I delved into the history of religions; you know the rest."

"But now, my dear Arcade," concluded young d'Esparvieu, "you have lost your position, your situation, you are entirely without resource. You have lost caste, you are o the lines, a vagabond, a bare-footed wanderer."

The Angel replied bitterly that, after all, he was a little better clad at present than when he was wearing the slops of a suicide.

Maurice alleged in excuse that when he dressed his naked angel in a suicide's slops, he was irritated with that angel's infidelity. But it was useless to dwell on the past or to recriminate. What was really needful was to consider what steps to take in future.

And he asked:

"Arcade, what do you think of doing?"

"Have I not already told you, Maurice? To fight with Him who reigns in the heavens, dethrone Him, and set up Satan in His stead."

"You will not do it. To begin with it is not the opportune moment. Opinion is not with you. You will not be in the swim, as papa says. Conservatism and authority are all the go nowadays. We like to be ruled, and the President of the Republic is going to parley with the Pope. Do not be obstinate, Arcade. You are not as bad as you say. At bottom you are like the rest of the world, you adore the good God."

"I thought I had already explained to you, Maurice, that He whom you consider God is actually but a demiurge. He is absolutely ignorant of the divine world above him, and in all good faith believes himself to be the true and only God. You will find in the History of the Church, by Monsignor Duchesne -- Vol.

I, page 162 -- that this proud and narrow-minded demiurge is named Ialdabaoth. My child, so as not to ruffle your prejudices and to deal gently with your feelings in future, that is the name I shall give him. If it should happen that I should speak of him to you, I shall call him Ialdabaoth. I must leave you. Adieu."

"Stay----"

"I cannot."

"I shall not let you go thus. You have deprived me of my guardian angel. It is for you to repair the injury you have caused me. Give me another one."

Arcade objected that it was difficult for him to satisfy such a demand. That having quarrelled with the sovereign dispenser of guardian Spirits, he could obtain nothing from that quarter.

"My dear Maurice," he added, smiling, "ask for one yourself from Ialdabaoth."

"No, -- no, -- no," exclaimed Maurice. "You have taken away my guardian angel, -- give him back to me."

"Alas! I cannot."

"Is it, Arcade, because you are a revolutionary that you cannot?"

"Yes."

"An enemy of God?"

"Yes."

"A Satanic spirit?"

"Yes."

"Well, then," exclaimed young Maurice, "I will be your guardian angel, -- I will not leave you."

And Maurice d'Esparvieu took Arcade to have some oysters at P---'s.

CHAPTER XXVI. THE CONCLAVE

THAT day, convoked by Arcade and Zita, the rebellious angels met together on the banks of the Seine at La Jonchère, in a deserted and tumble-down entertainment-hall that Prince Istar had hired from a pot-house keeper called Barattan. Three hundred angels crowded together in the stalls and boxes. A table, an arm-chair, and a collection of small chairs were arranged on the stage, where hung the tattered remnants of a piece of rustic scenery. The walls, coloured in distemper with flowers and fruit, were cracked and stained with damp, and were crumbling away in flakes. The vulgar and poverty stricken appearance of the place rendered the grandeur of the passions exhibited therein all the more striking.

When Prince Istar asked the assembly to form its Committee, and first of all to elect a President, the name that was renowned throughout the world entered the minds of all present, but a religious respect sealed their lips; and after a moment's silence, the absent Nectaire was elected by acclamation. Having been invited to take the chair between Zita and an angel of Japan, Arcade immediately began as follows:

"Sons of Heaven! My comrades! You have freed yourselves from the bonds of celestial servitude -- you have shaken off the thrall of him called Iahveh, but to whom we should here accord his veritable name of Ialdabaoth, for he is not the creator of the worlds, but merely an ignorant and barbarous demiurge, who having obtained possession of a minute portion of the Universe has therein sown suffering and death. Sons of Heaven, tell me, I charge you, whether you will combat and destroy Ialdabaoth?"

All with one voice made answer:

"We will!"

And many speaking all together swore they would scale the mountain of Ialdabaoth, and hurl down the walls of jasper and porphyry, and plunge the tyrant of Heaven into eternal darkness.

But a voice of crystal pierced through the sullen murmur.

"Tremble, ye impious, sacrilegious madmen! The Lord hath already lifted his dread arm to smite you!"

It was a loyal angel who, with an impulse of faith and love, envying the glory of confessors and martyrs, jealous and eager, like his God himself, to emulate man in the beauty of sacrifice, had flung himself in the midst of the blasphemers, to brave them, to confound them, and to fall beneath their blows. The assembly turned upon him with furious unanimity. Those nearest to him overwhelmed him with blows. He continued to cry, in a clear, ringing voice, "Glory to God! Glory to God! Glory to God!"

A rebel seized him by the neck and strangled his praises of the Almighty in his throat. He was thrown to the ground, trampled underfoot. Prince Istar picked him up, took him by the wings between his fingers, then rising like a column of smoke, opened a ventilator, which no one else could have reached, and passed the faithful angel through it. Order was immediately restored.

"Comrades," continued Arcade, "now that we have affirmed our stern resolve, we must examine the possible plans of campaign, and choose the best. You will therefore have to consider if we should attack the enemy in full force, or whether it were better, by a lengthy and assiduous propaganda, to win the inhabitants of Heaven to our cause."

"War! War!" shouted the assembled host.

And it seemed as if one could hear the sound of trumpets and the rolling of drums.

Théophile, whom Prince Istar had dragged to he meeting, rose, pale and unstrung, and, speaking with emotion, said:

"Brethren, do not take ill what I am about to say; for it is the friendship I have for you that inspires me. I am but a poor musician. But, believe me, all your plans will come to naught before the Divine Wisdom which has foreseen everything."

Théophile Belais sat down amid hisses. And Arcade continued:

"Ialdabaoth foresees everything. I do not contest it. He foresees everything, but in order to leave us our free will he acts towards us absolutely as if he foresaw nothing. Every instant he is surprised, disconcerted; the most probable events take him unawares. The obligation which he has undertaken, to reconcile with his prescience the liberty of both men and angels, throws him constantly into inextricable difficulties and terrible dilemmas. He never sees further than the end of his nose. He did not expect Adam's disobedience, and so little did he anticipate the wickedness of men that he repented having made them, and drowned them in the waters of he Flood, and all the animals as well, though he had no fault to find with the animals. For blindness he is only to be compared with Charles X, his favourite king. If we are prudent it will be easy to take him by surprise. I think that these observations will be calculated to reassure my brother."

Théophile made no reply. He loved God, but he was fearful of sharing the fate of the faithful angel.

One of the best-informed Spirits of the assembly, Mammon, was not altogether reassured by the remarks of his brother Arcade.

"Bethink you," said this Spirit, "Ialdabaoth has little general culture, but he is a soldier -- to the marrow of his bones. The organisation of Paradise is a thoroughly military organisation. It is founded on hierarchy and discipline. Passive obedience is imposed there as a fundamental law. The angels form an army. Compare this spot with the Elysian Fields which Virgil depicts for you. In the Elysian Fields reign liberty, reason, and wisdom. The happy shades hold converse together in the groves of myrtle. In the Heaven of Ialdabaoth there is no civil population. Everyone is enrolled, numbered, registered. It is a barracks and a field for manoeuvres. Remember that."

Arcade replied that they must look at their adversary in his true colours, and that the military organisation of Paradise was far more reminiscent of the villages of King Koffee than of the Prussia of Frederick the Great.

"Already," said he, "at the time of the first revolt, before the beginning of Time, the conflict raged for two days, and Ialdabaoth's throne was made to totter. Nevertheless, the demiurge gained the victory. But to what did he owe it? To the thunderstorm which happened to come on during the conflict. The thunderbolts falling on Lucifer and his angels struck them down, bruised and blackened, and Ialdabaoth owed his victory to the thunderbolts. Thunder is his sole weapon. He abuses its power. In the midst of thunder and lightning he promulgates his laws. 'Fire goeth before him,' says the Prophet. Now Seneca, the philosopher, said that the thunderbolt in its fall brings peril to very few, but fear to all. This remark was true enough for men of the first century of the Christian era; it is no longer so for the angels of the twentieth; all of which goes to prove that, in spite of his thunder, he is not very powerful; it was acute terror that made men rear him a tower of unbaked brick and bitumen. When myriads of celestial spirits, furnished with machines which modern science puts at their disposal, make an assault upon the heavens, think you, comrades, that the old master of the solar system surrounded with his angels, armed as in the time of Abraham, will be able to resist them? To this day the warriors of the demiurge wear helmets of gold and shields of diamond. Michael, his best captain, knows no other tactics than the hand-to-hand combat. To him Pharaoh's chariots are still the latest thing, and he has never heard of the Macedonian phalanx."

And young Arcade lengthily prolonged the parallel between the armed herds of Ialdabaoth and the intelligent fighting men of the rebel army. Then the question of pecuniary resources arose.

Zita asserted that there was enough money to commence war, that the electrophores were in order, that an initial victory would obtain them credit.

The discussion continued, amid turbulence and confusion. In this parliament of angels, as in the synods of men, empty words flowed in abundance. Disturbances grew more violent and more frequent as the time for putting the resolution drew near. It was beyond question that supreme command would be entrusted to him who had first raised the flag of revolt. But as everyone aspired to act as Lucifer's Lieutenant, each in describing the kind of fighting man to be preferred drew a portrait of himself. Thus Alcor, the youngest of the rebellious angels, arose and spoke rapidly as follows:

"In Ialdabaoth's army, happily for us, the officers obtain their posts by seniority. This being the case, there is little likelihood of the command falling into the hands of a military genius, for men are not made leaders by prolonged habits of obedience, and close attention to military is not a good apprenticeship for the evolution of vast plans of campaign. If we consult ancient and modern history, we shall see that the greatest leaders were kings like Alexander and Frederick, aristocrats like Cæsar and Turenne, or men impatient of red-tape like Bonaparte. A routine man will always be poor or second-rate. Comrades, let us appoint intelligent leaders, men in the prime of life, to command us. An old man may retain the habit of winning victories, but only a young man can acquire it!"

Alcor then gave place to an angel of the philosophic order, who mounted the rostrum and spoke thus:

"War never was an exact science, a clearly defined art. The genius of the race, or the brain of the individual, has ever modified it. Now how are we to define the qualities necessary for a general in command in the war of the future, where one must consider greater masses and a larger number of movements than the intelligence of man can conceive? The multiplication of technical means, by infinitely multiplying the opportunities for mistake, paralyses the genius of those in command. At a certain stage in the progress of military science, a stage which our models, the Europeans, are about to reach, the cleverest leader and the most ignorant become equalized by reason of their incapacity. Another result of great modern armaments is, that the law of numbers tends to rule with inflexible rigour. It is of course true that ten angels in revolt are worth more than ten angels of Ialdabaoth; it is not at all certain that a million rebellious angels are worth more than a million of Ialdabaoth's angels. Great numbers, in war as elsewhere, annihilate intelligence and individual superiority in favour of a sort of exceedingly rudimentary collective soul."

A buzz of conversation drowned the voice of the philosophic angel, and he concluded his speech in an atmosphere of general indifference.

The tribune then resounded with calls to arms and promises of victory. The sword was held up to praise, the sword which defends the right. The triumph of the angels in revolt was celebrated twenty times beforehand, to the plaudits of a delirious crowd.

Cries of "War!" rose to the silent heavens; "Give us war!"

In the midst of these transports Prince Istar hoisted himself on to the platform, and the floor creaked under his weight.

"Comrades," said he, "you wish for victory, and it is a very natural desire, but you must be mouldy with literature and poetry if you expect to obtain it from war. The idea of making war can nowadays only enter the brain of a sottish bourgeois or a belated romantic. What is war? A burlesque masquerade in the midst of which fatuous patriots sing their stupid dithyrambs. Had Napoleon possessed a practical mind he would not have made war; but he was a dreamer, intoxicated with Ossian. You cry, 'Give us war!' You are visionaries. When will you become thinkers? The thinkers do not look for power and strength from any of the dreams which constitute military art: tactics, strategy, fortifications, artillery, and all that rubbish. They do not believe in war, which is a phantasy; they believe in chemistry, which is a science. They know the way to put victory into an algebraic formula."

And drawing from his pocket a small bottle, which he held up to the meeting, Prince Istar exclaimed:

"Victory -- it is here!"

CHAPTER XXVII. WHEREIN WE SHALL SEE REVEALED A DARK AND SECRET MYSTERY AND LEARN HOW IT COMES ABOUT THAT EMPIRES ARE OFTEN HURLED AGAINST EMPIRES, AND RUIN FALLS ALIKE UPON THE VICTORS AND THE VANQUISHED; AND THE WISE READER (IF SUCH THERE BE -- WHICH I DOUBT) WILL MEDITATE UPON THIS IMPORTANT UTTERANCE: "A WAR IS A MATTER OF BUSINESS."

THE Angels had dispersed. At the foot of the slopes at Meudon, seated on the grass, Arcade and Zita watched the Seine flowing by the willows.

"In this world," said Arcade, "in this world, which we call a cosmos, though it is but a microcosm, no thinking being can imagine that he is able to destroy even one atom. At the utmost, all we can hope for is that we shall succeed in modifying, here and there, the rhythm of some group of atoms and the arrangement of certain cells. That, when one thinks of it, must be the limit of our great enterprise. And when we shall have set up the Contradictor in the place of Ialdabaoth, we shall have done no more.... Zita, is the evil in the nature of things or in their arrangement? That is what we ought to know. Zita, I am profoundly troubled----"

"Arcade," replied Zita, "if to act we had to know the secret of Nature, one would never act at all. And neither would one live -- since to live is to act. Arcade, is your resolution failing you already?"

Arcade assured the beautiful angel that he was resolved to plunge the demiurge into eternal darkness.

A motor-car passed by on the road, followed by a long trail of dust. It stopped before the two angels, and the hooked nose of Baron Everdingen appeared at the window.

"Good morning, my celestial friends, good morning," said the capitalist. "Sons of Heaven, I am pleased to meet you. I have a word of importance to say to you. Do not remain idle -- do not go to sleep. Arm! Arm! You may be surprised by Ialdabaoth. You have a big war-fund. Employ it without stint. I have just learnt that the Archangel Michael has given large orders in Heaven for thunder-bolts and arrows. If you take my advice you will procure fifty thousand more electrophores. I will take the order. Good day, angels. Long live the celestial country!"

And Baron Everdingen flew by the flowery shores of Louveciennes in the company of a pretty actress.

"Is it true that they are taking up arms at the demiurge's?" asked Arcade.

"It may be," replied Zita, "that up there another Baron Everdingen is inciting to arms."

The guardian angel of young Maurice remained pensive for some moments. Then he murmured:

"Can it be that we are the sport of financiers?"

"Pooh!" said the beautiful archangel. "War is a business. It has always been a business."

Then they discussed at length the means of executing their immense enterprise. Rejecting disdainfully the anarchistic proceedings of Prince Istar, they conceived a formidable and sudden invasion of the kingdom of Heaven by their enthusiastic and well-drilled troops.

Now Barattan, the innkeeper of La Jonchère, who had let the entertainment-hall to the rebellious angels, was in the employ of the secret police. In the reports he furnished to the Prefecture he denounced the members of this secret meeting as meditating an attack on a certain person whom they described as obtuse and cruel, and whom they called Alaballotte. The agent believed this to be a pseudonym denoting either the President of the Republic or the Republic itself. The conspirators had unanimously given voice to threats against Alaballotte, and one of them, a very dangerous individual, well-known in anarchist circles, who had already several convictions against him on account of writings and speeches of a seditious nature, and who was known as Prince Istar or the Queroube, had brandished a bomb of very small calibre which seemed to contain a formidable machine. The other conspirators were unknown to Barattan, notwithstanding the fact that he frequented revolutionary circles. Many among them were very young men, mere beardless youths. There were two who, it appeared, had spoken with conspicuous vehemence; a certain Arcade, dwelling in the Rue St. Jacques, and a woman of easy virtue called Zita, living at Montmartre, both without visible means of subsistence.

The affair seemed sufficiently serious to the Prefect of Police to make him think it necessary to confer without delay with the President of the Council.

The Third Republic was then going through one of those climacteric periods during which the French nation, enamoured of authority and worshipping force, gave itself up for lost because it was not governed enough, and clamoured loudly for a saviour. The President of the Council, and Minister of Justice, was only too eager to be that longed-for saviour. Still, for him to play that part it was first necessary that there should be a danger to face. Thus the news of a plot was highly welcome to him. He questioned the Prefect of Police on the character and importance of the affair. The Prefect of Police explained that the people seemed to have money, intelligence, and energy; but that they talked too much and were too numerous to undertake secret and concerted action. The Minister, leaning back in his armchair, pondered on the matter. The

Empire writing-table at which he was seated, the ancient tapestry which covered the walls, the clock and the candelabra of the Restoration period -- all, in this traditional setting, reminded him of those great principles of government which remain immutable throughout the succession of régimes, of stratagem and of bluff. After brief reflexion, he concluded that the plot must be allowed to grow and take shape, that it would even be fitting to nurse it, to embroider it, to colour it, and only to stifle it after having extracted every possible advantage from it.

He instructed the Prefect of Police to watch the affair closely, to render him an account of what went on from day to day, and to confine himself to the role of informer.

"I rely on your well-known prudence; observe, and do not intervene."

The Minister lit a cigarette. He quite reckoned, with the help of this plot, on silencing the Opposition, strengthening his own influence, diminishing that of his colleagues, humiliating the President of the Republic, and becoming the saviour of his country.

The Prefect of Police undertook to follow the ministerial instructions, vowing inwardly all the while to act in his own way. He had a watch put upon the individuals pointed out by Barattan, and commanded his agents not to intervene, come what might. Perceiving that he was a marked man, Prince Istar -- who united prudence with strength -- withdrew the bombs from the gutter outside his window where he had hidden them, and changing from motor 'bus to tube, from tube to motor 'bus, and choosing the most cunningly circuitous route, at length deposited his machines with the angelic musician.

Every time he left his house in the Rue St. Jacques, Arcade found a man of exaggerated smartness at his door, with yellow gloves and in his tie a diamond bigger than the Regent. Being a stranger to the things of this world, the rebellious angel paid no attention to the circumstance. But young Maurice d'Esparvieu, who had undertaken the task of guarding his guardian-angel, viewed this gentleman with uneasiness, for he equalled in assiduity and surpassed in vigilance that Monsieur Mignon who had formerly allowed his inquisitive gaze to wander from the rams' heads on the Hôtel de la Sordiere on the Rue Garancière to the apse of the church of St. Sulpice. Maurice came two and three times a day to see Arcade in his furnished rooms, warning him of the danger, and urging him to change his abode.

Every evening he took his angel to night restaurants, where they supped with ladies of easy virtue. There young d'Esparvieu would foretell the issue of some coming glove-fight, and afterwards exert himself to demonstrate to Arcade the existence of God, the necessity for religion, and the beauties of Christianity, and adjure him to renounce his impious and criminal undertakings wherefrom, he said, he would reap but bitterness and disappointment.

"For really," said the young apologist, "if Christianity were false it would be known."

The ladies approved of Maurice's religious sentiments, and when the handsome Arcade uttered some blasphemy in language they could understand, they put their hands to their ears and bade him be silent, for fear of being struck down with him. For they believed that God, in his omnipotence and sovereign goodness, taking sudden vengeance against those who insulted him, was quite capable of striking down the innocent with the guilty without meaning it.

Sometimes the angel and his guardian took supper with the angelic musician. Maurice, who remembered from time to time that he was Bouchotte's lover, was displeased to see Arcade taking liberties with the singer. She had allowed him to do so ever since the day when, the angelic musician having had the little flowery couch repaired, Arcade and Bouchotte had made it a foundation for their friendship. Maurice, who loved Madame des Aubels a great deal, also loved Bouchotte a little, and was rather jealous of Arcade. Now jealousy is a feeling natural to man and beast, and causes them, however slight the attack, keen unhappiness. Therefore, suspecting the truth, which Bouchotte's temperament and the angel's character made sufficiently obvious, he overwhelmed Arcade with sarcasm and abuse, reproaching him with the immorality of his ways. Arcade answered, tranquilly, that it was difficult to subject physiological impulses to perfectly defined rules, and that moralists encountered great difficulties in the case of certain natural necessities.

"Moreover," added Arcade, "I freely acknowledge that it is almost impossible systematically to constitute a natural moral law. Nature has no principles. She furnishes us with no reason to believe that human life is to be respected. Nature, in her indifference, makes no distinction between good and evil."

"You see, then," replied Maurice, "that religion is necessary."

"Moral law," replied the angel, "which is supposed to be revealed to us, is drawn in reality from the grossest empiricism. Custom alone regulates morals. What Heaven prescribes is merely the consecration of ancient customs. The divine law, promulgated amid fireworks on some Mount Sinai, is never anything but the codification of human prejudice. And from this fact -- namely, that morals change -- religions which endure for a long time, such as Judæo-Christianity, vary their moral law."

"At any rate," said Maurice, whose intelligence was swelling visibly, "you will grant me that religion prevents much profligacy and crime?"

"Except when it promotes crime -- as, for instance, the murder of Iphigenia."

"Arcade," exclaimed Maurice, "when I hear you argue, I rejoice that I am not an intellectual."

Meanwhile Théophile, with his head bent over the piano, his face hidden by the long fair veil of his hair, bringing down from on high his inspired hands on to the keys, was playing and singing the full score of Aline, Queen of Golconda.

Prince Istar used to come to their friendly reunions, his pockets filled with bombs and bottles of champagne, both of which he owed to the liberality of Baron Everdingen. Bouchotte received the Kerûb with pleasure, since she saw in him the witness and the trophy of the victory she had gained on the little flowered couch. He was to her as the severed head of Goliath in the hands of the youthful David. And she admired the prince for his cleverness as an accompanist, his vigour, which she had subdued, and his prodigious capacity for drink.

One night, when young d'Esparvieu took his angel home in his car from Bouchotte's house to the lodgings in the Rue St. Jacques, it was very dark; before the door the diamond in the spy's necktie glittered like a beacon; three cyclists standing in a group under its rays made off in divers directions at the car's approach. The angel took no notice, but Maurice concluded that Arcade's movements interested various important people in the State. He judged the danger to be pressing, and at once made up his mind. The next morning he came to seek the suspect, to take him to the Rue de Rome. The angel was in bed. Maurice urged him to dress and to follow him.

"Come," said he. "This house is no longer safe for you. You are watched. One of these days you will be arrested. Do you wish to sleep in gaol? No? Well, then, come. I will put you in a safe place."

The spirit smiled with some little compassion on his naive preserver.

"Do you not know," he said, "that an angel broke open the doors of the prison where Peter was confined, and delivered the apostle? Do you believe me, Maurice, to be inferior in power to that heavenly brother of mine, and do you suppose that I am unable to do for myself what he did for the fisherman of the lake of Tiberias?"

"Do not count on it, Arcade. He did it miraculously."

"Or by a stroke of luck, as a modern historian of the Church has it. But no matter. I will follow you. Just allow me to burn a few letters and to make a parcel of some books I shall need."

He threw some papers in the fire-place, put several volumes in his pockets, and followed his guide to the car, which was waiting for them not far off, outside the College of France. Maurice took the wheel. Imitating the Kerûb's prudence, he made so many windings and turnings, and so many rapid twists that he put all the swift and numerous cyclists, speeding in pursuit, off the scent. At length, having left wheelmarks in every direction all over the town, he stopped in the Rue de Rome, before the first-door flat, where the angel had first appeared.

On entering the dwelling which he had left eighteen months before to carry out his mission, Arcade remembered the irreparable past, and breathing in the scent used by Gilberte, his nostrils throbbed. He asked after Madame des Aubels.

"She is very well," replied Maurice. "A little plumper and very much more beautiful for it. She still bears you a grudge for your forward behaviour. I hope that she will one day forgive you, as I have forgiven you, and that she will forget your offence. But she is still very annoyed with you."

Young d'Esparvieu did the honours of his flat to his angel with the manners of a well-bred man and the tender solicitude of a friend. He showed him the folding bed which was opened every evening in the entrance hall and pushed into a dark cupboard in the morning. He showed him the dressing-table, with its accessories; the bath, the linen cupboard, the chest of drawers; gave him the necessary information regarding the heating and lighting; told him that his meals would be brought and the rooms cleaned by the concierge, and showed him which bell to press when he required that person's services. He told him also that he must consider himself at home, and receive whom he wished.

CHAPTER XXVIII. WHICH TREATS OF A PAINFUL DOMESTIC SCENE

SO long as Maurice confined his selection of mistresses to respectable women, his conduct had called forth no reproach. It was a different matter when he took up with Bouchotte. His mother, who had closed her eyes to liaisons which, though guilty, were elegant and discreet, was scandalised when it came to her ears that her son was openly parading about with a music-hall singer. By dint of much prying and probing, Berthe, Maurice's younger sister, had got to know of her brother's adventures, and she narrated them, without any indignation, to her young girl friends. His little brother Léon declared to his mother one day, in the presence of several ladies, that when he was big he, too, would go on the spree, like Maurice. This was a sore wound to the maternal heart of Madame d'Esparvieu.

About the same time there occurred a family event of a very grave nature which occasioned much alarm to Monsieur René d'Esparvieu. Drafts were presented to him signed in his name by his son. His writing had not been forged, but there was no doubt that it had been the son's intention to pass off the signature as his father's. It showed a perverted moral sense; whence it appeared that Maurice was living a life of profligacy, that he was running into debt and on the point of outraging the decencies. The paterfamilias talked the matter over with his wife. It was arranged that he should give his son a very severe lecture, hint at vigorous corrective measures, and that in due course the mother should appear with gentle and sorrowing mien and endeavour to soothe the righteous indignation of the father. This plan being agreed upon, Monsieur René d'Esparvieu sent for his son to come to him in his study. To add to the solemnity of the occasion, he had arrayed himself in his frock-coat. As soon as Maurice saw it he knew there was something serious in the wind. The head of the family was pale, and his voice shook a little (for he was a nervous man), as he declared that he would no longer put up with his son's irregular behaviour, and insisted on an immediate and absolute reform. No more wild courses, no more running into debt, no more undesirable companions, but work, steadiness, and reputable connexions.

Maurice was quite willing to give a respectful reply to his father, whose complaints, after all, were perfectly justified; but, unfortunately, Maurice, like his father, was shy, and the frock-coat which Monsieur d'Esparvieu had donned in order to discharge his magisterial duty with greater dignity seemed to preclude the possibility of any open and unconstrained intercourse. Maurice maintained an awkward silence, which looked very much like insolence, and this silence compelled Monsieur d'Esparvieu to reiterate his complaints, this time with additional severity. He opened one of the drawers in his historic bureau (the bureau on which Alexandre d'Esparvieu had written his "Essay on the Civil and Religious Institutions of the World"), and produced the bills which Maurice had signed.

"Do you know, my boy," said he, "that this is nothing more nor less than forgery? To make up for such grave misconduct as that----"

At this moment Madame d'Esparvieu, as arranged, entered the room attired in her walking-dress. She was supposed to play the angel of forgiveness, but neither her appearance nor her disposition was suitable to the part. She was harsh and unsympathetic. Maurice harboured with in him the seeds of all the ordinary and necessary virtues. He loved his mother and respected her. His love, however, was more a matter of duty than of inclination, and his respect arose from habit rather than from feeling. Madame René d'Esparvieu's complexion was blotchy, and having powdered herself in order to appear to advantage at the domestic tribunal, the colour of her face suggested raspberries sprinkled over with sugar. Maurice, being possessed of some taste, could not help realising that she was ugly and rather repulsively so. He was out of tune with her, and when she began to go through all the accusations his father had brought against him, making them out to be blacker than ever, the prodigal turned away his head to conceal his irritation.

"Your Aunt de Saint-Fain," she went on, "met you in the street in such disgraceful company that she was really thankful that you forbore to greet her."

"Aunt de Saint-Fain!" Maurice broke out. "I like to hear her talking about scandals! Everyone knows the sort of life she has led, and now the old hypocrite wants to----"

He stopped. He had caught sight of his father, whose face was even more eloquent of sorrow than of anger. Maurice began to feel as though he had committed murder, and could not imagine how he had allowed such words to escape him. He was on the point of bursting into tears, falling on his knees, and imploring his father to forgive him, when his mother, looking up at the ceiling, said with a sigh:

"What offence can I have committed against God, to have brought such a wicked son into the world?"

This speech struck Maurice as a piece of ridiculous affectation, and it pulled him up with a jerk. The bitterness of contrition suddenly gave place to the delicious arrogance of wrong-doing. He plunged wildly into a torrent of insolence and revolt, and breathlessly delivered himself of utterances quite unfit for a mother's ear.

"If you will have it, mamma, rather than forbid me to continue my friendship with a talented lyrical artist, you would be better employed in preventing my elder sister, Madame de Margy, from appearing, night after night, in society and at the theatres with a contemptible and disgusting individual that everybody knows is her lover. You should also keep an eye on my little sister Jeanne, who writes objectionable letters to herself in a disguised hand, and then, pretending she has found them in her prayer-book, shows them to you with assumed innocence, to worry and alarm you. It would be just as well, too, if you prevented my little brother Léon, a child of seven, from being quite so much with Mademoiselle Caporal, and you might tell your maid..."

"Get out, sir, I will not have you in the house!" cried Monsieur René d'Esparvieu, white with anger, pointing a trembling finger at the door.

CHAPTER XXIX. WHEREIN WE SEE HOW THE ANGEL, HAVING BECOME A MAN, BEHAVES LIKE A MAN, COVETING ANOTHER'S WIFE AND BETRAYING HIS FRIEND. IN THIS CHAPTER THE CORRECTNESS OF YOUNG D'ESPARVIEU'S CONDUCT WILL BE MADE MANIFEST

THE angel was pleased with his lodging. He worked of a morning, went out in the afternoon, heedless of detectives, and came home to sleep. As in days gone by, Maurice received Madame des Aubels twice or thrice a week in the room in which they had seen the apparition.

All went very well until one morning Gilberte, having, the night before, left her little velvet bag on the table in the blue room, came to find it, and discovered Arcade stretched on the couch in his pyjamas, smoking a cigarette, and dreaming of the conquest of Heaven. She gave a loud scream.

"You, Monsieur! Had I thought to find you here, you may be quite sure I should not... I came to fetch my little bag, which is in the next room. Allow me...." And she slipped past the angel, cautiously and quickly, as if he were a brazier.

Madame des Aubels that morning, in her pale green tailor-made costume, was deliciously attractive. Her tight skirt displayed her movements, and her every step was one of those miracles of Nature which fill men's hearts with amazement.

She reappeared, bag in hand.

"Once more I ask your pardon.... I never dreamt that..."

Arcade begged her to sit down and to stay a moment.

"I never expected, Monsieur," said she, "that you would be doing the honours of this flat. I knew how dearly Monsieur d'Esparvieu loved you.... Nevertheless, I had no idea that..."

The sky had suddenly grown overcast. A brownish glare began to steal into the room. Madame des Aubels told him she had walked for her health's sake, but a storm was brewing, and she asked if a carriage could be called for her.

Arcade flung himself at Gilberte's feet, took her in his arms as one takes a precious piece of china, and murmured words which, being meaningless in themselves, expressed desire.

She put her hands over his eyes and on his lips, and exclaimed, "I hate you!"

And shaking with sobs, she asked for a drink of water. She was choking. The angel went to her assistance. In this moment of extreme peril she defended herself courageously. She kept saying: "No!... No!... I will not love you. I should love you too well...." Nevertheless she succumbed.

In the sweet familiarity which followed their mutual astonishment she said to him:

"I have often asked after you. I knew that you were an assiduous frequenter of the playhouses at Montmartre, -- that you were often seen with Mademoiselle Bouchotte, who, nevertheless, is not at all pretty. I knew that you had become very smart, and that you were making a good deal of money. I was not surprised. You were born to succeed. The day of your" -- and she pointed at the spot between the window and the wardrobe with the mirror -- "apparition, I was vexed with Maurice for having given you a suicide's rags to wear. You pleased me.... Oh, it was not your good looks! Don't think that women are as sensitive as people say to outward attractions. We consider other things in love. There is a sort of---- Well, anyhow I loved you as soon as I saw you."

The shadows grew deeper.

She asked:

"You are not an angel, are you? Maurice believes you are; but he believes so many things, Maurice." She questioned Arcade with her eyes and smiled maliciously. "Confess that you have been fooling him, and that you are no angel?"

Arcade replied:

"I only aspire to please you; I will always be what you want me to be."

Gilberte decided that he was no angel; first, because one never is an angel; secondly, for more detailed reasons which drew her thoughts to the question of love. He did not argue the matter with her, and once again words were found inadequate to express their feelings.

Outside, the rain was falling thick and fast, the windows were streaming, lightning lit up the muslin curtains, and thunder shook the panes. Gilberte made the sign of the Cross and remained with her head hidden in her lover's bosom.

At this moment Maurice entered the room. He came in wet and smiling, confident, tranquil, happy, to announce to Arcade the good news that with his half-share in the previous day's race at Longchamps the angel had won twelve times his stake. Surprising the lady and the angel in their embrace, he became furious; anger gripped the muscles of his throat, his face grew red with blood, and the veins stood out on his forehead. He sprang with clenched fists towards Gilberte, and then suddenly stopped.

Interrupted motion was transformed into heat. Maurice fumed. His anger did not arm him, like Archilochus, with lyrical vengeance. He merely applied an offensive epithet to his unfaithful one.

Meanwhile she had recovered her dignified bearing. She rose, full of modesty and grace, and gave her accuser a look which expressed both offended virtue and loving forgiveness.

But as young d'Esparvieu continued to shower coarse and monotonous insults on her, she grew angry in her turn.

"You are a pretty sort of person, are you not?" she said. "Did I run after this Arcade of yours? It was you who brought him here, and in what a state, too! You had only one idea: to give me up to your friend. Well, Monsieur, you can do as you like -- I am not going to oblige you."

Maurice d'Esparvieu replied simply, "Get out of it, you trollop!" And he made a motion as if to push her out. It pained Arcade to see his mistress treated so disrespectfully, but he thought he lacked the necessary authority to interfere with Maurice. Madame des Aubels, who had lost none of her dignity, fixed young d'Esparvieu with her imperious gaze, and said:

"Go and get me a carriage."

And so great is the power of woman over a wellbred soul, in a gallant nation, that the young Frenchman went immediately and told the concierge to call a taxi. Madame des Aubels, with a studied exhibition of charm in every movement, took leave of them, throwing Maurice the contemptuous look that a woman owes to him whom she has deceived. Maurice witnessed her departure with an outward expression of indifference he was far from feeling. Then he turned to the angel clad in the flowered pyjamas which Maurice himself had worn the day of the apparition; and this circumstance, trifling in itself, added fuel to the anger of the host who had been thus shamefully deceived.

"Well," he said, "you may pride yourself on being a despicable individual. You have behaved basely, and all for nothing. If the woman took your fancy, you had but to tell me. I was tired of her. I had had enough of her. I would have willingly left her to you."

He spoke thus to hide his pain, for he loved Gilberte more than ever, and the creature's treachery caused him great suffering. He pursued:

"I was about to ask you to take her off my hands. But you have followed your lower nature -- you have behaved like a sweep."

If at this solemn moment Arcade had but spoken one word from his heart, Maurice would have burst into tears, and forgiven his friend and his mistress, and all three would have become content and happy once again. But Arcade had not been nourished on the milk of human kindness. He had never suffered, and did not know how to sympathise with suffering. He replied with frigid wisdom:

"My dear Maurice, that same necessity which orders and constrains the actions of living beings, produces effects that are often unexpected, and sometimes absurd. Thus it is that I have been led to displease you. You would not reproach me if you had a good philosophical understanding of nature; for you would then know that free-will is but an illusion, and that physiological affinities are as exactly determined as are chemical combinations, and, like them, may be summed up in a formula. I think that, in your case, it might be possible to inculcate these truths, but it would be a difficult task, and maybe they would not bring you the serenity which eludes you. It is fitting, therefore, that I should leave this spot, and----"

"Stay," said Maurice.

Maurice had a very clear sense of social obligations. He put honour, when he thought about it, above everything. So now he told himself very forcibly that the outrage he had suffered could only be wiped out with blood. This traditional idea instantly lent an unexpected nobility to his speech and bearing.

"It is I, Monsieur," said he, "who will quit this place, never to return. You will remain here, since you are a refugee. My seconds will wait upon you."

The angel smiled.

"I will receive them, if it gives you pleasure, but, bethink you, my dear Maurice, I am invulnerable. Celestial spirits even when they are materialised cannot be touched by point of sword or pistol shot. Consider, my dear Maurice, the awkward situation in which this fatal inequality puts me, and realise that in refusing to appoint seconds I cannot give as a reason my celestial nature, -- it would be unprecedented."

"Monsieur," replied the heir of the Bussart d'Esparvieu, "you should have thought of that before you insulted me."

Out he marched haughtily; but no sooner was he in the street than he staggered like a drunken man. The rain was still falling. He walked unseeing, unhearing, at haphazard, dragging his feet in the gutters through pools of water, through heaps of mud. He followed the outer boulevards for a long time, and at length, fordone with weariness, lay down on the edge of a piece of waste land. He was muddied up to the eyes, mud and tears smeared his face, the brim of his hat was dripping with rain. A passer-by, taking him for a beggar, tossed him a copper. He picked it up, put it carefully in his waistcoat pocket, and set off to find his seconds.

CHAPTER XXX. WHICH TREATS OF AN AFFAIR OF HONOUR, AND WHICH WILL AFFORD THE READER AN OPPORTUNITY OF JUDGING WHETHER, AS ARCADE AFFIRMS, THE EXPERIENCE OF OUR FAULTS MAKES BETTER MEN AND WOMEN OF US

THE ground chosen for the combat was Colonel Manchon's garden, on the Boulevard de la Reine at Versailles. Messieurs de la Verdelière and Le Truc de Ruffec, who had both of them constant practice in affairs of honour and knew the rules with great exactness, assisted Maurice d'Esparvieu. No duel was ever fought in the Catholic world without Monsieur de la Verdelière being present; and, in making application to this swordsman, Maurice had conformed to custom, though not without a certain reluctance, for he had been notorious as the lover of Madame de la Verdelière; but Monsieur de la Verdelière was not to be looked upon as a husband. He was an institution. As to Monsieur Le Truc de Ruffec, honour was his only known profession and avowedly his sole resource, and when the matter was made the subject of ill-natured comment in Society, the question was asked what finer career than that of honour Monsieur Le Truc de Ruffec could possibly have adopted. Arcade's seconds were Prince Istar and Théophile. The celestial musician had not voluntarily nor with a good grace taken a hand in this affair. He had a horror of every kind of violence and disapproved of single combat. The report of pistols and the clash of swords were intolerable to him, and the sight of blood made him faint. This gentle son of Heaven had obstinately refused to act as second to his brother Arcade, and to bring him to the starting-point the Kerûb had had to threaten to break a bottle of panclastite over his head.

Besides the combatants, the seconds, and the doctors, the only people in the garden were a few officers from the barracks at Versailles and several reporters. Although young d'Esparvieu was known merely as a young man of family, and Arcade had never been heard of at all, the duel had attracted quite a large crowd of inquisitive individuals, and the windows of the adjoining houses were crammed with photographers, reporters, and Society people. What had aroused much curiosity was that a woman was known to be the cause of the quarrel. Many mentioned Bouchotte, but the majority said it was Madame des Aubels. It had been remarked upon, moreover, that duels in which Monsieur de la Verdelière acted as second drew all Paris.

The sky was a soft blue, the garden all a-bloom with roses, a blackbird was piping in a tree. Monsieur de la Verdelière, who, stick in hand, conducted the affair, laid the points of the swords together, and said:

" Pas de ça, Messieurs."

Maurice d'Esparvieu attacked by doubling and beating the blade. Arcade retired, keeping his sword in line. The first engagement was without result. The seconds were under the impression that Monsieur d'Esparvieu was in a grievous state of nervous irritability, and that his adversary would wear him down. In the second encounter Maurice attacked wildly, spread out his arms, and exposed his breast. He attacked as he advanced, gave a straight thrust, and the point of his sword grazed Arcade on the shoulder. The latter was thought to be wounded. But the seconds ascertained with surprise that it was Maurice who had received a scratch on the wrist. Maurice asserted that he felt nothing, and Dr. Quille declared, after examination, that his client might continue the fight. After the regulation quarter of an hour the duel was resumed. Maurice attacked with fury. His adversary was obviously nursing him, and, what disturbed Monsieur de la Verdelière, seemed to be paying very little attention to his own defence. At the opening of the fifth bout, a black spaniel that had got into the garden no one knew how rushed out from a clump of rose-bushes, made its way on to the space reserved for the combatants, and, in spite of sticks and cries, ran in between Maurice's legs. The latter seemed as though his arm vere benumbed, merely gave a shoulder-thrust at his invulnerable opponent. He then delivered a straight lunge and impaled his arm on his adversary's sword, which made a deep wound just below the elbow.

Monsieur de la Verdelière stopped the fight, which had lasted an hour and a half. Maurice was conscious of a painful shock. They laid him down on a grassy bank against a wall covered with wistaria. While the surgeon was dressing the wound Maurice called Arcade and offered him his wounded hand. And when the victor, saddened with his victory, advanced, Maurice embraced him tenderly, saying:

"Be generous, Arcade; forgive my treachery. Now that we have fought, I can ask you to be reconciled with me."

He embraced his friend, weeping, and whispered in his ear:

"Come and see me, and bring Gilberte."

Maurice, who was still unreconciled with his parents, was taken to the little flat in he Rue de Rome. No sooner was he stretched on the bed at the far end of the bedroom where the curtains were drawn as on the day of the apparition, than he saw Arcade and Gilberte appear. He began to suffer greatly from his wound; his temperature was rising, but he was at peace, happy and contented. Angel and woman, both in tears, threw themselves at the foot of the bed. He took both their hands with his left, smiled on them. and kissed them tenderly.

"I am sure now that I shall never quarrel with either of you again; you will deceive me no more. I now know you are capable of anything "

Gilberte, weeping, swore that Maurice had been misled by appearances, that she had never betrayed him with Arcade, that she had never betrayed him at all. And in a great gush of sincerity she persuaded herself that this was so.

"You wrong yourself, Gilberte," replied the wounded man. "It did happen; it had to. And it is well. Gilberte, you were basely false to me with my best friend in this very room, and you were right. If you had not been we should not be here, reunited, all three of us, and I should not be at your side tasting the greatest happiness of my life. Oh, Gilberte, how wrong of you to deny a perfect and accomplished fact!"

"If you wish, my friend," replied Gilberte, a little acidly, "I will not deny it. But it will only be to please you."

Maurice made her sit down on the bed, and begged Arcade to be seated in the arm-chair.

"My friend," said Arcade, "I was innocent. I became man. Straightway I did evil. Then I became better."

"Do not let us exaggerate things," said Maurice. "Let's have a game of bridge."

Scarcely, however, had the patient seen three aces in his hand and called "no trumps," than his eyes began to swim, the cards slipped from his fingers, head fell heavily back on the pillow, and he complained of a violent headache. Almost immediately, Madame des Aubels went off to pay some calls, for she made a point of appearing in Society, in order that the calmness and confidence of her demeanour might give the lie to the various rumours that were current concerning her. Arcade saw her to the door, and, with a kiss, inhaled from her a delicate perfume which he brought back with him into the room where Maurice lay dozing.

"I am perfectly content," murmured the latter, "that things should have happened as they have."

"It was bound to be so," answered the Spirit. "All the other angels in revolt would have done as I did with Gilberte. 'Women,' saith the Apostle, 'should pray with their heads covered, because of the angels,' and the Apostle speaks thus because he knows that the angels are disturbed when they look upon them and see that they are beautiful. No sooner do they touch the earth than they desire to embrace mortal women and fulfil their desire. Their clasp is full of strength and sweetness, they hold the secret of those ineffable caresses which plunge the daughters of men into unfathomable depths of delight. Laying upon the lips of their happy victims a honey that burns like fire, making their veins flow with torrents of refreshing flames, they leave them raptured and undone."

"Stop your clatter, you unclean beast," cried the wounded one.

"One word more!" said the angel; "just one other word, my dear Maurice, to bear out what I say, and I will let you rest quietly. There's nothing like having sound references. In order to assure yourself that I am not deceiving you, Maurice, on this subject of the amorous embraces of angels and women, look up Justin, Apologies, I and II; Flavius Josephus, Jewish Antiquities, Book I, Chapter III; Athenagoras, Concerning the Resurrection ; Lactantius, Book II, Chapter XV; Tertullian, On the Veil of the Virgins ; Marcus of Ephesus in Psellus ; Eusebius, Præparatio Euangelica, Book V, Chapter IV; Saint Ambrose, in his book on Noah and the Ark, Chapter V; Saint Augustine, in his City of God, Book XV, Chapter XXIII; Father Meldonat, the Jesuit, Treatise on Demons, page 248; Pierre Lebyer the King's Counsellor----"

"Arcade, please, for pity's sake, be quiet; do, please do, and send this dog away," cried Maurice, whose face was burning, and whose eyes were starting from his head; for in his delirium he thought he saw a black spaniel on his bed.

Madame de la Verdelière, who was assiduous in every modish and patriotic practice, was reckoned, in the best French society, as one of the most gracious of the great ladies interested in good works. She came herself to ask for news of Maurice, and offered to nurse the wounded man. But at the vehement instigation of Madame des Aubels, Arcade shut the door in her face. Expressions of sympathy were showered upon Maurice. Piled on the salver, visiting cards displayed their innumerable little dogs' ears. Monsieur Le Truc de Ruffec was one of the first to show his manly sympathy at the flat in the Rue de Rome, and, holding out his loyal hand, asked young d'Esparvieu as one honourable man to another for twenty-five louis to pay a debt of honour.

"Of course, my dear Maurice, that is the sort of thing one could not ask of everybody."

The same day Monsieur Gaétan came to press his nephew's hand. The latter introduced Arcade.

"This is my guardian angel, whose foot you thought so beautiful when you saw the print it had made on the tell-tale powder, uncle. He appeared to me last year in this very room. You don't believe it? Well, it is true, nevertheless."

Then turning towards the Spirit he said:

"What say you, Arcade? The Abbé Patouille, who is a great theologian and a good priest, does not believe that you are an angel; and Uncle Gaétan, who doesn't know his catechism and hasn't a scrap of religion in him, doesn't think so either. They deny you, the pair of them; the one because he has faith, the other because he hasn't. After that you may be sure that your history, if ever it comes to be narrated, will scarcely appear credible. Moreover, the man that took it into his head to tell your story would not be a man of taste, and would not come in for much approval. For your story is not a pretty one. I love you, but I sit in judgment upon you, too. Since you fell into atheism, you have become an abominable scoundrel. A bad angel, a bad friend, a traitor, and a homicide, for

I suppose it was to bring about my death that you sent that black spaniel between my legs on the duelling-ground."

The angel shrugged his shoulders and, addressing Gaétan, said:

"Alas! Monsieur, I am not surprised at finding little credit in your eyes. I have been told that you have fallen out with the Judæo-Christian heaven, which is where I came from."

"Monsieur," answered Gaétan, "my faith in Jehovah is not sufficiently strong to enable me to believe in his angels."

"Monsieur, he whom you call Jehovah is really a coarse and ignorant demiurge, and his name is Ialdabaoth."

"In that case, Monsieur, I am perfectly ready to believe in him. He is a narrow-minded ignoramus, is he? Then belief in his existence offers me no further difficulty. How is he getting on?"

"Badly! We are going to lay him low next month."

"Don't make too sure of that, Monsieur. You remind me of my brother-in-law, Cuissart, who has been expecting to hear of the fall of the Republic for the past thirty years."

"You see, Arcade," exclaimed Maurice, "Uncle Gaétan thinks as I do. He knows you won't succeed."

"And, pray, Monsieur Gaétan, what makes you think I shall not succeed?"

"Your Ialdabaoth is still very powerful in this world, if he isn't in the other. In days gone by he used to be upheld by his priests, by those who believed in him. Now he is supported by those who do not believe in him, by the philosophers. A pedant of a fellow called Picrochole has recently come on the scene who wants to make a bankrupt of science in order to do a good turn to the Church. And just lately Pragmatism has been invented for the express purpose of gaining credit for religion in the minds of rationalists."

"You have been studying Pragmatism?"

"Not I! I was frivolous once, and I went in for metaphysics. I read Hegel and Kant. I have become serious with years, and now I only trouble myself about things evident to the senses: what the eye can see or what the ear can hear. Man is summed up in Art. All the rest is moonshine."

Thus the conversation went on until evening; it was marked by obscenities that would have brought a blush -- I will not say to a cuirassier, for cuirassiers are frequently chaste, but even to a Parisienne.

Monsieur Sariette came to see his old pupil. When he entered the room the bust of Alexandre d'Esparvieu seemed to take shape behind the librarian's bald head. He drew near the bed. In the place of blue curtains, mirrored wardrobe, and chimney-piece, there straightway came into view the heavy-laden bookcases of the room of the globes and busts, and the air was heavy with piles of papers, records, and files. Monsieur Sariette could not be dissociated from his library;

one could not conceive of him or even see him apart from it. He himself was paler, more vague, more shadowy, and more a creature of the fancy than the fancies he evoked.

Maurice, who had grown very quiet, was sensible of this mark of friendship.

"Sit down, Monsieur Sariette, -- you know Madame des Aubels. May I introduce Arcade to you, -- my guardian angel. It was he who, while yet invisible, pillaged your library for two years, made you lose all desire for food and drink, and drove you to the verge of madness. He it was who moved piles of books from the room of the busts to my summer-house one day; under your very nose, he took away I know not what precious volumes; and was the cause of your falling on the staircase; another day he took a volume of Salomon Reinach's, and, forced to go out with me (for he never left me, as I have learnt later), he let the volume drop in the gutter of the Rue Princesse. Forgive him, Monsieur Sariette, -- he had no pockets. He was invisible. I bitterly regret, Monsieur Sariette, that all your old books were not devoured by fire or swallowed up by a flood. They made my angel lose his head. He became man, and now knows neither faith nor obedience to laws. It is I, now, who am his guardian angel. God knows how it will all end."

While listening to this speech, Monsieur Sariette's face took on an expression of infinite, irreparable, eternal sadness; the sadness of a mummy. Rising to take his leave, the sorrowful librarian murmured in Arcade's ear:

"The poor child is very ill. He is delirious."

Maurice called the old man back.

"Do stay, Monsieur Sariette. You shall have a game of bridge with us. Monsieur Sariette, listen to my advice. Do not do as I did -- do not keep bad company. You will be lost. I shudder at the mere thought. Monsieur Sariette, do not go yet. I have something very important to ask you. When you come again, bring me a book on the truth of religion, so that I may study it. I must restore to my guardian-angel the faith which he has lost."

CHAPTER XXXI. WHEREIN WE ARE LED TO MARVEL AT THE READINESS WITH WHICH AN HONEST MAN OF TIMID AND GENTLE NATURE CAN COMMIT A HORRIBLE CRIME

PROFOUNDLY distressed by the dark utterances of young Maurice, Monsieur Sariette took a motor-omnibus, and went to see Père Guinardon, his friend, his only friend, the the whole world whom it gave him pleasure to see and hear. When Monsieur Sariette entered the shop in the Rue de Courcelles, Guinardon was alone, dozing in the depths of an antique armchair. His face, surrounded by his curly hair and luxuriant beard, was crimson in hue. Little violet filaments spread a network about the fleshy part of his nose, to which the wines of Burgundy had imparted a purple tint; for there was no longer any disguising the fact, Père Guinardon drank. Two feet away from him, on the fair Octavie's work-table, a rose, all but withered, drooped in an empty vase, and in a basket a piece of embroidery was lying unfinished and neglected. The young Octavie's absences from the shop were growing more and more frequent, and Monsieur Blancmesnil never called when she was not there. The reason of this was that they were meeting three times a week at five o'clock in a house close to the Champs Élysées Père Guinardon knew nothing of that. He did not know the full extent of his misfortune, but he suffered.

Monsieur Sariette shook his old friend by the hand; but he did not enquire for the young Octavie, for he refused to recognise the connexion. He would sooner have talked about Zéphyrine, who had been so cruelly deserted, and whom he hoped the old man would make his lawful wife. But Monsieur Sariette was prudent. He contented himself with asking Guinardon how he was.

"Perfectly well," was Guinardon's reply; but he felt ill, for either age and love-making had undermined his sturdy constitution, or else young Octavie's faithlessness had dealt her lover a fatal blow. "God be praised," he went on, "I still retain my powers of mind and body. I am chaste. Be chaste, Sariette. Chastity is strength."

That evening Père Guinardon had taken some specially valuable books out of the king-wood cabinet to show to a distinguished bibliophile, Monsieur Victor Meyer, and after the latter's departure he had dropped off to sleep without putting them back in their places. Books had an attraction for Monsieur Sariette, and seeing these particular volumes on the marble top of the cabinet, he began to examine them with interest. The first one he looked at was La Pucelle, in morocco, with the English continuation. Doubtless it pained his patriotic and Christian heart to admire its text and illustrations, but a good copy was always virtuous and pure in his sight. Continuing to chat very affectionately with

Guinardon, he picked up, one by one, the books which the antiquary had, for one reason or another -- binding, illustrations, distinguished ownership, or scarcity -- added to his stock.

Suddenly a glorious shout of joy and love broke from his lips. He had discovered the Lucretius of the Prior de Vendôme, his Lucretius, and he was clasping it to his bosom.

"Once again I behold you," he sighed, as he pressed it to his lips.

At first Père Guinardon could not quite make out what his old friend was talking about; but when the latter declared to him that the volume was from the d'Esparvieu collection, that it belonged to him, Sariette, and that he was going to take it away without further ado, the antiquary completely woke up, got on his legs, declared emphatically that the book belonged to him, Guinardon, by right of true and lawful purchase, and that he would not part with it unless he got five thousand francs for it cash down."You don't take in what I am telling you," answered Sariette. "The book belongs to the d'Esparvieu library; I must restore it to its place."

"Pas de ca, Lisette"---- hummed Guinardon.

"The book belongs to me, I tell you!"

"You are crazy, my good Sariette!"

And noticing that, as a matter of fact, the librarian had a wandering look in his eye, he took the book from him, and tried to change the conversation.

"Have you seen, Sariette, that the rascals are going to rip up the Palais Mazarin, and cover up the very heart and centre of the Old Town, the finest and most venerable place in the whole of Paris, with the deuce knows what works of art of theirs? They are worse than the Vandals, for the Vandals, although they destroyed the buildings of antiquity, did not replace them with hideous and disgusting erections and atrocious bridges like the Pont d'Alexandre. And your poor Rue Garancière, Sariette, has fallen a prey to the barbarians. What have they done with the pretty bronze mask of the Palace fountain?"

Monsieur Sariette never listened to a word of all this.

"Guinardon, you have not understood me. Now listen. This book belongs to the d'Esparvieu library. It was taken away, how or by whom I know not. Dreadful and mysterious things went on in that library. But, anyhow, the book was stolen. I need scarcely appeal to your sentiments of scrupulous probity, my dear friend. You would not like to be regarded as the receiver of stolen goods. Give me the book. I will return it to Monsieur d'Esparvieu, who will duly requite you; of that you may be sure. Rely on his generosity, and you will be acting like the downright good fellow that you are."

The antiquary smiled a bitter smile.

"Catch me relying on the generosity of that old curmudgeon of a d'Esparvieu. Why, he'd skin a flea to get its coat. Look at me, Sariette, old boy, and tell me if I look like a dunderhead. You know perfectly well that d'Esparvieu refused to give fifty francs in a second-hand shop for a portrait of Alexandre d'Esparvieu, the founder of the family, by Hersent, and that consequently the founder of the family has had to remain on the Boulevard Montparnasse, propped against a Jew hawker's stall, just opposite the cemetery, where all the dogs of the neighbourhood come and make water on him. Catch me trusting to Monsieur d'Esparvieu's liberality! You've got some bright ideas in your head, you have!"

"Very well, Guinardon, I myself will undertake to pay you any indemnity that a board of arbitrators may fix upon. Do you hear?"

"Now don't go and do the handsome for people who won't give you so much as a thank-you. This man, d'Esparvieu, has taken your knowledge, your energies, your whole life for a salary that even a valet wouldn't accept. So leave that idea alone. In any case it is too late. The book is sold."

"Sold? To whom" asked Sariette in agonized tones.

"What does that matter? You'll never see it again. You'll hear no more about it; it's off to America."

"To America! The Lucretius with the arms of Philippe de Vendôme and marginalia in Voltaire's own hand! My Lucretius off to America!"

Père Guinardon began to laugh.

"My dear Sariette, you remind me of the Chevalier des Grieux when he learns that his darling mistress is to be transported to the Mississippi. 'My dear mistress going to the Mississippi!' says he."

"No! no!" answered Sariette, very pale, "this book shall not go to America. It shall return, as it ought, to the d'Esparvieu library. Let me have it, Guinardon."

The antiquary made a second attempt to put an end to an interview that now looked as if it might take an ugly turn.

"My good Sariette, you haven't told me what you think of my Greco. You never so much as glanced at it. It is an admirable piece of work all the same."

And Guinardon, putting the picture in a good light, went on:

"Now just look at Saint Francis here, the poor man of the Lord, the brother of Jesus. See how his fuliginous body rises heavenward like the smoke from an agreeable sacrifice, like the sacrifice of Abel."

"Give me the book, Guinardon," said Sariette, without turning his head; "give me the book."

The blood suddenly flew to Père Guinardon's head.

"That's enough of it," he shouted, as red as a turkey-cock, the veins standing out on his forehead.

And he dropped the Lucretius into his jacket pocket.

Straightway old Sariette flew at the antiquary, assailed him with sudden fury, and, frail and weakly as he was, butted him back into young Octavie's armchair.

Guinardon, in furious amazement, belched forth the most horrible abuse on the old maniac and gave him a punch that sent him staggering back four paces against the Coronation of the Virgin, by Fra Angelico, which fell down with a crash. Sariette returned to the charge, and tried to drag the book out of the pocket in which it lay hid. This time Père Guinardon would really have floored him had he not been blinded by the blood that was rushing to his head, and hit sideways at the work-table of his absent mistress. Sariette fastened himself on to his bewildered adversary, held him down in the armchair, and with his little bony hands clutched him by the neck, which, red as it was already, became a deep crimson. Guinardon struggled to get free, but the little fingers, feeling the mass of soft, warm flesh about them, embedded themselves in it with delicious ecstasy. Some unknown force made them hold fast to their prey. Guinardon's throat began to rattle, saliva was oozing from one corner of his mouth. His enormous frame quivered now and again beneath the grasp; but the tremors grew more and more intermittent and spasmodic. At last they ceased. The murderous hands did not let go their hold. Sariette had to make a violent effort to loose them. His temples were buzzing. Nevertheless he could hear the rain falling outside, muffled steps going past on the pavement, newspaper men shouting in the distance. He could see umbrellas passing along in the dim light. He drew the book from the dead man's pocket and fled.

The fair Octavie did not go back to the shop that night. She went to sleep in a little entresol underneath the bric-a-brac stores which Monsieur de Blancmesnil had recently bought for her in this same Rue de Courcelles. The workman whose task it was to shut up the shop found the antiquary's body still warm. He called Madame Lenain, the concierge, who laid Guinardon on the couch, lit a couple of candles, put a sprig of box in a saucer of holy water, and closed the dead man's eyes. The doctor who was called in to certify the death ascribed it to apoplexy.

Zéphyrine, informed of what had happened by Madame Lenain, hastened to the house, and sat up all night with the body. The dead man looked as if he were sleeping. In the flickering light of the candles El Greco's Saint mounted upwards like a wreath of smoke, the gold of the Primitives gleamed in the shadows. Near the deathbed a little woman by Baudouin was plainly discernible giving herself a douche. All through the night Zéphyrine's lamentations could be heard fifty yards away.

"He's dead, he's dead!" she kept saying. "My friend, my divinity, my all, my love---- But no! he is not dead, he moves. It is I, Michel; I, your Zéphyrine. Awake, hear me! Answer me; I love you; if ever I caused you pain, forgive me.

Dead! dead! O my God! See how beautiful he is. He was so good, so clever, so kind. My God! My God! My God! If I had been there he would not now be lying dead. Michel! Michel!"

When morning came she was silent. They thought she had fallen asleep. She was dead too.

CHAPTER XXXII. WHICH DESCRIBES HOW NECTAIRE'S FLUTE
WAS HEARD IN THE TAVERN OF CLODOMIR

MADAME DE LA VERDELIÈRE having failed to force an entrée as
sick-nurse, returned after several days had elapsed, -- during the absence of
Madame des Aubels, -- to ask Maurice d'Esparvieu for his subscription to the
French churches. Arcade led her to the bedside of the convalescent. Maurice
whispered in the angel's ear:

"Traitor, deliver me from this ogress immediately, or you will be
answerable for the evil which will soon befall."

"Be calm," said Arcade, with a confident air.

After the conventional complimentary flourishes, Madame de la Verdelière
signed to Maurice to dismiss the angel. Maurice feigned not to understand. And
Madame de la Verdelière disclosed the ostensible reason of her visit.

"Our churches," she said, "our beloved country churches, -- what is to
become of them?"

Arcade gazed at her angelically and sighed.

"They will disappear, Madame; they will fall into ruin. And what a pity!
I shall be inconsolable. The church amid the villagers' cottages is like the hen
amidst her chickens."

"Just so!" exclaimed Madame de la Verdelière with a delighted smile. "It
is just like that."

"And the spires, Madame?"

"Oh, Monsieur, the spires!..."

"Yes, the spires, Madame, that stick up into the skies towards the little
Cherubim, like so many syringes."

Madame de la Verdelière incontinently left the place.

That same day Monsieur l'Abbé Patouille came to offer the wounded man
good counsel and consolation. He exhorted him to break with his bad
companions and to be reconciled to his family.

He drew a picture of the sorrowful father, the mother in tears, ready to
receive their long-lost child with open arm. Renouncing with manly effort a life
of profligacy and deluding joys, Maurice would recover his peace and strength
of mind, he would free himself from devouring chimeras, and shake off the Evil
Spirit.

Young d'Esparvieu thanked Abbé Patouille for all his kindness, and made
a protestation of his religious feelings.

"Never," said he, "have I had such faith. And never have I been in such
need of it. Just imagine, Monsieur l'Abbé, I have to teach my guardian angel his
catechism all over again, for he has quite forgotten it!"

Monsieur l'Abbé Patouille heaved a deep sigh, and exhorted his dear child
to pray, there being no other resource but prayer for a soul assailed by the Devil.

"Monsieur l'Abbé," asked Maurice, "may I introduce my guardian angel
to you? Do stay a moment; he has gone to get me some cigarettes."

"Unhappy child!"

And Abbé Patouille's fat cheeks drooped in token of affliction. But almost
immediately they plumped up again, as a sign of light-heartedness. For in his
heart there was matter for rejoicing. Public opinion was improving. The
Jacobins, the Freemasons, the Coalitionists were everywhere in disgrace. The
Smart Set led the way. The Academie Franfaise was of the right way of
thinking. The number of Christian schools was increasing by leaps and bounds.
The young men of the Quartier Latin were submitting to the Church, and the
École Normale exhaled the perfume of the seminary. The Cross was gaining the
day; but money was wanted, -- more money, always money.

After six weeks' rest, Maurice was allowed by his doctor to take a drive.
He wore his arm in a sling. His mistress and his friend went with him. They
drove to the Bois, and took a gentle pleasure in looking upon the grass and the
trees. They smiled on everything and everything smiled on them. As Arcade had
said, their faults had made them better. By the unlooked-for ways of jealousy
and anger, Maurice had attained to calm and kindliness. He still loved Gilberte
and he loved her with an indulgent love. The angel still desired her as much as
ever, but having once possessed her, his desire had lost the sting of curiosity.
Gilberte forbore trying to please, and thereby pleased the more. They drank milk
at the Cascade, and found it good. They were all three innocent. Arcade forgot
the injustice of the old tyrant of the world. But he was soon to be reminded of
it.

On entering his friend's house, he found Zita awaiting him, looking like a
statue in ivory and gold.

"You excite my pity," she said to him. "The day is at hand the like of
which has never dawned since the beginning of Time, and perhaps will never
dawn again before the Sun enters with all its train into the constellation of
Hercules. We are on the eve of surprising Ialdabaoth in his palace of porphyry,
and you, who are burning to deliver the heavens, who were so eager to enter in
triumph into your emancipated country, -- you suddenly forget your noble
purpose and fall asleep in the arms of the daughters of men. What pleasure can
you find in intercourse with these unclean little animals, composed, as they are,
of elements so unstable that they may be said to be in a state of constant

evanescence? O Arcade! I was indeed right to distrust you. You are but an intellectual; you do but feel idle curiosity. You are incapable of action."

"You misjudge me, Zita," replied the angel. "It is the nature of the sons of heaven to love the daughters of men. Corruptible though it be, the material part of women and of flowers charms the senses none the less. But not one of these little animals can make me forget my hatred and my love, and I am ready to rise up against Ialdabaoth."

Zita expressed her satisfaction at seeing him in this resolute mood. She urged him to pursue the accomplishment of this vast undertaking with undiminished ardour. Nothing must be hurried or deferred.

"A great action, Arcade, is made up of a multitude of small ones; the most majestic whole is composed of a thousand minute details. Let us neglect nothing."

She had come to take him to a meeting where his presence was required. They were to take a census of the revolutionaries.

She added but one word:

"Nectaire will be there."

When Maurice saw Zita, he deemed her lacking in attraction. She failed to please him because she was perfectly beautiful and because true beauty always caused him painful surprise. Zita inspired him with antipathy when he learned that she was an angel in revolt and that she had come to seek Arcade to take him away among the conspirators.

The poor child tried to retain his companion by all the means that his wit and the circumstances afforded him. If his guardian angel would only remain with him, he would take him to a magnificent boxing-match, to a "revue" where he would witness the apotheosis of Poincare, or, lastly, to a certain house he knew of where he would behold women remarkable for their beauty, talents, vices, or deformities. But the angel would not allow himself to be tempted, and said he was going with Zita.

"What for?"

"To plot the conquest of the skies."

"Still the same nonsense! The conquest of---- but there, I proved to you that it was neither possible nor desirable."

"Good night, Maurice."

"You are going? Well, I will accompany you."

And Maurice, his arm in a sling, went with Arcade and Zita all the way to Clodomir's restaurant at Montmartre, where the tables were laid in an arbour in the garden.

Prince Istar and Théophile were already there, with a little creature who looked like a child, and was, in fact, a Japanese angel.

"We are only waiting for Nectaire," said Zita.

And at that moment the old gardener noiselessly appeared. He took his seat, and his dog lay down at his feet. French cooking is the best in the world. It is a glory that will transcend all others when humanity has grown wise enough to put the spit above the sword. Clodomir served the angels, and the mortal who was with them, with a soup made of cabbages and bacon, a loin of pork and kidneys-cooked in wine, thereby proving himself a real Montmartre cook, and showing that he had not been spoilt by the Americans, who corrupt the most excellent chefs of the City of Restaurants.

Clodomir brought forth some Bordeaux, which, though unrecorded among the renowned vintages of Médoc, gave evidence by its choice and delicate aroma of the high nobility of its origin. We must not omit to chronicle that, after this wine and many others had been drunk, the cellarman, in solemn state, produced a Bergundy choice and rare, full-bodied yet not heavy, generous yet delicate, rich with the true Burgundian mellowness, a noble and, withal, a somewhat heady wine, that brought delight alike to mind and sense.

"Hail to thee, Dionysus, greatest of the Gods!" cried old Nectaire, raising his glass on high. "I drink to thee who wilt restore the Golden Age, and give again to mortal men, who will become heroes as of old, the grapes which the Lesbians used to cull, long since, from the vines of Methymna; who wilt restore the vineyards of Thasus, the white clusters of Lake Mareotis, the storehouses of Falernus, the vines of the Tmolus, and the wine of Phanae, of all wines the king. And the juice thereof shall be divine, and, as in old Silenus' day, men shall grow drunk with Wisdom and with Love."

When the coffee was served, Prince Istar, Zita, Arcade, and the Japanese angel took it in turns to give an account of the forces assembled against Ialdabaoth. Angels, in exchanging eternal bliss for the sufferings of an earthly life, grow in intelligence, acquire the means of going astray and the faculty of self-contradiction. Consequently their meetings, like those of men, are tumultuous and confused. Did one of them deal in figures, the others immediately called them in question. They could not add one number to another without quarrelling, and arithmetic itself, subjected to passion, lost its certitude. The Kerûb, who had brought with him the pious Théophile, waxed indignant when he heard the musician praising the Lord, and rained down such blows on his head as would have felled an ox. But the head of a musician is harder than a bucranium, and the blows which Théophile received did not avail to modify that angel's notion of divine providence. Arcade, having at great length set up his scientific idealism in opposition to Zita's pragmatism, the beautiful archangel told him that he argued badly.

"And you are surprised at that!" exclaimed young Maurice's guardian angel. "I argue, like you, in the language of human beings. And what is human language but the cry of the beasts of the forests or the mountains, complicated and corrupted by arrogant anthropoids. How then, Zita, can one be expected to argue well with a collection of angry or plaintive sounds like that? Angels do not reason at all; men, being superior to the angels, reason imperfectly. I will not mention the professors who think to define the absolute with the aid of cries that they have inherited from the pithecanthropoid monkeys, marsupials, and reptiles, their ancestors! It is a colossal joke! How it would amuse the demiurge, if he had any brains!"

It was a beautiful starlight night. The gardener was silent.

"Nectaire," said the beautiful archangel, "play to us on your flute, if you are not afraid that the Earth and Heaven will be stirred to their depths thereby."

Nectaire took up his flute. Young Maurice lighted a cigarette. The flame burnt brightly for a moment, casting back the sky and its stars into the shadows, and then died out. And Nectaire sang of the flame on his divine flute. The silvery voice soared aloft and sang:

"That flame was a whole universe which fulfilled its destiny in less than a minute. Suns and planets were formed therein. Venus Urania apportioned the orbits of the wandering spheres in those infinite spaces. Beneath the breath of Eros -- the first of the gods, -- plants, animals, and thoughts sprang into being. In the twenty seconds which hurried by betwixt the life and death of those worlds, civilizations were unfolded, and empires sank in long decline. Mothers shed tears, and songs of love, cries of hatred, and sighs of victims rose upward to the silent skies.

"In proportion to its minuteness, that universe lasted as long as this one -- whereof we see a few atoms glittering above our heads -- has lasted or will last. They are, one no less than the other, but a gleam in the Infinite."

As the clear, pure notes welled up into the charmed air, the earth melted into a soft mist, the stars revolved rapidly in their orbits, the Great Bear fell asunder, its parts flew far and wide. Orion's belt was shattered; the Pole Star forsook its magnetic axis. Sirius, whose incandescent flame had lit up the far horizon, grew blue, then red, flickered, and suddenly died out. The shaken constellations formed new signs which were extinguished in their turn. By its incantations the magic flute had compressed into one brief moment the life and the movement of this universe which seems unchanging and eternal both to men and angels. It ceased, and the heavens resumed their immemorial aspect. Nectaire had vanished. Clodomir asked his guests if they were pleased with the cabbage soup which, in order that it might be strong, had been kept simmering for twenty-four hours on the fire, and he sang the praises of the Beaujolais which they had drunk.

The night was mild. Arcade, accompanied by his guardian angel, Théophile, Prince Istar, and the Japanese angel, escorted Zita home.

CHAPTER XXXIII. HOW A DREADFUL CRIME PLUNGES PARIS INTO A STATE OF TERROR

The city was asleep. Their footsteps rang loudly on the deserted pavement. Having reached the corner of the Rue Feutrier, half-way up Montmartre, the little company halted before the dwelling of the beautiful angel. Arcade was talking about the Thrones and Dominations with Zita, who, her finger on the bell, could not make up her mind to ring. Prince Istar was tracing the mechanism of a new sort of bomb on the pavement with the end of his stick, and bellowed so loudly that he woke the sleeping citizens and stirred into activity the amatory passions of the neighbouring Pasiphaës. Théophile was singing the barcarole from the second act of Aline, Queen of Golconda at the top of his voice. Maurice, his arm in a sling, was fencing left-handed with the Japanese, striking sparks from the pavement, and crying "A hit! a hit!" in a piercing voice.

Meanwhile Inspector Grolle at the corner of the next street was dreaming. He had the bearing of a Roman legionary and displayed all the characteristics of that proudly servile race, who, ever since men first took to building cities, have been the mainstay of Empires and the support of ruling houses. Inspector Grolle was very strong, but very tired. He suffered from an arduous profession and from lack of food. He was a man devoted to duty, but still a man, and he was unable to resist the wiles, the charms, and the blandishments of the gay ladies whom he met in swarms in the shadows along the empty streets and round about pieces of waste ground; he loved them. He loved like a soldier under arms. It tired him, but courage conquered fatigue. Though he had not yet reached the middle of Life's way, he longed for sweet repose and peaceful country pursuits. At the corner of the Rue Muller, on this mild night, he stood lost in thought. He was dreaming of the house where he was born, of the little olive wood, of his father's bit of ground, of his old mother, bent with long and heavy labour, whom he would never see again. Roused from his reverie by the nocturnal tumult, Inspector Grolle turned the corner of the street, and looked rather unfavourably at the band of loiterers, wherein his social instinct suspected enemies of law and order. He was patient and resolute. After a lengthy silence, he said, with awe-inspiring calm:

"Move on, there!"

But Maurice and the Japanese angel were fencing and heard nothing. The musician heard nothing but his own melodies. Prince Istar was absorbed in the explanation of explosive formulæ. Zita was discussing with Arcade the greatest enterprise that had ever been conceived since the solar system issued from its original nebula, -- and thus they all remained unconscious of their surroundings.

"Move on, I tell you!" repeated Inspector Grolle.

This time the angels heard the solemn word of warning, but either through indifference or contempt, they neglected to obey, and continued their talk, their songs, and their cries.

"So you want to be taken up, do you" shouted Inspector Grolle, clapping his great hand on Prince Istar's shoulder.

The Kerûb was indignant at this vile contact, and with one blow from his formidable fist sent the Inspector flying into the gutter. But Constable Fesandet was already running to his comrade's aid, and they both fell upon the Prince, whom they belaboured with mechanic fury, and whom, notwithstanding his strength and weight, they would perchance have dragged all bleeding to the police station, had not the Japanese angel overset them one after the other without effort, and reduced them to writhing and shreiking in the mud, before Maurice, Arcade, and Zita had time to intervene. As to the angelic musician, he stood apart trembling, and invoked the heavens.

At this moment two bakers who were kneading their dough in a neighbouring cellar ran out at the noise, in their white aprons, stripped to the waist. With an instinctive feeling for social solidarity they took the side of the downfallen police. Théophile conceived a just fear at the sight of them, and fled away; they caught him and were about to hand him over to the guardians of the peace, when Arcade and Zita tore him from their hands. The fight continued, unequal and terrible, between the two angels and the two bakers. Like an athlete of Lysippus in strength and beauty, Arcade smothered his heavy adversary in his arms. The beautiful archangel drove her dagger into the baker who had attacked her. A dark stream of blood flowed down over his hairy chest, and the two white-capped supporters of the law sank to the ground.

Constable Fesandet had fainted face downwards in the gutter. But Inspector Grolle, who had got up, blew a blast on his whistle loud enough to be heard at the neighbouring police-station, and sprang upon young Maurice, who, having but one arm with which to defend himself, fired his revolver with his left hand at the inspector, who put his hand to his heart, staggered, and dropped down. He gave a long sigh, and the shadows of eternity darkened his eyes.

Meanwhile, windows opened one by one, and heads looked out on the street. A sound of heavy steps approached. Two policemen on bicycles debouched upon the street. Thereupon Prince Istar flung a bomb which shook the ground, put out the gas, shattered some of the houses, and enveloped the flight of young Maurice and the angels in a dense smoke.

Arcade and Maurice came to the conclusion that the safest thing to do after this adventure was to return to the little flat in the Rue de Rome. They would certainly not be sought for immediately and probably not at all, the bomb thrown by the Kerûb having fortunately wiped out all witnesses of the affair. They fell asleep towards dawn, and they had not yet awoke at ten o'clock in the morning when the concierge brought their tea. While eating his toast and butter and slice of ham, young d'Esparvieu remarked to the angel:

"I used to think that a murder was something very extraordinary. Well, I was mistaken. It is the simplest, the most natural action in the world."

"And of most ancient tradition," replied the angel. "For long centuries it was both usual and necessary for man to kill and despoil his fellows. It is still recommended in warfare. It is also honourable to attempt human life in certain definite circumstances, and people approved when you wanted to assassinate me, Maurice, because it appeared to you that I had been intimate with your mistress. But killing a police-inspector is not the action of a man of fashion."

"Be silent," exclaimed Maurice, "be silent, scoundrel! I killed the poor Inspector instinctively, not knowing what I was doing. I am grieved to my heart about it. But it is not I, it is you who are the guilty one; you who are the murderer. It was you who lured me along this path of revolt and violence which leads to the pit. You have been my undoing. You have sacrificed my peace of mind, my happiness, to your pride and your wickedness, and all in vain; for I warn you, Arcade, you will not succeed in what you are undertaking."

The concierge brought in the newspapers. On seeing them Maurice grew pale. They announced the outrage in the Rue de Ramey in huge headlines:

"An Inspector killed -- Two cyclist policemen and two bakers seriously wounded -- Three houses blown up, numerous victims."

Maurice let the paper drop, and said in a weak, plaintive voice:

"Arcade, why did you not slay me in the little garden at Versailles amidst the roses, to the song of the blackbirds?"

Meanwhile terror reigned in Paris. In the public squares, and in the crowded streets, housewives, string-bag in hand, grew pale as they listened to the story of the crime, and consigned the perpetrators to the most dreadful punishment. Shopkeepers, standing at the doors of their shops, put it all down to the anarchists, syndicalists, socialists, and radicals, and demanded that special measures should be taken against them.

The more thoughtful people recognized the handiwork of the Jew and the German, and demanded the expulsion of all aliens. Many vaunted the ways of America and advocated lynching. In addition to the printed news sinister rumours became current. Explosions had been heard at various places; everywhere bombs had been discovered; everywhere individuals, taken for malefactors, had been struck down by the popular arm and given up to justice, torn to ribbons. On the Place de la République a drunkard who was crying "Down with the police" was torn to pieces by the crowd.

The President of the Council and Minister of Justice held long conferences with the Prefect of Police, and they agreed to take immediate action. In order to allay the excitement of the Parisians, they arrested five or six hooligans out of the thirty thousand which the Capital contains. The chief of the Russian police, believing he recognised in this attack the methods of the Nihilists, demanded, on behalf of his Government, that a dozen refugees should be given up. The demand was immediately granted. Proceedings were also taken for certain individuals to be extradited to ensure the safety of the King of Spain.

On learning of these energetic measures, Paris breathed once more, and the evening papers congratulated the Government. There was excellent news of the wounded. They were out of danger and identified as their assailants all who were brought before them.

True, Inspector Grolle was dead; but two Sisters of Mercy kept vigil at his side, and the President of the Council came and laid the Cross of Honour on the breast of this victim of duty.

At night there were panics. In the Avenue de la Revolte the police, noticing a travelling acrobat's caravan on a piece of waste ground, took it for the retreat of a band of robbers. They whistled for help, and when they were a goodly number, attacked the caravan. Some worthy citizens joined them; fifteen thousand revolver-shots were fired, the caravan was blown up with dynamite, and among the debris they found the corpse of a monkey.

CHAPTER XXXIV. WHICH CONTAINS AN ACCOUNT OF THE ARREST OF BOUCHOTTE AND MAURICE, OF THE DISASTER WHICH BEFELL THE D'ESPARVIEU LIBRARY AND OF THE DEPARTURE OF THE ANGELS

Maurice D'esparvieu passed a terrible night. At the least sound he seized his revolver that he might not fall alive into the hands of justice. When morning came he snatched the newspapers from the hands of the concierge, devoured them greedily, and gave a cry of joy; he had just read that Inspector Grolle having been taken to the Morgue for the postmortem, the police-surgeons had only discovered bruises and contusions of a very superficial nature, and stated that death had been brought about by the rupture of an aneurism of the aorta.

"You see, Arcade," he exclaimed triumphantly; "you see I am not an assassin. I am innocent. I could never have imagined how extremely agreeable it is to be innocent."

Then he grew thoughtful, and -- no unusual phenomenon -- reflection dissipated his gaiety.

"I am innocent, -- but there is no disguising the fact," he said, shaking his head, "I am one of a band of malefactors. I live with miscreants. You are in your right place there, Arcade, for you are deceitful, cruel, and perverse. But I come of good family and have received an excellent education, and I blush for it."

"I also," said Arcade, "have received an excellent education."

"Where was that?"

"In Heaven."

"No, Arcade, no; you never had any education. If good principles had been inculcated into you, you would still hold them. Such principles are never lost. In my childhood I learnt to revere my family, my country, my religion. I have not forgotten the lesson and I never shall. Do you know what shocks me most in you? It is not your perversity, your cruelty, your black ingratitude; it is not your agnosticism, which may be borne with at a pinch; it is not your scepticism, though it is very much out of date (for since the national awakening there is no longer any scepticism in France); -- no, what disgusts me in you is your lack of taste, the bad style of your ideas, the inelegance of your doctrines. You think like an intellectual, you speak like a freethinker, you have theories which reek of radicalism and Combeism and all ignoble systems. Get along with you! you disgust me. Arcade, my old friend, Arcade, my dear angel, Arcade, my beloved child, listen to your guardian angel! Yield to my prayers, renounce your mad ideas; become good, simple, innocent, and happy once more. Put on your hat, come with me to Nôtre-Dame. We will say a prayer and burn a candle together."

Meanwhile public opinion was still active in the matter; the leading papers, the organs of the national awakening, in articles of real elevation and real depth, unravelled the philosophy of this monstrous attack which was revolting to the conscience. They discovered the real origin, the indirect but effective cause in the revolutionary doctrines which had been disseminated unchecked, in the weakening of social ties, the relaxing of moral discipline, in the repeated appeals to every appetite, to every greedy desire. It would be needful, so as to cut down the evil at its root, to repudiate as quickly as possible all such chimeras and Utopias as syndicalism, the income-tax, etc., etc., etc. Many newspapers, and these not the least important, pointed out that the recrudescence of crime was but the natural fruit of impiety and concluded that the salvation of society lay in an unanimous and sincere return to religion. On the Sunday which followed the crime the congregations in the churches were noticed to be unusually large.

Judge Salneuve, who was entrusted with the task of investigation, first examined the persons arrested by the police, and lost his way among attractive but illusory clues; however, the report of the detective Montremain, which was laid before him, put him on the right road, and soon led him to recognise the miscreants of La Jonchère as the authors of the crime of the Rue de Ramey. He ordered a search to be made for Arcade and Zita, and issued a warrant against Prince Istar, on whom the detectives laid hands as he was leaving Bouchotte's, where he had been depositing some bombs of new design. The Kerûb, on learning the detectives' intentions, smiled broadly and asked them if they had a powerful motor-car. On their replying that they had one at the door, he assured them that was all he wanted. Thereupon he felled the two detectives on the stairs, walked up to the waiting car, flung the chauffeur under a motor-'bus which was opportunely passing, and seized the steering wheel under the eyes of the terrified crowd.

That same evening Monsieur Jeancourt, the Police Magistrate, entered Théophile's rooms just when Bouchotte was swallowing a raw egg to clear her voice, for she was to sing her new song, "They haven't got any in Germany," at the "National Eldorado" that evening. The musician vas absent. Bouchotte received the Magistrate, and received him with a hauteur which intensified the simplicity of her attire; Bouchotte was en déshabille. The worthy Magistrate seized the score of Aline, Queen of Golconda, and the love-letters which the singer carefully preserved in the drawer of the table by her bed, for she was an orderly young woman. He was about to withdraw when he espied a cupboard, which he opened with a careless air, and found machines capable of blowing up half Paris, and a pair of large white wings, whose nature and use appeared inexplicable to him. Bouchotte was invited to complete her toilette, and, in spite of her cries, was taken off to the police-station.

Monsieur Salneuve was indefatigable. After the examination of the papers seized in Bouchotte's house, and acting on the information of Montremain, he issued a warrant for the arrest of young d'Esparvieu, which was executed on Wednesday, the 27th May, at seven o'clock in the morning, with great discretion. For three days Maurice had neither slept nor eaten, loved nor lived. He had not a moment's doubt as to the nature of the matutinal visit. At the sight of the police magistrate a strange calm fell on him. Arcade had not returned to sleep in the flat. Maurice begged the magistrate to wait for him, dressed with care, and then accompanied the magistrate to the taxi that was waiting at the door. He felt a calmness of mind which was barely disturbed when the door of the Conciergerie closed on him. Alone in his cell, he climbed upon the table to look out His tranquillity was due to his weariness of spirit, to his numbed senses, and to the fact that he no longer stood in fear of arrest. His misfortune endowed him with superior wisdom. He felt he had fallen into a state of grace. He did not think too highly or too humbly of himself, but left his cause in the hands of God. With no desire to cover up his faults, which he would not hide even from himself, he addressed himself in mind to Providence, to point out that if he had fallen into disorder and rebellion it was to lead his erring angel back into the straight path. He stretched himself on the couch and slept in peace.

On hearing of the arrest of a music-hall singer and of a young man of fashion, both Paris and the provinces felt painful surprise. Deeply stirred by the tragic-accounts which the leading newspapers were bringing out, the general idea was that the sort of people the authorities ought to bring to justice were ferocious anarchists, all reeking and dripping from deeds of blood and arson; but they failed to understand what the world of Art and Fashion should have to do with such things. At this news, which he was one of the last to hear, the President of the Council and keeper of the Seals started up in his chair. The Sphinxes that adorned it were less terrible than he, and in the throes of his angry meditation he cut the mahogany of his imperial table with his penknife, after the manner of Napoleon. And when Judge Salneuve, whose attendance he had commanded, appeared before him, the President flung his penknife in the grate, as Louis XI flung his cane out of the window in the prescence of Lauzun; and it cost him a supreme effort to master himself and to say in a voice of suppressed fury:

"Are you mad? Surely I said often enough that I meant the plot to be anarchist, anti-social, fundamentally anti-social and anti-governmental, with a shade of syndicalism. I have made it clear enough that I wanted it kept within these lines; and what do you go and make of it?... The vengeance of anarchists and aspirants to freedom? Whom do you arrest? A singer adored of the nationalist public, and the son of a man highly esteemed in the Catholic party, who receives our bishops and has the entrée to the Vatican; a man who may be one day sent as ambassador to the Pope. At one blow you alienate one hundred and sixty Deputies and forty Senators of the Right on the very eve of a motion to discuss the question of religious pacification; you embroil me with my friends of to-day, with my friends of to-morrow. Was it to find out if you were in the same dilemma as des Aubels that you seized the love-letters of young Maurice d'Esparvieu? I can put your mind at rest on that point. You are, and all Paris knows it. But it is not to avenge your personal affronts that you are on the Bench."

"Monsieur le Garde des Sceaux," murmured the Judge, nearly apoplectic and in a choked voice. "I am an honest man."

"You are a fool... and a provincial. Listen to me; if Maurice d'Esparvieu and Mademoiselle Bouchotte are not released within half an hour I will crush you like a piece of glass. Be off!"

Monsieur René d'Esparvieu went himself to fetch his son from the Conciergerie and took him back to the old house in the Rue Garancière. The return was triumphant. The news had been disseminated that Maurice had with generous imprudence interested himself in an attempt to restore the monarchy, and that Judge Salneuve, the infamous freemason, the tool of Combes and Andre, had tried to compromise the young man by making him out to be an accomplice of a band of criminals.

That was what Abbé Patouille seemed to think, and he answered for Maurice as for himself. It was known, moreover, that breaking with his father, who had rallied to the support of the Republic, young d'Esparvieu was on the high road to becoming an out-and-out Royalist. The people who had an inside knowledge of things saw in his arrest the vengeance of the Jews. Was not Maurice a notorious anti-Semite? Catholic youths went forth to hurl imprecations at Judge Salneuve under the windows of his residence in the Rue Guénégaud, opposite the Mint.

On the Boulevard du Palais a band of students presented Maurice with a branch of palm. Maurice made a charming reply.

Maurice was overcome with emotion when he beheld the old house in which his childhood had been spent, and fell weeping into his mother's arms.

It was a great day, unhappily marred by one painful incident. Monsieur Sariette, who had lost his reason as a consequence of the shocking events that had taken place in the Rue de Courcelles, had suddenly become violent. He had shut himself up in the library, and there he had remained for twenty-four hours, uttering the most horrible cries, and, turning a deaf ear alike to threats and entreaties, refused to come out. He had spent the night in a condition of extreme restlessness, for all night long the lamp had been seen passing rapidly to and fro behind the curtains. In the morning, hearing Hippolyte shouting to him from the court below, he opened the window of the Hall of the Spheres and the

Philosophers, and heaved two or three rather weighty tomes on to the old valet's head. The whole of the domestic staff -- men, women, and boys -- hurried to the spot, and the librarian proceeded to throw out books by the armful on to their heads. In view of the gravity of the situation, Monsieur René d'Esparvieu did not disdain to intervene. He appeared in night-cap and dressing-gown, and attempted to reason with the poor lunatic, whose only reply was to pour forth torrents of abuse on the man whom till then he had worshipped as his benefactor, and to endeavour to crush him beneath all the Bibles, all the Talmuds, all the sacred books of India and Persia, all the Greek Fathers, and all the Latin Fathers, Saint John Chrysostom, Saint Gregory Nazianzen, Saint Augustine, Saint Jerome, all the apologists, ay! and under the Histoire des Variations, annotated by Bossuet himself! Octavos, quartos, folios came crashing down, and lay in a sordid heap on the courtyard pavement. The letters of Gassendi, of Père Mersenne, of Pascal, were blown about hither and thither by the wind. The lady's-maid who had stooped down to rescue some of the sheets from the gutter got a blow on the head from an enormous Dutch atlas. Madame René d'Esparvieu had been terrified by the ominous sounds, and appeared on the scene without waiting to apply the finishing touches of powder and paint. When he caught sight of her, old Sariette became more violent than ever. Down they came one after another as hard as he could pelt them; the busts of the poets, philosophers, and historians of antiquity -- Homer, Æschylus, Sophocles, Euripides, Herodotus, Thucydides, Socrates, Plato, Aristotle, Demosthenes, Cicero, Virgil, Horace, Seneca, Epictetus -- all lay scattered on the ground. The celestial sphere and the terrestrial globe descended with a terrifying crash that was followed by a ghastly hush, broken only by the shrill laughter of little Léon, who was looking down on the scene from a window above. A locksmith having opened the library door, all the household hastened to enter, and found the aged Sariette entrenched behind piles of books, busily engaged in tearing and slashing away at the Lucretius of the Prior de Vendôme annotated in Voltaire's own hand. They had to force a way through the barricade. But the maniac, perceiving that his stronghold was being invaded, fled away and escaped on to the roof. For two whole hours he gave vent to shouts and yells that were heard far and wide. In the Rue Garancière the crowd kept growing bigger and bigger. All had their eyes fixed on the unhappy creature, and whenever he stumbled on the slates, which cracked beneath him, they gave a shout of terror. In the midst of the crowd, the Abbé Patouille, who expected every moment to see him hurled into space, was reciting the prayers for the dying, and making ready to give him the absolution in extremis. There was a cordon of police round the house keeping order. Someone summoned the fire-brigade, and the sound of their approach was soon heard. They placed a ladder against the wall of the house, and after a terrific struggle managed to secure the maniac, who in the course of his desperate resistance had one of the muscles of his arm torn out. He was immediately removed to an asylum.

Maurice dined at home, and there were smiles of tenderness and affection when Victor, the old butler, brought on the roast veal. Monsieur l'Abbé Patouille sat at the right hand of the Christian mother, unctuously contemplating the family which Heaven had so plentifully blessed. Nevertheless, Madame d'Esparvieu was ill at ease. Every day she received anonymous letters of so insulting and coarse a nature that she thought at first they must come from a discharged footman. She now knew they were the handiwork of her youngest daughter, Berthe, a mere child! Little Léon, too, gave her pain and anxiety. He paid no attention to his lessons, and was given to-bad habits. He showed a cruel disposition. He had plucked his sister's canaries alive; he stuck innumerable pins into the chair on which Mademoiselle Caporal was accustomed to sit, and had stolen fourteen francs from the poor girl, who did nothing but cry and dab her eyes and nose from morning till night.

No sooner was dinner over than Maurice rushed of to the little dwelling in the Rue de Rome, impatient to meet his angel again. Through the door he heard a loud sound of voices, and saw assembled in the room where the apparition had taken place, Arcade, Zita, the angelic musician, and the Kerûb, who was lying on the bed, smoking a huge pipe, carelessly scorching pillows, sheets, and coverlets. They embraced Maurice, and announced their departure. Their faces shone with happiness and courage. Alone, the inspired author of Aline, Queen of Golconda, shed tears and raised his terrified gaze to heaven. The Kerûb forced him into the party of rebellion by setting before him two alternatives: either to allow himself to be dragged from prison to prison on earth, or to carry fire and sword into the palace of Ialdabaoth.

Maurice perceived with sorrow that the earth had scarcely any hold over them. They were setting out filled with immense hope, which was quite justifiable. Doubtless they were but a few combatants to oppose the innumerable soldiers of the sultan of the heavens; but they counted on compensating for the inferiority of their numbers by the irresistible impetus of a sudden attack. They were not ignorant of the fact that Ialdabaoth, who flatters himself on knowing all things, sometimes allows himself to be taken by surprise. And it certainly looked as if the first attack would have taken him unawares had it not been for the warning of the archangel Michael. The celestial army had made no progress since its victory over the rebels before the beginning of Time.

As regards armaments and material it was as out of date as the army of the Moors. Its generals slumbered in sloth and ignorance. Loaded with honours and riches, they preferred the delights of the banquet to the fatigues of war. Michael, the commander-in-chief, ever loyal and brave, had lost, with the passing of centuries, his fire and enthusiasm. The conspirators of 1914, on the other hand, knew the very latest and the most delicate appliances of science for the art of destruction. At length all was ready and decided upon. The army of revolt, assembled by corps each a hundred thousand angels strong, on all the waste places of the earth -- steppes, pampas, deserts, fields of ice and snow -- was ready to launch itself against the sky. The angels, in modifying the rhythm of the atoms of which they are composed, are able to traverse the most varied mediums. Spirits that have descended on to the earth, being formed, since their incarnation, of too compact a substance, can no longer fly of themselves, and to rise into ethereal regions and then insensibly grow volatilized, have need of the assistance of their brothers, who, though revolutionaries like themselves, nevertheless, stayed behind in the Empyrean and remained, not immaterial (for all is matter in the Universe), but gloriously untrammelled and diaphanous. Certes, it was not without painful anxiety that Arcade, Istar, and Zita prepared themselves to pass from the heavy atmosphere of the earth to the limpid depths of the heavens. To plunge into the ether there is need to expend such energy that the most intrepid hesitate to take flight. Their very substance, while penetrating this fine medium, must in itself grow fine-spun, become vaporised, and pass from human dimensions to the volume of the vastest clouds which have ever enveloped the earth. Soon they would surpass in grandeur the uttermost planets, whose orbits they, invisible and imponderable, would traverse without disturbing.

In this enterprise -- the vastest that angels could undertake -- their substance would be ultimately hotter than the fire and colder than the ice, and they would suffer pangs sharper than death.

Maurice read all the daring and the pain of the undertaking in the eyes of Arcade.

"You are going?" he said to him, weeping.

"We are going, with Nectaire, to seek the great archangel to lead us to victory."

"Whom do you call thus?"

"The priests of the demiurge have made him known to you in their calumnies."

"Unhappy being," sighed Maurice.

Arcade embraced him, and Maurice felt the angel's tears as they dropped upon his cheek.

CHAPTER XXXV. AND LAST, WHEREIN THE SUBLIME DREAM OF SATAN IS UNFOLDED

Climbing the seven steep terraces which rise up from the bed of the Ganges to the temples muffled in creepers, the five angels reached, by half-obliterated paths, the wild garden filled with perfumed clusters of grapes and chattering monkeys, and, at the far end thereof, they discovered him whom they had come to seek. The archangel lay with his elbow on black cushions embroidered with golden flames. At his feet crouched lions and gazelles. Twined in the trees, tame serpents turned on him their friendly gaze. At the sight of his angelic visitors his face grew melancholy. Long since, in the days when, with his brow crowned with grapes and his sceptre of vine-leaves in his hand, he had taught and comforted mankind, his heart had many times been heavy with sorrow; but never yet, since his glorious downfall, had his beautiful face expressed such pain and anguish.

Zita told him of the black standards assembled in crowds in all the waste places of the globe; of the deliverance premeditated and prepared in the provinces of Heaven, where the first revolt had long ago been fomented.

"Prince," she went on, "your army awaits you. Come, lead it on to victory."

"Friends," replied the great archangel, "I was aware of the object of your visit. Baskets of fruit and honeycombs await you under the shade of this mighty tree. The sun is about to descend into the roseate waters of the Sacred River. When you have eaten, you will slumber pleasantly in this garden, where the joys of the intellect and of the senses have reigned since the day when I drove hence the spirit of the old Demiurge. To-morrow I will give you my answer."

Night hung its blue over the garden. Satan fell asleep. He had a dream, and in that dream, soaring over the earth, he saw it covered with angels in revolt, beautiful as gods, whose eyes darted lightning. And from pole to pole one single cry, formed of a myriad cries, mounted towards him, filled with hope and love. And Satan said:

"Let us go forth! Let us seek the ancient adversary in his high abode." And he led the countless host of angels over the celestial plains. And Satan was cognizant of what took place in the heavenly citadel. When news of this second revolt came thither, the Father said to the Son:

"The irreconcilable foe is rising once again. Let us take heed to ourselves, and in this, our time of danger, look to our defences, lest we lose our high abode."

And the Son, consubstantial with the Father, replied:

"We shall triumph under the sign that gave Constantine the victory."

Indignation burst forth on the Mountain of God. At first the faithful Seraphim condemned the rebels to terrible torture, but afterwards decided on doing battle with them. The anger burning in the hearts of all inflamed each countenance. They did not doubt of victory, but treachery was feared, and eternal darkness had been at once decreed for spies and alarmists.

There was shouting and singing of ancient hymns and praise of the Almighty. They drank of the mystic wine. Courage, over-inflated, came near to giving way, and a secret anxiety stole into the inner depths of their souls. The archangel Michael took supreme command. He reassured their minds by his serenity. His countenance, wherein his soul was visible, expressed contempt for danger. By his orders, the chiefs of the thunderbolts, the Kerûbs, grown dull with the long interval of peace, paced with heavy steps the ramparts of the Holy Mountain, and, letting the gaze of their bovine eyes wander over the glittering clouds of their Lord, strove to place the divine batteries in position. After inspecting the defences, they swore to the Most High that all was in readiness. They took counsel together as to the plan they should follow. Michael was for the offensive. He, as a consummate soldier, said it was the supreme law. Attack, or be attacked, -- there was no middle course.

"Moreover," he added, "the offensive attitude is particularly suitable to the ardour of the Thrones and Dominations."

Beyond that, it was impossible to obtain a word from the valiant chief, and this silence seemed the mark of a genius sure of himself.

As soon as the approach of the enemy was announced, Michael sent forth three armies to meet them, commanded by the archangels Uriel, Raphael, and Gabriel. Standards, displaying ail the colours of the Orient, were unfurled above the ethereal plains, and the thunders rolled over the starry floors. For three days and three nights was the lot of the terrible and adorable armies unknown on the Mountain of God. Towards dawn on the fourth day news came, but it was vague and confused. There were rumours of indecisive victories; of the triumph now of this side, now of that. There came reports of glorious deeds which were dissipated in a few hours.

The thunderbolts of Raphael, hurled against the rebels, had, it was said, consumed entire squadrons. The troops commanded by the impure Zita were thought to have been swallowed up in the whirlwind of a tempest of fire. It was believed that the savage Istar had been flung headlong into the gulf of perdition so suddenly that the blasphemies begun in his mouth had been forced backwards with explosive results. It was popularly supposed that Satan, laden with chains of adamant, had been plunged once again into the abyss. Meanwhile, the commanders of the three armies had sent no messages. Mutterings and murmurs, mingling with the rumours of glory, gave rise to fears of an indecisive battle, a precipitate retreat. Insolent voices gave out that a spirit of the lowest category, a guardian angel, the insignificant Arcade, had checked and routed the dazzling host of the three great archangels.

There were also rumours of wholesale defection in the Seventh Heaven, where rebellion had broken out before the beginning of Time, and some had even seen black clouds of impious angels joining the armies of the rebels on Earth. But no one lent an ear to the odious rumours, and stress was laid on the news of victory which ran from lip to lip, each statement readily finding confirmation. The high places resounded with hymns of joy; the Seraphim celebrated on harp and psaltery Sabaoth, God of Thunder. The voice of the elect united with those of the angels in glorifying the Invisible and at the thought of the bloodshed that the ministers of holy wrath had caused among the rebels, sighs of relief and jubilation were wafted from the Heavenly Jerusalem towards the Most High. But the beatitude of the most blessed, having swelled to the utmost limit before due time, could increase no more, and the very excess of their felicity completely dulled their senses.

The songs had not yet ceased when the guards watching on the ramparts signalled the approach of the first fugitives of the divine army; Seraphim on tattered wing, flying in disorder, maimed Kerûbs going on three feet. With impassive gaze, Michael, prince of warriors, measured the extent of the disaster, and his keen intelligence penetrated its causes. The armies of the living God had taken the offensive, but by one of those fatalities in war which disconcert the plans of the greatest captains, the enemy had also taken the offensive, and the effect was evident. Scarcely were the gates of the citadel opened to receive the glorious but shattered remnants of the three armies, when a rain of fire fell on the Mountain of God. Satan's army was not yet in sight, but the walls of topaz, the cupolas of emerald, the roofs of diamond, all fell in with an appalling crash under the discharge of the electrophores. The ancient thunderclouds essayed to reply, but the bolts fell short, and their thunders were lost in the deserted plains of the skies.

Smitten by an invisible foe, the faithful angels abandoned the ramparts. Michael went to announce to his God that the Holy Mountain would fall into the hands of the demon in twenty-four hours, and that nothing remained for the Master of the Heavens but to seek safety in flight. The Seraphim placed the jewels of the celestial crown in coffers. Michael offered his arm to the Queen of Heaven, and the Holy Family escaped from the palace by a subterranean passage of porphyry. A deluge of fire was falling on the citadel. Regaining his post once more, the glorious archangel declared that he would never capitulate, and straightway advanced the standards of the living God. That same evening the rebel host made its entry into the thrice-sacred city. On a fiery steed Satan led his demons. Behind him marched Arcade, Istar, and Zita. As in the ancient revels of Dionysus, old Nectaire bestrode his ass. Thereafter, floating out far behind, followed the black standards.

The garrison laid down their arms before Satan. Michael placed his flaming sword at the feet of the conquering archangel.

"Take back your sword, Michael," said Satan. "It is Lucifer who yields it to you. Bear it in defence of peace and law." Then letting his gaze fall on the leaders of the celestial cohorts, he cried in a ringing voice:

"Archangel Michael, and you, Powers, Thrones, and Dominations, swear all of you to be faithful to your God."

"We swear it," they replied with one voice.

And Satan said:

"Powers, Thrones, and Dominations, of all past wars, I wish but to remember the invincible courage that you displayed and the loyalty which you rendered to authority, for these assure me of the steadfastness of the fealty you have just sworn to me."

The following day, on the ethereal plain, Satan commanded the black standards to be distributed to the troops, and the winged soldiers covered them with kisses and bedewed them with tears.

And Satan had himself crowned God. Thronging round the glittering walls of Heavenly Jerusalem, apostles, pontiffs, virgins, martyrs, confessors, the whole company of the elect, who during the fierce battle had enjoyed delightful tranquillity, tasted infinite joy in the spectade of the coronation.

The elect saw with ravishment the Most High precipitated into Hell, and Satan seated on the throne of the Lord. In conformity with the will of God which had cut them off from sorrow they sang in the ancient fashion the praises of their new Master.

And Satan, piercing space with his keen glance, contemplated the little globe of earth and water where of old he had planted the vine and formed the first tragic chorus. And he fixed his gaze on that Rome where the fallen God had founded his empire on fraud and lie. Nevertheless, at that moment a saint ruled over the Church. Satan saw him praying and weeping. And he said to him:

"To thee I entrust my Spouse. Watch over her faithfully. In thee I confirm the right and power to decide matters of doctrine, to regulate the use of the sacraments, to make laws and to uphold purity of morals. And the faithful shall be under obligation to conform thereto. My Church is eternal, and the gates of hell shall not prevail against it. Thou art infallible. Nothing is changed."

And the successor of the apostles felt flooded with rapture. He prostrated himself, and with his forehead touching the floor, replied:

"O Lord, my God, I recognise Thy voice! Thy breath has been wafted like balm to my heart. Blessed be Thy name. Thy will be done on Earth, as it is in Heaven. Lead us not into temptation, but deliver us from evil."

And Satan found pleasure in praise and in the exercise of his grace; he loved to hear his wisdom and his power belauded. He listened with joy to the canticles of the cherubim who celebrated his good deeds, and he took no pleasure in listening to Nectaire's flute, because it celebrated nature's self, yielded to the insect and to the blade of grass their share of power and love, and counselled happiness and freedom. Satan, whose flesh had crept, in days gone by, at the idea that suffering prevailed in the world, now felt himself inaccessible to pity. He regarded suffering and death as the happy results of omnipotence and sovereign kindness. And the savour of the blood of victims rose upward towards him like sweet incense. He fell to condemning intelligence and to hating curiosity. He himself refused to learn anything more, for fear that in acquiring fresh knowledge he might let it be seen that he had not known everything at the very outset. He took pleasure in mystery, and believing that he would seem less great by being understood, he affected to be unintelligible. Dense fumes of Theology filled his brain. One day, following the example of his predecessor, he conceived the notion of proclaiming himself one god in three persons. Seeing Arcade smile as this proclamation was made, he drove him from his presence. Istar and Zita had long since returned to earth. Thus centuries passed like seconds. Now, one day, from the altitude of his throne, he plunged his gaze into the depths of the pit and saw Ialdabaoth in the Gehenna where he himself had long lain enchained. Amid he everlasting gloom Ialdabaoth still retained his lofty mien. Blackened and shattered, terrible and sublime, he glanced upwards at the palace of the King of Heaven with a look of proud disdain, then turned away his head. And the new god, as he looked upon his foe, beheld the light of intelligence and love pass across his sorrow-stricken countenance. And lo! Ialdabaoth was now contemplating the Earth and, seeing it sunk in wickedness and suffering, he began to foster thoughts of kindliness in his heart. On a sudden he rose up, and beating the ether with his mighty arms, as though with oars, he hastened thither to instruct and to console mankind. Already his vast shadow shed upon the unhappy planet a shade soft as a night of love.

And Satan awoke bathed in an icy sweat.

Nectaire, Istar, Arcade, and Zita were standing round him. The finches were singing.

"Comrades," said the great archangel, "no -- we will not conquer the heavens. Enough to have the power. War engenders war, and victory defeat.

"God, conquered, will become Satan; Satan, conquering, will become God. May the fates spare me this terrible lot; I love the Hell which formed my genius. I love the Earth where I have done some good, if it be possible to do any good in this fearful world where beings live but by rapine. Now, thanks to us, the god of old is dispossessed of his terrestrial empire, and every thinking being on this globe disdains him or knows him not. But what matter that men should be no longer submissive to Ialdabaoth if the spirit of Ialdabaoth is still in them; if they, like him, are jealous, violent, quarrelsome, and greedy, and the foes of the arts and of beauty? What matter that they have rejected the ferocious Demiurge, if they do not hearken to the friendly demons who teach all truths; to Dionysus, Apollo, and the Muses? As to ourselves, celestial spirits, sublime demons, we have destroyed Ialdabaoth, our Tyrant, if in ourselves we have destroyed Ignorance and Fear."

And Satan, turning to the gardener, said:

"Nectaire, you fought with me before the birth of the world. We were conquered because we failed to understand that Victory is a Spirit, and that it is in ourselves and in ourselves alone that we must attack and destroy Ialdabaoth."

CPSIA information can be obtained
at www.ICGtesting.com
Printed in the USA
LVHW051231030622
720443LV00001B/44